WRIGHT & WRONG

A RAFFERTY P.I. NOVEL
BOOK 8

BILL DUNCAN

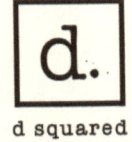
d squared
publishing.

THE RAFFERTY P.I. SERIES

Rafferty's Rules

Last Seen Alive

Poor Dead Cricket

Wrong Place, Wrong Time

Cannon's Mouth

Fatal Sisters

False Gods

Wright & Wrong

Down The Barrel

———

Scan the QR code below for more details and
the up-to-date list of all books in the series.

Published in 2020 by d squared publishing.

Cover Design by d squared publishing

Edited by Amanda Spedding - Phoenix Editing

Ebook ISBN: 978-0-6482234-7-4

P'back ISBN: 978-0-6459470-0-7

For enquiries regarding this book, please email: bill@duncanandlee.com

For Mum and Dad,

Your choices let me be the man I am today.

Thanks.

1

For a long time after I would wonder if I'd done the right thing.

But I couldn't worry about that now, because the kid was fast, and I needed every bit of energy I could muster just to keep him in sight.

I'd first noticed him slouching in the doorway of a disused office building on South Harwood, as I was walking back to the office— figuring him for just another kid cutting class and hoping he realized how lucky he was.

Me? Too focused on that bottle of scotch in my desk drawer. I made it a hundred yards farther before my brain kicked in and I realized where I'd seen the kid before.

By the time I retraced my steps, he was on the move, turning the corner at Wood Street.

Not wanting to spook him, I kept a loose tail as he headed out of the city towards Deep Ellum.

Kept my eyes open for a working phone booth as we walked.

Normally did my following in the Mustang, but that was a

no-go today. I could have tried to get back to the lot near the office, get the car, and pick him up further down the road, but it's hard to use a vehicle to tail a person on foot. They have too many options: heading into a store and out the back door, or worse, pausing for a minute just inside the front door and then heading back out while I'm wasting tire rubber trying to make it around the block.

It'd also have been a lot easier if I could have called DPD and got a dispatcher to put me through to Ed so he could send a blue and white to pick up the kid, but we'd passed three non-operational payphones already.

Bottom line, I had to tail this kid on my own two feet, no matter where he went or how far he decided to go, and I wasn't looking forward to it. It's hard for a guy my size to effectively follow someone on an open street.

For a start, I'm bigger than your average Dallas city dweller, so I tend to get spotted too easily. For another thing, I'm not as fast as your typical high schooler, so if he decided to turn up the heat, I could be shit out of luck.

As I found out.

He had made me as he came back out of an alley off Elm Street. I'd picked up my speed and jogged towards the mouth of the alley as he turned off the sidewalk and disappeared from view. I got there, stuck my head around the corner, and hoped to catch a glimpse of which door he entered or get an idea on which way he went from the other end of the alley.

What I hadn't expected was to bump into him coming back out to the sidewalk and turning right into me.

"Ohh … excuse me … sir," he stammered.

I tried to get my game face on, but I was too damn slow.

He saw that I knew, and then he knew.

He whirled and I grabbed for him. Missed the first two times—Christ he was slippery!—before I got my fist around his upper arm and wrestled him back into the alley. He thrashed and flailed, and I hung on.

"Okay, kid. Settle down. Hey!"

He pushed and wriggled and swung a skinny arm at me. I had a couple of inches and probably sixty pounds on him, so he wasn't going to win if we started going head to head, but I didn't want him to get lucky with a random fist.

"I said, settle the fuck *down!*" Pushed him into a corner between a filthy dumpster and the even grimier brick wall of the alley. Pulled the .38 from my shoulder holster and started to feel better about the situation.

He bounced off the dumpster, got his feet back underneath him, bent over and put his hands on his knees. His breathing was ragged, and I tried not to let him see that mine was the same.

"I didn't do it," he panted.

"Uh huh."

It looked like he realized that I wasn't who he was expecting, and decided to try a different tack. "Who the fuck are you, anyway? Why'd you drag me in here? Fucking pervert." Looked up at me through a shock of dirty-blond hair and gave me a sneer that only a teenager could pull off.

"Saw what you did down at Columbus. Figured the cops might be interested, too."

The glare turned to a look of fear so strong that I thought maybe I'd collared the wrong kid.

Nope.

Same black leather jacket and denim jeans as I'd seen earlier that morning. Same white sneakers, too. I had misjudged his height—he was taller than I'd originally thought. But if there had been any remaining question, the T-shirt that I had thought was browny-red was actually a lighter shade of something now unrecognizable beneath a whole lotta drying blood.

Gotcha.

I stepped back a foot or two, gave myself a little extra space. Not that I wanted to use my gun against a kid, no matter what I'd seen him do less than two hours ago, but it was good to be prepared.

The kid sniffed. "I didn't do it," he said again. Softer, and without the attitude this time.

"Twenty-five to life says you did, pal."

Another sniff.

"Okay kid. We're gonna walk outta this alley, you and I, and we're going to head down to DPD. I know a lieutenant who's gonna be real interested in talking to you. So stand up. Nice and slow."

A car went past the mouth of the alley, someone yelled something, and I saw the glint of green in the kid's hand too late.

The bottle came flying at me, and by the time I'd ducked, felt the thump as it hit my shoulder and the relief that it hadn't been my head, and looked back, the kid was hoofing it to the other end of the alley.

Damn it, he was fast.

He beat me to the back end of the alley by twenty feet and, by the time I'd made it around the corner, he'd increased that to twenty-five.

We ran down a narrow laneway squeezed between the back of old brick buildings and a disused industrial lot.

I ran hard, tried to ignore the pain in my ankle, and did my best to not trip over the piles of garbage and detritus, or get tangled in the overgrowth doing its best to pull down the ten-foot-high chain-link fence on our left.

Looked like this laneway continued for a hundred yards

or so before it ended against another brick wall with a steel roof rusting into oblivion above. Couldn't tell if there was another alley at that point so I wasn't sure whether I had the kid boxed in or not.

Kept pushing, just in case.

Vines and leaves slapped at my face and something harder —loose wire maybe—scratched my left arm. I pounded through a puddle and my feet threatened to get out from under me, but I held it together and kept running.

About fifty yards short of the end of the laneway the kid disappeared, and I had to grab at the wall to help angle myself into the shoulder-width alley he'd found. He hurdled a pile of pallets and sprinted toward the light at the street end.

I slipped as I climbed over the pallets, barked my shin, and was thirty feet behind as I hit the slimy pavement again.

But he was slipping and sliding too, and I wasn't losing any ground. I was breathing hard, though, so unless I ended this thing soon, the kid was too likely to outrun me.

"Stop!" I yelled.

The kid snapped a look over his shoulder as he bolted for the mouth of the alley.

"Don't make me shoot."

I wasn't going to shoot a kid, but he didn't need to know that particular detail.

I found a little patch of dry ground and skidded to a halt just as the kid stepped onto the sidewalk, bathed in sunlight.

"Stop right there. I shit you not. I will shoot you."

He stopped. Turned to face me.

"So what? So fucking what? How much more can that hurt?" he said. I could see the tears and sweat dripping down his cheeks. He spread his arms wide. "Do it then. If you're gonna. Fucking DO IT!" he screamed.

I pulled the trigger, loosed a round over his head, and he flinched. Looked down at his chest. Back at me.

"I thought so."

He stepped off the curb.

I heard the horn and squealing tires a split second before the front end of a Greyhound bus sent the kid flying out of view.

2

efore all that excitement had erupted, it had been just another typical Monday.

In the office, feet on the desk, and into my second cup of hot black heart-starter. Spring was starting to show signs of being ready to arrive, and I was enjoying the warm breeze from the street on the back of my neck. Loafing with the newspaper and eyeballing the hell out of a pre-lunch nap.

Not everyone was sharing my sunny disposition and positive outlook.

A tanker, the *Exxon Valdez*, had run aground a couple days earlier in Alaska, someplace called Prince William Sound, and the aerial photos of the resultant oil spill looked like a depraved Christo installation.

Behold, Ladeez and Gentlemen, I give you 'Ze Earth ... in Black-face.' Thunderous applause and don't forget to visit the gift shop on the way out.

Hundreds of oil-skinned volunteers were already at the scene, doing their best to contain the threatening slick and limit damage to the surrounding wilderness. Only time would tell how successful those efforts would be.

I was trying to visualize the reports of how much oil had made it outside the boat, when I heard the first shot.

My brain tried to downshift straight from barrels of crude to threat assessment, got caught somewhere in the middle, and lurched into a call and response routine—

That was a gunshot.

Don't be stupid, it was a car backfire.

No, I'm certain it was a gunshot.

—before I told the cerebral combatants to shut the hell up and got myself to the open window.

Looked up and down Jackson street.

Usual morning traffic. People running late for work jockeying with those go-getters headed to the second or third meeting for the day. Lots of cars. No obvious clunkers.

Strike the car backfire.

Another shot

Two.

Three.

The city tableau laid out before me gave no clues to who was firing, where they were, or what I could do about it.

I turned and bulled my way through the office door, thundered down the hallway and heaved myself up the fire escape to the roof. Just as I got to the low brick parapet at the edge, a three-shot burst rang out.

Now with a clear line of hearing, and maybe a bit of oxygen debt, my brain gave up arguing with itself and started triangulating.

Slantwise, through a gap between brick buildings and over past The Scottish Rite Cathedral on the other side of Young Street, I could see figures running around the school rec-area there, wheeling in unison, like a flock of birds startled into flight.

Screams, shouts, and a chorus of "Oh my God"s pleaded their way to me before a volley of shots cut them off.

Two teenagers at the rear edge of the flock—a boy and girl —fell like puppets with slashed strings. The rest of the bodies surged to the left and out of my sight.

It was all happening in front of me.

And there wasn't a damn thing I could do about it.

An overcoated and backwards-baseball-cap-wearing figure strode into my view slot. He stood next to the two bodies, cradled his AR-15, and cocked his head. He brought the gun up to his shoulder and fired at the sprawled carcasses. They twitched and sprouted crimson haloes.

Blood angels on the pavement.

The figure toed both bodies with a booted foot, then turned towards me and lifted his arm. For a second I thought he was going to wave, then another member of the Overcoat Club stepped into view, and they high-fived before the new arrival checked the magazine on a gun that looked like a black capital letter T. I couldn't tell from that distance, but probably a TEC-9 or MAC-10.

Not that the exact designation of weapon would make the slightest bit of difference to the kids being murdered in their schoolyard.

I noticed for the first time that my hands were clenched, nails digging into my palms. I wanted—needed—to do something, but the best I could do right now was stop edging forward and accidentally pitch myself headfirst off the roof.

Thought about the weapons I had in the office a floor below. Nothing that could throw a slug far enough to make a difference. Considered for a split second taking a leaf from

Mimi's book and adding a sniper rifle to my arsenal, then snapped myself back into observation mode.

It wasn't much, but it was all I had, and it might help later on.

Uh huh.

Overcoat One smiled, reached into the khaki duffel bag hanging from his shoulder, pulled out a flat black magazine. He ejected the one from the gun like he was in the middle of his third tour, and slammed the new one home.

Overcoat Two swung his duffel bag around to his back, raised his gun, braced his feet, and squeezed off a series of shots. The reverberations reached me a split second later.

More screams and shouts.

The two Overcoats moved left out of my sight line. Rattling gunfire, and strangled shrieks bent around the buildings and stung my ears.

Another movement.

Over the top of the shorter building in front of me, and at the far edge of the school rec-area, a figure crept around the bottom of a short flight of brick stairs.

Boy. Skinny. Black leather jacket and denim jeans. Brown, or browny-red T-Shirt. White sneakers. Medium height, probably five-nine though it was hard to tell while he was crouched. Dirty-blond hair. Handgun in one fist.

His hair whipped around his face as he looked side to side.

He lifted the gun in front of his face, looked at it a few seconds. Wrapped his hand around it more tightly and crouch-walked out of my view.

A knot of kids ran back through the nearer view slot. One of them actually tripped over the bodies of the two blood angels and couldn't get her feet back under her before she sprawled out of sight. I willed her to get up and the hell out of there.

The Overcoat Club were there again. Looked like they were laughing as they walked back out of view, both firing short bursts from the hip.

Good fire control.

I mentally pistol-whipped my brain for such a thought.

Before I could continue my internal flagellation, Skinny Boy walked into view, pistol outstretched, lined up a shot, didn't take it, then followed his buddies out of sight.

And there I was, standing ineffectually on a roof watching the whole thing play out before me. I was only a hundred twenty, hundred thirty yards away, but I might as well have been in Alaska for all the good I could do at that moment.

Felt vaguely schizophrenic knowing that the best thing I could do was keep watching in case I could help the cops once they got hold of the situation, but also not wanting to look at it anymore.

I'd seen a lot in my forty-plus years on this rock, but violence against kids still hit me the hardest. Not that I thought adults were more deserving of pain just for being older, but I was able to set that aside more easily. I'm sure Hilda would be able to tell me exactly what it was.

Maybe I'd just seen too many kids get hurt. Vivian, Kimberly, Edie …

A bunch of kids—fewer in number this time—ran screaming through my view slot again, closely followed by the Overcoats, in a weird parody of a sideshow alley shooting game. This time though, there wouldn't be any kewpie dolls for a knocking down all the targets.

Overcoat Two changed magazines, dropping the empty right next to the lifeless bodies at his feet. Craned his head back and let out a war-whoop that I heard over the traffic noise, grabbed his buddy around the shoulders and gave him a healthy shake. Cycled the action on his weapon and nodded to Overcoat One.

They brought their weapons up to hip height and blazed fire—no short bursts now—and moved after the running students.

About ten seconds after they were out of sight, Skinny Boy crept back into view. He stopped, half-kneeled, hesitated, looked like he sucked in half a dozen breaths and then squeezed off a shot. It was a big gun, more than he was used to, judging by how he had to bring the recoil down from over his head.

More screaming collided with rattling gunfire and covered the echoes of the handgun's report.

In the background, I could dimly hear sirens cutting through the traffic.

Not quickly enough.

Skinny Boy cocked his head, looked around, and ran out of sight.

Long seconds passed as I waited for something else to happen.

Shorter bursts of gunfire now.

Louder sirens.

Fewer screams.

As a cop car careered down the wrong side of Jackson below me, another blue and white slid through my view slot, all four wheels locked. I guessed that was the Young Street school frontage and that someone in blue serge was about to have his chance to be a hero.

A long burst of fire counterpointed the squealing tires, and I hoped it was towards the cruiser and not directed at any of the kids who might still be alive.

A series of small pops, sounding ridiculous in comparison

to the rifle shots, told me the cop had unholstered his police-issue .38 and was doing what he could to keep the three gun-toting teenagers' heads down.

That was my cue to stop being a passive spectator, get my ass down there, and see what I could do.

The boom of a shotgun bounced off buildings and streets as I bolted for the fire escape and the street below.

3

"It's a fucking mess," Lieutenant Ed Durkee said, like it wasn't obvious.

The cops had done a good job securing the site and keeping the media—damn they were fast!—away from the school perimeter, allowing them only oblique views from each end of the street to the killing fields in front of us.

That wouldn't be enough to deter them.

I'd have been surprised if there wasn't more than one eager reporter and camera crew already knocking on doors in the apartment block on the opposite side of Young Street, hoping to get an elevated view of the carnage and their network logo plastered coast-to-coast for the next news cycle.

Ed had been good enough to let me stay inside the police cordon. Probably too busy to throw me out but I repaid the favor by doing my best not to get in the way.

"What happened, Ed?"

"Looks like a couple of kids decided they were Rambo and the rest of the students were Charlies. Fucked if I know why, though."

Ed's description was accurate. The asphalt rec-area beyond the fence did look like an urban war movie.

Police and paramedics jockeyed with each other as they moved in and out of the schoolyard through a breach where a fence panel had been hastily snipped open and pulled to the side.

Like an open wound.

Inside the fence, bodies lay on the hard, dark bitumen like fallen leaves. The lucky were wrapped in blankets and being tended to, and simultaneously questioned, by the uniforms but there were too many silent, misshapen lumps under white sheets.

Two in a V-formation where I'd first seen the Overcoat Club.

Three lined up like piano keys on the main steps into the school building. Which way they'd been facing in their last moment, I couldn't tell.

One crumpled outside a doorway at the top of the steps. Trying to barricade the door, maybe.

A few scattered single sheets behind steel-gray outdoor furniture.

Too many lined up side-by-side for their last assembly.

A few strands of straw-colored hair escaped from under the nearest shroud and wafted around. I knew it was only the breeze. Knew that there was no point pushing past Ed to rip the sheet off the poor girl and do my best to bring her back to life.

Knew it as well as I knew my own name.

But it still took everything I had to keep my feet rooted. I hacked and spat at the base of the fence. "I heard it happen, Ed. Lots of semi-auto rifle fire."

"Yeah. There're casings from one end of this yard to the

other. It's gonna take a lot of time to catalog it all. They musta been armed to the teeth."

"Uh huh. Two were carrying duffel bags with spare ammo. The third one had a handgun, but coulda had something else under his jacket, too."

"You saw them?" Ed eyebrows reached for the sky. "When? Where?"

"After it all started to go down. Didn't see much, no more than a glimpse between buildings. There was a single big-bore shot, too. That was late in the piece, after your guys arrived on the scene."

"Two, actually. You musta missed the other one. At this point we think there were two who took the coward's way out. Least, that what it looks like. There're a couple of bodies, still with weapons, and the duffel bags you saw, slung around their torsos."

"Let me guess. Wearing overcoats and backwards baseball caps?"

"Negative on the caps. Neither one has enough of their head left to be wearing anything up top, but overcoats is right. Looks like they took turns eating the shotgun. I expect the first on scene'll confirm that for us, if what you say about the timing is right."

I swallowed. Ed continued.

"We'll get a report from you. As a witness. But it might be a while. At this rate, Sergeant Ricco's gonna be taking statements for the next few weeks. At the very least."

I nodded and looked over Ed's shoulder to where Ricco squatted on his haunches next to a dark-haired girl. In his natty pinstripe suit, wingtips and fedora, Ricco could have been at the craps game from *Guys and Dolls*.

Luck be a lady.

The girl streamed tears and whipped her corn-rowed head

from side to side as she talked to Ricco. I caught a few words. "... in class, with everyone else ... came outside ... running back and forth ... chasing ... shooting ... we were trying to hide ... but there was nowhere to go ... I was so lucky ..." Looked like she'd lost control of her eyes; they rolled and bounced, dark and red and raw, reliving everything that she never wanted to see in the first place.

Ricco nodded, said, "Okay, Imani, what else?" and scribbled in a black notebook. So began the long and winding road of evidence collection.

I turned back. "How many, Ed?"

Ed mashed his face under both palms and let loose the biggest sigh I'd ever heard.

"Twenty-two dead. We figure two of those to be the shooters, though if what you say is right, there's another one of them under a sheet back there." He scrabbled inside his suit jacket and extracted a spiral notepad. "What'd he look like?"

"Like any other teenage kid, Ed." He wrote down my description and nodded.

"We'll confirm that soon enough." He sighed again. "Only speck of good news is that there were only sixteen injured, but a shitload of kids and teachers traumatized to hell and back."

"I'll bet."

"Listen, Rafferty, I gotta talk to the principal and Mayor Strauss wants an update in ..." Ed checked a watch under his brown suit sleeve. "Shit, less than thirty minutes. I gotta go."

"No problems, Ed. Let me know if there's anything I can do."

Ed flapped an arm at me and weaved his way between the uniforms, between wailing kids and quiet sheets, and trudged up the stairs into the school.

———

I packed a pipe and got it blazing. Eased my way through the opening in the fence.

My first footfall onto the school asphalt was like treading on hallowed ground. I tiptoed like a thief to avoid bullet casings glittering in the sun.

Though it had been less than an hour since I'd heard that first shot, DPD was already swinging from containing the scene and treating the injured to attempting to find out what the hell had happened, and to answer the bigger question.

Why?

Investigators were starting their work, a small group clustered around a senior detective to get briefed on the situation which would ensure they missed a lot of home-cooked dinners for the next few months. A young guy with a buzzcut locked eyes with me and I jerked my chin at him. He grimaced a thin smile, shook his head twice, and turned back to his briefing.

Looked back across Young Street. Between the apartment building—balconies filled with rubber-neckers—and the back of a weathered concrete office building, I could see my office building and roof top viewing position. From this end of the perspective, the distance appeared farther away than the reverse view had looked earlier in the morning.

Rafferty's Rule Thirty-eight: There's nothing like automatic gunfire to sharpen the senses and tighten the sphincter.

Lined up with the view I'd had from the roof and let myself drift back.

The first shot.

Impossible to tell where it had come from, or which direction it had been going. Wondered if that shot had been preceded by others. No way for me to even guess at that;

DPD would have to put the timeline together from interviews.

I needed to start with what I could know, not what I couldn't.

Okay.

Three shots spaced two to three seconds apart.

Then a three-shot burst.

The wheeling flock of terrified teenagers. Swooping right to left in front of me, from over there—where the three sheets pointed the way back into the school—and headed towards that corner, where the girl with the straw-colored hair lay on the hard ground underneath a white sh—

Breathe, Rafferty.

Okay.

The two slowest in the flock were hit *here*, and Overcoat stood *there* while he wasted another half-dozen rounds shooting at kids who were already dead. The crimson blot creeping from underneath the shrouds told the story loud enough.

After that, the Overcoat Club had chased after the screaming kids while Skinny Boy came out the doors and down the steps to join in the fun.

I clamped my pipe in my teeth and headed across the rec-area.

Avoided the four shrouds as I climbed the steps. Peered in through the glass panels in the doors, and answered the question of whether there were any shots fired inside the school buildings. The hallway didn't quite befit a scene from *Carrie*, but John Carpenter would have been proud.

Four more shrouds lay in the space, and all the walls I could see would need some heavy-duty cleaning before anyone other than cops could set foot in the hallway without tasting bile. There were a couple of techs taking photos and scribbling notes and doing their best not to trip over the bodies or each other.

I wondered how long it would take the Medical Examiner's office to get moving, realized they wouldn't know how to deal with this any better than the rest of us. Had the morgue ever had to deal with this many bodies at once?

"Hey you!"

I turned to see a patrol cop with a thick neck and razor burn heaving his bulk up the steps.

"Yeah?"

"This ain't no peep show, buddy. Get the hell outta here."

I pulled out my wallet and showed him my license. He stabbed it with a thick finger and read every word. I knew he did, I could see his lips moving.

"Private dick, huh? Don't matter. Piss off."

"Ed knows I'm here."

"Well, don't that change things? Since Ed knows you're here, I guess you can ... piss off. Now." He moved to stand in front of the door and folded his arms across his chest. Must be nice to have a gut big enough to rest your arms on.

I could have pushed it, but I didn't think there was much more to see without getting into the hallway itself, and that was already too crowded with bodies.

Headed down the stairs, didn't give the fat cop the satisfaction of seeing me look back at him, and worked my way towards the street. Leaned on the chain-mesh fence and looked over the scene.

Kids still being comforted, questioned, and then escorted towards the police barricades where it looked like hysterical parents and hysterical media personnel heaved in equal numbers. For those unable to make the journey on their own feet, the occasional blart of an ambulance running the media gauntlet chronicled their progress.

Cops shuffled around on the street alongside the rec-area, sipped coffee, smoked, and shook their heads. More than one peeled back the scab to let their feelings out. "Goddamn it!" and more. Radios crackled.

Inside the fence, the investigators had broken from their huddle and started the tedious process of taking notes, placing crime scene markers, and photographing everything in sight. All while weaving between the sheets laying on the cold ground.

Stark. Silent. Still.

I'd have bet my favorite .45 that the two sheets slightly separated from the others would be covering two boys in overcoats and a pair of matching duffel bags.

But if that was the case, it meant the third shooter, the one that Ed hadn't known about, wasn't with those two. And, although I had faith that my favorite lieutenant would get back to the details after his mayoral audience, I was left wondering why the third shooter didn't end up with his buddies.

And, assuming I was right, where the hell did he go?

Levered myself off the fence and shuffled around the perimeter of the rec-area to the left, keeping my back to the street and watching my feet. Headed towards the shrouds draped over my assumed shooters, see if I could sneak a look and confirm my thoughts. Was almost there before one of the techs taking pictures stepped out of the way, the fat cop saw me, and started down the stairs.

I held up a hand and backed away.

Not that he worried me, I just wasn't in the mood for going head-to-head with a numb-nuts today. There'd already been too much violence for the morning and I didn't feel like adding to it.

But I needed to do something. All I'd done while this shit-show played out was stand around and watch.

I felt useless.

Impotent.

To keep moving was all I had at the moment, so I headed the other way. Passed the bodies of the first two kids I saw get killed then weaved around four other sheets to get to the quiet corner at the opposite end of the rec-area.

Where the street-side fence turned back at right angles toward the school building, an elm tree soared overhead, dappling soft light on metal benches and a gaggle of backpacks and soft bags that might never be tossed carelessly in the living room corner again.

Looked like it could have been a smoker's corner, the way it was tucked around a protruding brick wall and out of sight from all classroom and hallway windows.

An eight-foot-high green wall of out of control ivy sat behind the benches. The ground staff really needed to get onto that, the ivy was starting to pile up in the corner and a healthy crop of tendrils were making a move towards taking over the benches too.

I stepped up on the nearest bench. Couldn't see over the wall, so pulled my way through enough ivy to find another chain link fence buried deep in the greenery. Kept pulling vines apart like I was looking for Dr Livingstone until I could see through to a service area behind. A scratched and rusted black dumpster took up most of the service area, the rest of the stained and cracked concrete driveway lay covered with ripped cardboard packing, some broken pallets, and ankle-deep piles of dead elm leaves.

Stepped off the bench and parked my butt while I relit my pipe. The wind shifted and I had to cock my head and cover the lighter close. As I pulled in a lungful of smoke, the pile of ivy in the corner lifted, hovered, and a dozen dead leaves came drifting out from underneath, got sucked up into a little vortex, and went spinning away over the schoolyard.

I sat and watched the nature show for a few minutes. With each gust of wind, the ivy in the corner lifted and moved. I'd never seen ivy do that before, but then who the hell was I, David Attenborough?

I looked around the rest of the scene. The investigators were busy concentrating in the opposite quarter of the rec-area. Fat cop was still at the top of the steps into the school and glaring at the world.

I stepped to the corner, dropped to my haunches, and grabbed a fistful of ivy.

It came off the asphalt easily and the higher I lifted, the more the ivy came away from the fence. Unlike when I was trying to see through to the service area, the ivy in this area wasn't twisted and tangled through the wire. Like a living curtain, it pulled back to reveal an opening in the fence about three feet square.

Lifted the ivy as high as it would go and duck-walked into the opening. A pallet lay slant on the ground in front of me. I moved around it, made sure my head was clear, and stood.

I was in the service area and if I lifted the pallet and leaned it against the fence, no-one would be any the wiser as to how I got there. Neat little way in and out of the school. Perfect for cutting class without being seen. Definitely something I would have made use of back in my high school days when I would have rather been out with my friends than in another trig lesson.

I stepped over the pallet, lifted it back into place to see how well the hidey-hole would be concealed, and uncovered a familiar looking duffel bag.

Thought for a second that one of the shooters must have got over here and pitched the bag over the fence before eating his gun. Nope, Ed had said that the duffel bags were still with them. Maybe this was a different bag, just garbage to be thrown away.

A shotgun barrel poking up from one end said differently.

The Mossberg 500 was nicked, spotted with rust, and unloaded but two full boxes of shells underneath would have solved those problems without hassle. A KA-BAR knife and a two-foot length of lead pipe lay ready to take care of any others that might arise.

Lotta weaponry and ammo to leave behind. Not that the Overcoats had looked like they needed the extra supplies. But the other kid; why leave all this behind and head out armed only with a handgun? That didn't make sense.

Voices and rustling noises came from behind the pallet and I just got my fingers clear before it fell, covering the duffel bag again, and a young cop hauled himself through.

"Don't you let him get away, you hear me?" The voice of the fat cop from the rec-area. No prizes for guessing why he wasn't the first one through the hole.

"Yes sir!" The young cop in front of me put his hand on the butt of his gun and tried for his best sneer. I rolled my eyes at him and leaned against the dumpster.

It was two or three minutes later when Ed and the fat cop came hustling down the sidewalk and turned into the service area. I wouldn't have called Ed fit, but the way that the fat cop was breathing and gasping as he tried to keep up made Ed look like he was ready for the Olympic marathon team.

"Rafferty," Ed sighed. "I did you a solid by letting you stay on scene. Can't you at least stay outta the way? Huh?"

"Don't see why you need to do anything with me, but Jabba the Hutt there could do with a Richard Simmons video. Or a defibrillator." The fat cop tried to glare at me but seemed to be fully occupied with standing upright and breathing right then.

"Already … told him to … leave the scene … once …," he wheezed, "Sir."

"Yeah, he's a pain in the ass, all right," said Ed. "Doesn't take direction."

"Character assassinations aside, Ed," I replied, "you might be interested in this." I gestured at the young cop, who was now trying a scowl, and he almost jumped. "Settle down. I just need you to step away from …" I pointed at the pallet. He moved and I lifted the pallet back against the fence.

Three sets of DPD eyes saw the duffel bag and contents and started their responses at the same time.

"Shit! Oh, sorry, sir …"

"… we … we … already had that … identified … sir."

"Chrissake, Rafferty."

I looked at Ed with raised eyebrows. He shook his head and sighed. Hoisted his official face on.

"I know you think this is exciting, Rafferty, playing with the professionals, but do you have any idea how big this thing is going to get? Do you?" I caught his look and declined to respond. "The last thing I need is you getting in the way with this one. The mayor is already all over my ass and I don't have time to fix your usual fuck-ups at the same time."

"My fuck-ups?" I nodded at the shotgun and ammo.

Ed looked at both the cops and back to me.

"You heard me. Get the hell outta here. I've got work to do. Sergeant? Make sure he is no longer on the property." He turned on his heel and walked back towards the rec-area.

"With pleasure, Lieutenant." Fat cop's heart rate was obviously falling back towards normal and he relished the opportunity to take it into the red again. He turned to the young cop. "You stay right there. Make sure that no-one, and I mean no-fucking-one, goes near that bag, or it's your ass.

"Now you ..." He reached for my arm and I shrugged away. Thought about punching him in the throat. He took a step back and lowered his hand to his holster. "Ohh, yeah, boy howdy. That's it. Now, you can either get the hell out of here like the lieutenant said, or ..." His eyes twinkled and he unsnapped his holster. "Or you can resist. Your choice."

The other cop twitched, looked around like he expected to have to defend the evidence from an invading force of paratroopers.

Good grief. If they didn't want my help, then I could deal with that just fine; I had plenty of other things to do. It's not like they were doing me any favors. I turned to the sidewalk.

Fat cop followed me out of the service area, stood about ten feet away, and smirked his way through watching me get my pipe started again. Mock saluted me as I walked away.

Fuck 'em.

I shoved more smoke in the direction of my nerves and walked back to the office, now set on a date with a bottle of scotch. Didn't care that it wasn't yet noon. Any morning that involved watching the killing of innocent kids deserved an afternoon of hard drinking.

4

ut you already know how that turned out.

Instead of sitting in my office with my feet on the windowsill and the second or third glass of scotch in my fist, there I was standing on the sidewalk watching more paramedics do their best to keep another kid alive.

The bus had knocked him a good thirty feet down the street, whereupon his fall had been cushioned by the hood and windshield of a '81 Mercury Lynx. Damn if the car didn't look better afterwards.

Couldn't say the same thing for the kid, though. There was a lot of blood on the paint, and the glass, and the asphalt and —correspondingly—not a lot of movement from the teenager.

The rest of the street heaved with people and I leaned against a wall and watched the good folk of Big D come together in the face of a horrific accident.

The bus had slewed to a stop, already braking hard at the point of impact, and the driver was one of the first to the kid. A bike messenger slid sideways to a halt near the Mercury and checked on the driver and passenger. Shaken, but not injured, he called to a guy on the sidewalk with a house brick-sized cellphone pressed against his ear. Two construction workers had parked their pickup behind the bus and were now waving drivers around the accident scene.

I heard someone shout, "I'm a doctor," and then she was kneeling next to the kid, checking vitals and telling the bus driver to keep the growing crowd back. "Give me some room." It seemed a fair enough request to me, given that most of the assembled multitude had come streaming out from the bus—an entire complement of Japanese tourists by the look of it, all snapping pictures, lighting cigarettes, and doing their best to get in the way.

An ambulance rolled to a stop next to the bus two minutes later, the paramedics piled out and set up next to the kid. "Who is he? Anybody know his name?" Head shakes all around. The bus driver lifted his head and met my eye. The doctor gave the paramedics a brief run-down, then she moved to the side and let them do their thing.

"Hey, kid. Can you hear me?"

No response.

"Kid. Hey kid. I've got nothing here. You?"

"There's a pulse. Weak. Rapid and thready."

"Okay. Let's get a C collar on him. Check his pockets too … Gently! Gently."

"I found a wallet."

"Okay. Any details? Name? Blood type? Allergies?"

"His name's Bradley. Bradley Wright. Student card says he's from Columbus High."

The paramedics glanced at each other and shook their heads.

"This isn't your lucky day now, is it Bradley? Come on, stay with us now."

"Gotta get him ready to transport, or we're gonna lose him."

"No, we're not. You stay here, Bradley. This is not your day. Don't you give up on me, you hear!"

Two cruisers pulled up, strangling their sirens as they parked, but leaving the flashers on. One cop took over from the construction workers and started traffic control, his partner checked on the paramedics while the other two cops flipped open notepads and started working the crowd.

I'd already had enough speaking to cops, but I needed to know what was gonna happen to the kid. The paramedics might have thought he'd drawn a lucky hand earlier in the day, but I knew better.

Knew he'd been the one dealing the cards and now it had come time to cash out.

The house always wins.

I wasn't ready to walk away. No way this kid should get the easy way out like his buddies. Three asswipes who left a trail of pain and death and innocent schoolkids in their wake and they all get away with it? Life couldn't be that unfair.

Needed to stay around to make sure the paramedics did their duty and patched the kid up to live another day, so he could get what was coming to him.

But me hovering on the street wasn't going to change their result, so I decided to take up a more strategic position while I waited and watched.

I crossed the street, pushed through the scratched door, and entered O'Rileys Irish Bar.

———

The dark wood paneling, cracked leather stools, and Irish

Rovers with their folky harmonies and down-home whimsy relaxed me in no time at all.

I'm sure the glass of Jameson's had nothing to do with it.

Sat at the window and watched the scene continue to unfold outside. A tow truck had arrived, hooked up the Mercury, and dragged it off to the tow truck driver's brother's auto shop. Or a scrap yard.

The paramedics worked on the kid for long enough that I started to get concerned he wasn't going to make it. But they finally had him strapped to a gurney and packed up their bags. Almost ready to load him the back of the ambulance when one of them shouted, "He's vomiting!" and they had to tip the gurney—with kid attached—sideways to let him vomit without drowning. So it took few more minutes until they had the ambulance buttoned up and were easing away down the street towards Parkland Memorial.

The bus still hadn't moved—the driver chasing down some of his passengers who had decided to wander I guessed —but the crowd was thinning. Saw one cop flip his notepad closed and get back into his cruiser.

Heard the bell over the pub door tinkle and a voice say, "That's him, officer. And I saw him with a gun, too." And the day threatened to go downhill even further. I glared at the bus driver; he gave me a wink, then stepped back on to the sidewalk, no doubt pleased with having done his civic duty.

Nodded at the bartender. Sure as shit I was going to need another drink to deal with this.

"Excuse me, sir." I watched the uniform approach and made sure that he could see my hands the whole way in. I wasn't up for going toe-to-toe with another cop, especially not with a couple of drinks already under my belt.

"Top o' the mornin' to you," I said. "Sure it be a bonny day to be alive, to be sure, to be sure." Hilda says my Irish accent is one of my worst, and with good reason. Which made me think right then that the Rafferty forebears might be a little disappointed in the last of their line.

No time to dwell on that. The cop stood with his head cocked and reached for his radio. So I tried another tack.

"How can I help you, officer?" I hoisted a disarming smile to my face just to show I had no hard feelings about him interrupting my drinking time.

"You can start by telling me who you are and why you happen to be in this bar today, sir." He was more comfortable now that I wasn't trying leprechaun impersonations, but not enough to step within reach. Or burden his hands with a notebook and pen.

"Feller can't have a drink in the middle of the day?"

"The bus driver says he saw you near the kid when he got hit."

"Hell, there were a lotta people on the street when—"

"Says he also saw you with a gun. Would you care to explain that?"

Thought about the options I had at this point of what had become one of the shittiest starts to a week that I could remember.

Watching a bunch of kids get gunned down in cold blood and being unable to do anything about it.

Helping the cops with working out what the hell had happened, or at least how it had happened, and being unceremoniously thrown off the crime scene by a cop who didn't look smart enough to find the missing doughnut hiding in his own roll of neck fat.

Having a good drinking session ruined by recognizing the third shooter from the scene and trying to apprehend him.

Succeeding in chasing the only living perp from the shooting right in front of a speeding bus and watching him hover between life and death, the final outcome still undecided.

I don't like Mondays.

I hesitated so long that the cop had stepped back and started his hands moving toward his utility belt.

"I'm a P.I.," I said.

"Uh huh. So how about we start with some ID."

I shifted in the seat and reached for my pocket.

"Slowly there, buddy," said the cop, about the same time his hand reached the butt of his pistol. He glanced out the front window and nodded to his partner, who tinkled his way inside and took up a position near the bar. Nice triangulation.

I shrugged, finger-and-thumbed my wallet out from my back pocket, and laid it down on the countertop. Flipped it open, and pushed it toward the cop.

Like his overweight buddy from earlier in the day, he stabbed my license with a finger while he read all the details. Must have been a routine implemented after I left the force.

"Uh huh," he said. "And you're carrying?"

"Yep." I wanted to take a slug of the Jameson's but didn't want to move my hands. This cop still wasn't relaxed enough to make me feel relaxed enough. And the other guy near the bar looked a little too twitchy for comfort. So I just nodded.

"Okay. Let's see it. Again, nice and slow."

I opened the jacket with my left hand, let him see the holster and reached in—again with finger and thumb— extracted the .38 and laid it carefully on the countertop.

The cop used a pen to pick it up by the trigger guard, sniffed the barrel.

"It's been fired recently."

I thought of a hundred smart-ass remarks I could have used at this point but decided against them. Maybe I was starting to grow up. Sounded like something Hilda might be happy to hear about.

"Yeah. I was at the range earlier. Haven't had a chance to clean it yet."

"Uh huh," he said.

That was all he had, no way for him to prove otherwise. He knew it and so followed up by pulling out his notebook and pen.

"So why don't you tell me all about what happened here today?"

The bartender chose that moment to arrive with my fresh drink and I damn near could have kissed him.

I leaned back in my chair, took a swallow of some more of Jameson's finest work, and did one of the things I do best.

I lied to a cop.

5

"What an absolute bitch of a day," Hilda said as she came through the door and slung her bag on the countertop. "If it wasn't bad enough that I had to spend two whole hours with the Smithsons and they *still* couldn't make a decision on the Edwardian dining suite, then Ramon dropped a cast iron shoemakers form. You know, I'm beginning to think you might be right about him, Rafferty. He dropped it right onto the edge of an eighteenth-century ..."

She seemed to notice for the first time that I was sitting, slouched actually, on the sofa. I hadn't bothered to turn a light on after the sun went down, and the blue glow suffusing the house came from the TV, where I'd mercifully strangled the sound about an hour ago.

"Rafferty? What's wrong?"

"I take it you haven't heard the news?"

"What news? After the day I've had, I just wanted some peace and quiet on the way home. What's going on?"

I turned the volume up, stood, and headed for the kitchen.

Heard the breathless tones of the reporter of the moment fill the room behind me.

"... just tuning in, KTVT can confirm the following from today's shooting at Columbus High School. Twenty dead, including eighteen students and two teachers. Sixteen others injured, with six of those listed as critical and two still in surgery ..."

I looked up from refilling my glass to see Hilda's face illuminated by the TV. Her mouth was shaped like a big O and, if I hadn't seen it, I wouldn't have thought it was possible for someone to cry that quickly. I picked a bottle of wine out of the fridge, grabbed a glass from the cupboard, and returned to the sofa as she kept watching.

"... two other bodies in the schoolyard, also students, Kevin McKinley and Randy Wilson, believed at this time to be the perpetrators. We'll be back with more of our rolling coverage of this tragic story after this short word from our sponsor."

Hilda hugged herself and backed into the sofa beside me about the same time that her legs gave out.

"Oh my god," she breathed.

I poured wine and handed her a glass. Her hands shook.

"Uh huh," I said.

"That's near your office, isn't it?"

"Yep."

"Did you ... could you hear it?"

"Heard it," I said. "Saw it." A breath. "Couldn't do a damn thing about it."

"What?"

"Yeah. Turns out that you can see from the office roof right into the schoolyard where it happened. And I did."

"Oh, Rafferty." Hilda gave me a look I'd never seen before. The colors in her eyes flashed and I saw a thousand emotions in that look. Couldn't even think about choosing one to respond to.

But she didn't need anything from me. She drained her wineglass, reached for the bottle, topped up, and fumbled a cigarette out of a packet.

There wasn't anything to say.

The local Very Very Serious Talking Heads from KTVT came back after we had managed to resist the "latest door-busting deals on quality mattresses" and introduced a replay of an earlier interview with one of the survivors.

Hilda leaned forward. I busied myself with my scotch. Good scotch. Was glad I'd made the switch to Glenfiddich.

"Imani Laweles," a bottle-blond reporter said at us from a tight close-up, *"is one of the lucky students here at Columbus High School. She had no idea when she arrived for class this morning that she might never get to go home. But while her classmates lie fallen in the schoolyard, she lived to tell the tale. Describe for our viewers, in your own words, Imani, how you survived this horrific tragedy."*

The camera pulled out to show a girl with corn-rowed hair, a chubby face, and impossibly red eyes, wrapped in a blanket and barely keeping her feet next to the reporter. In the background, the techs were starting to work the scene, and I thought I could see the corner of a white sheet just creeping into shot. The cameraman must have noticed it too, and shifted a little further left. I automatically looked for Ricco amongst the crowd behind the reporter, but didn't see him.

"Umm. Well, we were all in class this morning, and ... and ..." Imani sniffed.

"I saw her," I said. "In the schoolyard."

"You were there? At the school?" Hilda asked. "No. Don't tell me now. I want to hear this."

"Well ... when we heard the ... the first shot we wasn't sure what it was. We ... my girlfriends and I ... one of us said maybe it was a ... was a car backfiring or something ..."

"It's okay, Imani," the reporter said. *"Take your time."*

"There were some more ... umm more bangs and we knew ... we knew ... it couldn't be a car or nothing. It had to be someone ... someone shooting ... we didn't want it to be, but it musta been."

"What did you do then?" the reporter said, obviously no longer willing to let Imani stick to her own timetable.

"Someone, I don't remember who, said ... umm ... that we should stay in the classroom and then ... then someone else said ... umm ... no we needed to ... umm ... to get out of there because if someone ... umm ... someone with a gun came in they'd be able to shoot us easy and ..."

I drained my glass, reached for the bottle. Refilled, took a bite, and sank deeper into the sofa. That was my fifth. Or sixth. Or ... what the hell, who gave a fuck.

"... and then ... I don't know who it was ... said that we ..."

I watched Hilda's face, hanging on every traumatized word coming from Imani's mouth and wished like hell for about the thousandth time that I'd been able to do something useful with my day.

"... so we ran out into the hallway ..."

"That must have been terrifying."

I thought about all the bodies and the blood in that hallway and didn't need the reporter's prompting to take that feeling of terror right to my gut.

"Uh huh. And then we ran out into the rec-area ..."

I knew what happened once everyone made it safely into the rec-area, and I didn't want to think about it any more, so I stopped listening.

———

The interview must have been over, or they'd gone to another commercial break, because Hilda was talking to me.

"What, babe?"

She finished lighting another cigarette and turned to face me.

"How did this happen, Rafferty?" She blew an angry stream of smoke at the ceiling. "Why would someone want to do this? I don't understand. Those poor kids. They must have been terrified."

"I suspect so. It's no fun being shot at. Especially without a way to fight back. Only happened to me a couple of times—"

"That's you, Rafferty! You're used to it. Those kids weren't. They were more worried about whether there'd be an Economics pop quiz or if Johnny was going to break up with them after school."

"I know, babe. I know."

Didn't know what she wanted from me.

Hilda dragged hard on her cigarette and butted it out.

I shrugged.

Another swallow, throat burning. Good.

A bright red banner scrolled across the TV screen.

"BREAKING NEWS"

The local VVSTH gave us a second and a half of steely eyes and perfect hair before intoning, *"We're cutting away from our coverage of the Columbus High School Massacre for a few moments to cross to Brian Adams live at Parkland Memorial Hospital with the latest on Bradley Wright. What can you tell us, Brian?"*

"You've got to be kidding," I muttered. Stood to pack a pipe and pace.

"What is it, Rafferty?"

I shook my head.

Brian gave us his best somber look down the lens and brought us all up to the minute.

"Thanks Steve and Tracey. The doctors have just told us that Bradley Wright is now out of surgery but remains in a critical

condition in the Surgical Intensive Care Unit. You'll remember from our report at the top of the hour that he's the student from Columbus High School who was lucky enough to survive today's horrendous carnage only, in a cruel twist of fate, to be struck by a bus later in the day."

"The poor boy," Hilda said.

"What's his prognosis?" asked the VVSTH.

"Yeah, it's a real sad story," I said.

"The doctors have told us he's stable, but critical. For the moment, he remains in a coma. This is a heartbreaking story, as you can imagine, Steve. To have survived the shooting ..."

"For fuck's sake!"

"What's your problem?"

"My problem? Nothing. Nothing at all. Peachy fucking keen, thank you!" I fired up my pipe and tried to ignore Hilda's stares.

"... keep you updated throughout the night as we hold vigil here alongside this brave —"

I puffed and paced and tried to hold it together.

Hilda's eyes followed me around the room.

The TV continued.

"I'm sorry to interrupt you, Brian, but the President is about to speak. So, we're crossing now to the White House. Do we have the feed? Yes? Okay, here we are. Ladies and gentlemen, the President of the United States."

The screen flickered, Hilda decided she would rather watch the TV than me, and President Bush started his address to the nation.

I paced and smoked and watched.

The first national tragedy that Bush had to face since moving from Reagan's VP to the head of the table and he did a passable job. Usual leader-of-the-country stuff: he avoided detail, talked up the need to remain calm until all the facts were to hand, and told us that he shared our sympathy for the victims and their families. He didn't take any questions.

The VVSTH came on to recap the speech. Unlike Bush, they waded into the details and wallowed in them like a baby hippopotamus.

Did my best to ignore them. Already knew more than I wanted to.

Hilda was a more willing participant and imbibed her wine and every fact about the shooting that the VVSTH were prepared to share. All neatly packaged in colorful charts and maps and tables and numbers. All of which contained one glaring error that kept burrowing under my skin.

I must have been muttering under my breath, because Hilda also gave me more than one sidelong glance over the next ten minutes.

The graphics and voice overs gave way to another recap, which didn't say anything more than we'd heard for the last three hours.

Hilda sat very upright, very still, and worked extra hard to control her breathing. Took tiny sips of her wine, her lips tight and horizontal.

Finally turned to me.

"So, what's—"

Ed Durkee appeared front and center on the TV. Looked like a replay from earlier in the day, a gang of reporters collaring him outside Police Headquarters.

"Hang on. I want to see this."

"What's so important—"

"Shhh."

Hilda flopped against the back of the sofa and I sat down, leaned forward.

"...tenant Durkee, what can you tell us about the police investigation."

"At the moment, the DPD has dozens of officers collecting hundreds, possibly thousands, of pieces of evidence from Columbus High and other locations. Over the next days and weeks, we will be in a position to share our findings with you, but it's too early right now to speculate."

Ed did a good job on camera. He even restrained himself from using the language that normally peppered our conversations. The camera did add twenty pounds, but I reminded myself not to mention it next time we met.

"Lieutenant. Lieutenant! Is there any risk of another attack? Are other schools, other kids, in any danger?"

"I can tell you that all the perpetrators of today's heinous attack were stopped at the scene. There is no reason to believe that—"

"What do you say about reports that the DPD was aware of today's attack as long ago as last month? Is there any truth to that?"

"Jane, there is absolutely no truth whatsoever to that. I don't know where you heard—"

"A very reliable source, Lieutenant."

"Uh huh. Well, Jane, it's highly irresponsible to throw around accusations such a—"

"It would seem irresponsible of the DPD to keep details from the public when those details are directly linked to the deaths of innocent children, Lieutenant. The public needs to know that terror stalks their children. They have a right to know how scared they should b—"

"I'm going to stop you right there, Jane. I don't care what you think is irresponsible or not. The DPD will be working around the clock to uncover all the evidence related to this tragedy and will continue in our duty to protect and serve the citizens of Dallas. That's all. Thank you."

Ed turned, shouldered his way through the reporters who had taken up station behind him, and entered the DPD building, leaving cries of *"Lieutenant. Lieutenant."* floundering in his wake.

The VVSTH came back to wrap things up.

"That was the response from Lieutenant Edmund Durkee earlier today when asked about reports that the DPD was aware of today's attack before it happened. We here at KTVT will keep you informed with every detail of this story as it continues to unfold."

And speaking of informed, a scrolling graphic started showing yearbook photographs of the deceased school-children while the VVSTHs announced the name and age of each and we in TV-land looked at the faces of kids who would never celebrate another birthday.

"Poor Ed," said Hilda.

"Uh huh."

The Glenfiddich got me to the end of the honor roll, but when the VVSTHs came back and started up the next round of *"Is your child next?"*, I'd had as much as I could stand. Got up and turned off the set.

We sat in silence and sipped.

Refilled, and sipped.

"So, are you going to tell me what's going on?"

"What'd you mean?"

"What's got you so upset?"

"What have you been watching for the last hour? Did you not listen to a word they said?"

"Of course I di—"

"Twenty killed, Hilda. Doesn't that mean anything to you?"

"Of course it mea—"

"Eighteen kids! There are eighteen innocent kids in the morgue tonight. That's eighteen kids who won't ever go home again. Who'll never pull on a football jersey again. Who'll never get another kiss, let alone their first. Who will never get the chance to fix things that they messed up. Who ... who just won't ..."

I ran down, swallowed the last of my scotch, knocked it back so fast that a couple drops ran down my chin.

Hilda's eyes were dark, but her fingers were soft as she reached out and gently, tentatively, wiped the drops away with her thumb.

"I'm sorry, Rafferty."

"What for?"

"For snapping. I don't know any of those kids, but I can't stop thinking about how frightened they must have been while it all happened."

"Uh huh."

"I'm sorry for you, too." I raised an eyebrow. She squeezed my hand. "You can relate to what they went through. More than most people."

"Yeah."

"I'm sorry that you had to watch it and couldn't do anything to stop it."

I wriggled on the sofa.

I hated that feeling.

And right then, I hated myself, too.

"I know that hurts. And that there's nothing you can do about it."

I wanted to hurt someone very badly right then.

"So why don't we do this instead? You have another drink, then we'll go to bed, and I'll rub your back."

I did, we did, she did, and it helped somewhat. By the time we fell asleep, nestled together safe and warm, my anger had cooled and I was no longer thinking of wanting to punch someone.

But, as I drifted off, I was thinking something else entirely.

Why was Ed lying?

6

"Can we at least turn the siren off, guys? My head is killing me."

"No chance. The lieutenant wanted you downtown asap. That means 'As Soon As Possible'. Not whenever the guy riding in the back seat feels like it. So maybe you just shut the hell up in case I decide to put the cuffs on you instead, all right?"

The two young cops in the front seat of the police cruiser were too enthusiastic for my taste. Of course, it was only seven a.m. and I hadn't had coffee yet, so that might have accounted for our differing views of the morning.

Starsky and Hutch had hammered on my door about twenty minutes earlier and didn't take it well when I told them to fuck off. We'd danced as a trio along the edges of resisting an officer for a few minutes before they agreed to let me get Ed on the phone to confirm what was going on.

"Get your ass in here," he told me. "Not soon. Not sometime today. NOW!"

I was in no shape to drive so I gratefully accepted their kind offer of accompanying them in the blue and white.

Until Hutch hit the lights and sirens.

But it was clear that he wasn't gonna change his mind on that aspect of our caravan of fun, so I sat in the back and did my best to keep my stomach contents where they belonged.

Starsky sped up at that point and put a little more emphasis into each turn.

Prick.

We finally rolled in to the parking lot at DPD headquarters where they then marched me down hallways and up stairs, and soon we were standing outside the glass-paneled door of my favorite lieutenant.

Starsky knocked.

"Yeah," Ed growled from inside.

"Finally," he said as Hutch opened the door and shouldered me through. "Thanks, Hawkins." Ed jerked his chin, the cop grinned at me and closed the door. I picked a stack of files off the only chair I could see, placed them on top of a bigger pile of papers on Ed's desk and sat. Didn't bother trying to hoist up a smile for him. If he was gonna haul me downtown this early, he could be his own damn moral support.

"What am I gonna do with you, Rafferty?" He rubbed his face. His jowls wobbled. He stabbed a button on his phone. "He's here."

Bent himself to signing files and ignoring me and I kicked myself for not grabbing my pipe and tobacco pouch as I was hustled out of the house. Maybe I could use my one phone call to Hilda and she could smuggle them to me in the false bottom of a cake.

Ed's door swung open and Ricco peacocked his way in, leaned against the wall, and made sure the crease on his trousers fell just so.

"Didn't ever think I'd see Rafferty this hour of the morning," Ricco said. "Looks like he got pulled out of a dumpster."

"Dave and Taylor picked him up from his house, so it's an easy mistake to make."

"What?" I said. "Those kids in the dress-up outfits are actually cops? I thought they were kidnapping me for your stag weekend, Ricco. Seriously Ed, you should look into that. I don't think they're old enough to have driver's permits, let alone carry weapons."

Not some of my best work, I'll admit, but it was early and I still was without coffee. Ed wasn't interested in playing the other side to my scintillating repartee. Instead, he got the ball rolling.

"Something you'd like to tell us, Rafferty?"

I said the ball was rolling. I didn't say I knew which direction.

"Well … yeah," I said, leaning in conspiratorially. "It'll be good to tell someone and get it off my chest. It's been a big burden to carry." Ed and Ricco both shifted their weight forward. "But first, can I get a cup of coffee? Then I'll tell you anything you want to know about how Frank Morris and I made it off Alcatraz back in '62."

Ed blew out a breath and glared at me. Ricco busied himself with a toothpick, looked down, and tried to hide his grin.

"Ricco, stop looking at your reflection in your shoes and get us coffee." Ricco's grin soured and I gave Ed's peripheral vision more credit. "And if you hear screaming when you come back … don't open the door."

It was statements like that, combined with Ed's borderline inability to smile, that caused me some discontent from time to time. I tried to ignore that feeling, looked around the room and raised my eyebrows. Nodded. "It looks like there's enough phone books here, Ricco, and I'm sure Ed has the rubber hoses stashed in a desk drawer somewhere, so don't hurry back. We'll get started without you."

Ricco raised a mock guffaw and eased his way into the hallway. Ed gave me the silent treatment and I tried to look bored.

Soon enough, we were all gripping mugs and the day— despite the paltry excuse for coffee served by the DPD— looked up for the first time.

Ed seemed determined to ruin it.

"When were you planning to come in and tell us about it?"

I held up a finger and took another sip of coffee.

Ahh.

"I'd love to help, I really would guys, but I don't have the faintest idea what you're talkin—"

"Cut the crap, Rafferty! Bradley Wright. Huh?"

"You found him?"

"Uh huh. And I also found a statement from a certain P.I., listed as a witness at the scene, which says that he ... let me find the line, yeah here it is, 'was passing the scene of the accident during his morning constitutional, before heading to his shift at a West Dallas soup kitchen. Mr. Rafferty stated that it was important to give back to the comm—', I can't read any more of this or I'm gonna puke. What the hell were you doing there when Bradley Wright tried to catch the bus?"

I couldn't help it. Ed's delivery was so serious and earnest, as a backdrop for the imagery he'd unwittingly painted, it was comedic genius. I burst out laughing.

He watched me, his lip curling.

"'Cept I ain't laughing, Rafferty. Notice that?"

"Actually, I did. What gives, Ed?"

"What gives is that when Sergeant Ricco's team finished checking the Columbus enrollment records against the students we identified at the scene yesterday, there was a name missing. One Bradley Wright."

"Huh."

"So, imagine my surprise," Ed said, "when I see his name crop up on an accident report from earlier in the day. Got me thinking. Why would this kid not be where he should have been? Would have been worth interviewing him to find out what he could tell us about the shooting, if only he wasn't in a coma."

"Yeah," I agreed. "That's gonna make it tough to get a statement."

Ed ignored that and rolled on. "If you can grasp all of that so far, imagine my fucking incredulity when I see your name on the report, too. I've been a cop for thirty-two years, Rafferty, and I've long since given up on the idea of coincidence. Since I can't get anything out of Bradley Wright, I pulled on the next thread—you. Now, cut the crap and tell me what you know about the accident."

I sipped bad coffee and thought about what I should share with Ed and how much I wanted to keep to myself.

I'd been happy enough to lie to the patrol cop in O'Rileys the day before, but Ed was different. We'd been through a lot together. And while it was true I'd been judicious with my use of the truth around Ed in the past, those decisions were usually based around when I thought that letting Ed know the truth, the whole truth, and nothing but the truth, would have slowed me down.

And speaking of lying, what was going on with Ed? He'd been holding something back during yesterday's interview, guaranteed, but I wasn't sure yet what that was. Looked him in the eye and tried to read what was floating around back there. He just glared at me.

Good thing I wasn't planning on adding clairvoyance to my list of marketable skills.

"Well?" he said.

I wondered why I was even bothering to think about the angles on this thing; this wasn't my case. Hell, this wasn't a case at all.

Two of the shooters were accounted for and wouldn't bother anyone again, ever.

The third was lying in Parkland walking the fine line between this life and the next.

No-one was in danger at the moment, and I'd missed the only opportunity I had to make a difference while I was standing on the roof the day before.

So I drained my coffee and told Ed the truth.

"Bradley Wright was the third shooter, Ed."

"The hell you say," Ricco said.

"Interesting theory, Rafferty." Ed leaned back in his chair. "Convince me."

So I started to lay it out, then stopped. "Ricco, you'd better take notes, 'cause I'm not coming in to do this again."

He shook his head and blinked at me. Looked at Ed for support, but only received raised eyebrows in return.

As the door was about to close behind him, I cleared my throat. "And another cup of coffee would be appreciated, too."

Ricco gave me the finger.

———

But he did bring more coffee back with his notepad, so I thought about forgiving him. He found another chair hiding under a stack of files in the corner and tried three different positions for relocating the files before happening on one that Ed gave a small nod to.

He perched the legal pad on his leg and the toothpick in the corner of his mouth pointed right at me and never wavered—*Don't mess with me, pal. I'm watchin' you.*

"If we're gonna do this," he said, "we're gonna do it right. What time was it when you heard the first shot?"

"Hell if I know, Ricco," I said. "I didn't stop to make notes." I picked up his sour look and toned it down a notch. "I was drinking coffee, hadn't started any work to speak of … say nine-twenty."

Ricco made another note on the pad. He had neat, and diabolically small, writing. As good as impossible for anyone else to read. Especially upside down.

"What then?"

"I got to the window, then to the roof, looked around, trying to find the source. Couldn't tell where until I heard the next shots. About the time I had the direction pegged, I saw the crowd of kids running through the schoolyard."

"Uh huh." More scratching in his tiny cuneiform. Toothpick leveled at me like a sniper rifle. "Then?"

I recalled all that I had seen from my building, and down at the schoolyard.

By the time I'd walked him and Ed along Jackson and then Elm Street, through the alleyway, past the results of Bradley and the bus trying to occupy the same time and space, and into O'Rileys, I had no more to add.

Ricco finished up with the formalities while I reflexively reached for my pipe.

Dammit.

"Rafferty, we're done here," Ricco said.

"Not yet," Ed said. "Let's say for the moment I believe you about Bradley Wright being one of the shooters. I still wanna know why you didn't think to pick up the phone yesterday and tell me all this then. Or better yet, earlier than that. When you first saw him, for instance."

"First off, Ed, the vandalism done to public phones in the downtown area is scandalous. I think it's time to establish a taskforce to get to the bottom of it."

"Uh huh."

"And, anyway, you made it clear at the schoolyard that you didn't need my help." Ed sucked in a breath and I rolled on before I got showered with a torrent of self-justification. "Truth be told, Ed, I was trying to bring him in when he got hit."

"So, how come you didn't get hit, too?" Ricco looked like he enjoyed the prospect. "You push him in front at the last second to cushion the blow?"

"I didn't have hold of him, smartass. I was about thirty yards back in the alley when he stepped into the street."

Ricco chuckled.

"I'd like to see you trying to catch the kid. Especially in *those* shoes. 'Sides, he was fast. Probably ran track."

"And you still thought it was better for me to find out about this on my own?" Ed said.

"It was already too late. By the time I could have done anything, the paramedics were trying to stop Bradley from leaking into the street drains. What difference would it have made?" I shrugged.

Ed leaned forward and stabbed a finger at me.

"The difference it would have made, *smartass,* is that we would have been on the front foot with this kid and any involvement he may or may not have had in the shooting. We could have been putting the screws to him to find out what actually happened, not playing catch up with our dicks in our hands, like a pack of fucking amateurs. Got it?!"

"Geez, Ed, I'll have to check, but I'm pretty certain I left the force back in 'seventy-one, so I'm not sure why you think you get to bawl me out. But, hell, it's funny, so have at it." Then the caffeine got my system up to full operating temperatures and the penny dropped. "You guys knew this was coming, didn't you?"

"Don't change the subject. You should have let us know about Bradley."

"C'mon Ed. It's me. Those reporters were right yesterday, weren't they? DPD knew about this."

Ricco looked like the front row at a tennis match. Ed gave me ten seconds of eye contact, then decided to let me in. "There was a report made a couple of weeks ago."

I let loose a low whistle. "No wonder you guys are feeling the heat."

He nodded. "You've no idea, Rafferty, but yeah, a neighbor of the Whites called in. Said she overheard the teenager talking with someone about stashing guns and 'shooting up a school.' The desk sergeant who took the call, he recognized the woman, she'd made a few nuisance calls in the past, he thought this was just the latest and so he didn't bother to do anything with it. And now, I'm the one who's gonna be left holding the shit sandwich when the music stops."

I didn't think that was the way the saying went, but it didn't seem like a good time to bring it up.

"But you've got the two kids of the Overcoat Club—"

"That ain't gonna be enough. The mayor is blowing a fuse about this, Rafferty and, consequently, the Chief is too. And you're sitting there telling me that this Bradley kid was one of the shooters."

I nodded.

"And that would give me something for the Chief and the

Mayor that would get them off my back and maybe save my job."

"Why Ed, you don't need to thank me, I'm just doing what any right—"

Ed rolled right over me.

"Which would be great, except I've only got your word that he's one of the bad guys. 'Course, I could live with that if I could put him in a room for a couple hours to soften him up, try to get a confession, or at least a better understanding of what the hell happened on the day but nooo, I can't do that, because he's almost dead. And why? Because you chased him in front of a goddamned bus!"

"You saw it yourself, Ed. Three duffel bags, three shooters. Plus, if he hadn't been trying to get away, I wouldn't have been chasing him. Think about that. I don't know what you want from me. I can't wave my hands and magically bring the kid out of his coma to face judgment."

"I'd settle for being able to put a gun in his hand," Ricco said.

"Check the alley," I said. "He may have dumped it. If not there, then—"

Ed sighed. "Of course, we'll check the alley, Rafferty. And the path you both took between the school and where he got hit. And his locker. And the third duffel. And … and why am I wasting my time telling you all this?"

I didn't know either.

Ed ranted a bit more, Ricco smirked, and then I was free to go.

My Starsky and Hutch valet service didn't arrive for the return trip, so I stepped out DPD's front door and into the center of downtown Dallas.

Buildings sparkled in the sunlight and the trees in Main Street Park beckoned me to sit under them, relax, and listen to the breeze through their leaves. The office was only a couple of blocks away if I was ready to throw myself back into my work, hitting the phones and chasing down leads. The rest of the city could be mine, too. Rush Diner if I wanted coffee and any number of bars for an early drink all within easy walking distance.

Decisions, decisions.

I hailed a cab, went home, and took a nap.

7

I wandered through the rest of the week, accomplishing nothing, just grinding towards normal.

Tuesday and Wednesday were two of the quietest days in Dallas that I could remember and, as far as I could tell, the rest of the country followed our lead.

Some of the less seriously injured were out of hospital, at home and taking the first tentative steps down the long road of rebuilding their lives. Columbus High wouldn't be open for a while to come, so other arrangements had been made for returning students, a bunch of remembrance ceremonies were planned, and there'd be counseling on tap for any and all who wanted to partake.

Funerals for the handful of victims released by the M.E. were being planned.

Vigils were being held. Fundraisers organized.

Side stories sprouted about Bradley Wright, the poor kid who survived the shooting only to be hit by a bus on his walk home. No-one bothered to ask the question why Bradley wasn't at school in the first place.

Gun sales were up.

By the end of the week, news of the Alaskan oil spill crept back in to the news—turned out the boat's skipper had been blind drunk when it hit the reef—traffic began honking outside my window, and people on the street were scowling at each other again. The city was finding itself.

All in all, it seemed like we might be getting back on an even keel. It would take longer for some than others, but the trajectory was upwards.

———

The Mustang shat itself on Thursday morning.

Correction. Shat itself *again*.

I didn't love the car, not in the same way that people who say they love their car do, just found that it was handy to have an old car that I didn't worry about so much when I drove it over things.

That being said, while standing by the side of the road trying to keep my pipe lit in a howling wind, watching the steam curling out from under the hood and waiting for a tow, I may have thought about junking it this time instead of repairing—again—and buying something newer.

At least built in the last decade.

But then how would Peter McLeod, the guy who did all my repair work, feed his family? I couldn't let him down like that.

After listening to the tow-truck driver complain about the heat on the way to McLeod Motors, cooling my heels for an hour in the grease-stained hall closet Peter called a waiting room, and amusing myself by wondering if the *Hustler* center-folds on the wall had fathers who were proud of them, he came in and gave me the good news.

"Gonna need it for a week or two this time, Rafferty."

"And that's the good news?"

Peter took off his *Pennzoil* cap, ran a greasy hand through his hair. "Yeah, I managed to track down a '67 in San Antone that got itself firebombed. The body's a write-off, but my buddy says the engine's okay. I'll get it up here to do the rebuild, but it's gonna take some time. Other than that, I got to get a new one from Ford, and that's gonna be a whole lot more time and money for ya."

"So what's the bad news?" I asked, despite not wanting to be anywhere in the vicinity for the answer.

"Hard to know right now, you unnerstand, until we get all the work done, but prob'ly gonna be fifteen, sixteen hundred bucks. Plus tax, a'course."

"Fuck me, Peter. The car's not worth that much."

"You're telling me. You want a trade-in instead? I could give ya ..." Peter slicked his hair again. "... say three hundred, you wanted to get rid of it. It's still got a few parts I could use."

"So I can spend another thirty-five hundred buying something else? No thanks."

Peter tilted his head. *Your call, Rafferty.*

"But you can help me with something in the meantime."

"Uhhh huhh." Peter suddenly sounded like he preferred to cough up the three hundred bucks and see me walk away.

"I can't be off the road for the next two weeks. You got a loaner?"

"Oh, that all? Shoot, no problem. Not here right now, but you come back in a couple hours, say 'bout three, and I'll have it all ready and waiting for ya."

Peter shot me a smile.

See, good guy like that, I was pleased I'd decided to keep helping him out. Even if it was going to cost me a small fortune.

We shook hands—Peter even rubbed his on a cloth before-hand, so I'd only need a light degrease later—and I headed back out in the general direction of the office.

———

I grabbed the mail from under the slot, looked without much hope for checks and ignored the bills, before I dropped the whole pile into the wastebasket. Set the coffee pot perking and leaned back in the chair to read the newspaper.

Imani Laweles had become the face of the survivors with her tell-all interview starting on page one and continuing on pages two, three, and twenty-nine.

There was more detail and fewer "umms" in this inter-view—one of the benefits of editing—and a smattering of backstory of the home life she was lucky enough to return to, but the main thrust was the same as the TV version on Monday evening.

She was in class when the shooting started, all the students were unsure what to do, then someone decided that they needed to get out, and so they flooded the hallway and made their burst for freedom into the rec-area.

I'd seen it live; I didn't need to read the play-by-play again.

There were pieces on the dead shooters, too. 'No comment' and 'Get the hell off my porch' from the families. Pictures of cops with serious faces hauling bags of who knew what out of the homes, all ready to be cataloged and pawed through downtown as investigators continued their hunt for answers.

The phone rang.

"Rafferty," I said, wedging the receiver in my shoulder.

"Hey, big guy," Hilda said. "You haven't forgotten about the party tonight, have you?"

Shit.

Hilda had teamed up with one of her clients to host a fundraiser for the families of the victims, and I'd scored an invitation by proximity.

"Absolutely not, babe. It's written right here on my desk planner, in black marker with a big red circle around it."

"Liar."

She knew me too well.

"I've got to help with the final setup, so I'll meet you there."

"No problem."

"Seven thirty. Don't be late. Love you."

"You too, babe."

And she was gone.

Looked at my watch, saw that I still had a couple hours before I needed to pick up the loaner from McLeod, and figured I should try to get some work done for the day, so I turned my focus to a little business development.

Called my service, where the gum-snapping voice on the other end only confirmed what I was expecting. "No messages, Mr. Rafferty. And we still haven't received last month's paymen—"

The declining quality of telecommunications these days is outrageous.

I did my secretary thing and got ready to mail the invoice for that hardware store theft job a couple of weeks ago. Who knew, when that four hundred bucks came in, I might be able to retire, move to Mexico, and spend the rest of my days sitting on the beach drinking Coronas.

Right.

Took a moment to think about my other cases.

I worked at it, and it almost took the full sixty seconds.

Aside from Duane and the ongoing Curious Case of the Missing Leg—which didn't take up a whole lot of my time—there weren't any other cases.

So I pulled out a legal pad and started scribbling notes on phone calls I could make to drum up some new clients.

Hell, old clients would do, so long as they paid.

Sid Parker always needed a hand with something or other. But then, those something or others never turned out to be as easy as they sounded. And getting Sid to part with his cash was even harder. Save Sid for later.

The phone rang. Ah hah! Things were looking up already.

"Yeah."

"Mr. Rafferty?"

"I believe he's in the billiards room. I'll have him paged. Who shall I say is calling?"

Turns out that the ladies in the Southwestern Bell collections department don't have much of a sense of humor. Who knew?

Back to the legal pad.

Wrote down Snowy's name.

Scratched out Snowy's name. Going to him cap in hand was not my idea of fun. Oh, I could handle his ego and the song and dance he made about helping me out, but I'd rather save Snowy for when I really needed his resources.

I could check in with Des Bickle, see if he was still having problems with those neighbors.

Uh huh.

Before I realized it, I'd written down Don Sweetham's name. *Repos?* Goddamn it, Rafferty! You're at the point of calling Don and *asking him for repos!* Get a grip. Things aren't that bad.

I was right. Things weren't that bad. And there was something I could do about it right there and then.

I had a nap.

———

The late afternoon sun on my face woke me. I levered myself upright and eased out the kink in my neck as I walked to McLeod's to pick up the car Peter had organized for me.

Got there and wished I hadn't.

"A Pacer? That's your idea of a loaner? An AMC *Pacer*?"

Peter couldn't respond to my indignation; he was too busy laughing.

Tried to ignore him as I got in the clown-mobile and headed out on to South Riverfront Boulevard. Peter was still doubled over in the driveway when I lost sight of him in the rearview mirror.

At least the air conditioning seemed to work. Not that I needed it yet, but good to know in case summer started to bite early.

I drove towards home, thinking that I probably should have had the suit dry-cleaned for Hilda's party, but a quick steam in the shower might work, and doing my best to not look at the reflection of me and the stupid car in the passing storefronts.

8

"You're joking," I said, but, reaching up to feel the swelling around my right eye, I knew she wasn't. Even without a mirror, I could tell that much.

"I only wish I was, Rafferty." Hilda stood in the bedroom doorway, hands on hips, and answered me through tight lips. "You even threw the first punch."

So the pounding in my brain wasn't just from a few too many drinks the previous night.

I shook my head. Bad idea.

Tried, but couldn't recall much from the party.

That sort of thing wasn't my usual scene and I knew Hilda was going to be busy all night schmoozing and getting people to part with their money for a good cause, so I'd loosened my tie soon after we'd arrived and headed straight to the bar.

Least I could do was to offer my respects to the host's excellent taste in scotch.

I was three or four in and having a good conversation with the hired bartender about whether the Cowboys had a chance at the playoffs. He thought the new coach Johnson could make the difference. I'd always been a Landry man though and, as far as I was concerned, we'd wasted our draft pick because there was not a chance in hell that the Aikman kid was ever going to amount to anything.

"Did I get into it with the bartender?"

That didn't sound like me; I'm a fan like anyone else but I didn't care enough to get into a fight about it. At least, I didn't think I did. And the guy had been serving great scotch, so I would have thought I'd have cut him a break on that fact alone.

"No. In fact, you're lucky he was there. I think he was the one who stepped in and stopped security beating you up."

"Wow, I'm sure glad that didn't happen." Reached up and fingered my brow. "So I can assume this wasn't deliberately inflicted. And what do you mean, security? Was I still at the party? Did we go somewhere afterwards?"

"Of course we were still at the party, Rafferty!" Hilda shook her head. "And now I'm going to spend time I don't have smoothing over your little *incident* if I ever want to be able to sell anything to David ever again." She sighed. "I can see it now; he'll talk me all the way back down on that Louis-the-fifteenth-style Duchesse Brisée en Trois. I've been working him up to my price for months, and now I'll have to take a bath on it. But if I know him, it's the only thing that'll get me back on his good side." She turned on her heel.

I got out of bed and stood. Balance was okay, but the sight in my right eye wasn't the best. Shucked on a pair of shorts and followed Hilda out to the living room. She stood in the kitchen, sipping coffee and looking sideways at me. I sat on one of the stools, with the counter between us, and asked, "What the hell happened?"

"You really don't remember?"

Shook my head. Still a bad idea. "It's all pretty hazy."

Hilda sighed.

"You took a swing at one of the guests. You'd already had too much to drink and, apparently, you missed."

"Who was the lucky guy?"

"His name is Richard, he's one of my best customers, which makes two people I've got to make happy this week, but after all that, it turns out you're the lucky one."

"How so?"

"Because Richard is in his late seventies and you'd have probably killed him if you'd connected."

Rafferty's Rule Two: Be lucky.

Rafferty's Rule Three: If you're going to be stupid, see Rule Number Two.

Hilda continued. "By the time I got there, you were mumbling something about a mysterious shooter, Richard's wife Mildred was screaming to high heaven about the drunk attacking her husband, and one of the security guys had already grabbed you around the neck and was dragging you towards the front door."

"Why?"

"I assume to stop you swinging at him a second time."

"No, why would I do something like that?"

"That's what I'd like to know!" Hilda huffed. She didn't often huff, but if she put her mind to it, Hilda could have been world-class. "Last night was meant to be where we could all come together and do something good for the victims of Columbus High. And you had to go and act like ... like an idiot!"

I got up, walked around the counter and wrapped my arms around Hilda. She kept her back to me and stiffened, but I held tough and leaned my head down into her neck. "I'm sorry, babe," I whispered. "I didn't mean to make things tough for you."

She relaxed a little and we stood there for a few minutes before she broke away.

"We can talk more about this tonight, but I've really got to go." She grabbed her bag off the counter. Turned to me, and her eyes were deep and dark. "Will you be okay?"

"I might put a little ice on the eye, but other than that, I'll be fine. Why?"

"Because last night, on the way home, you kept mumbling about calling Cowboy and Mimi and heading down to Parkland Hospital to 'do something' about Bradley Wright."

Huh.

Conjured up a fuzzy memory of the bartender starting to talk about the kid who'd survived the shooting only to get hit by a bus. *It's been kind of hard to miss, what with being the story in the newspapers all week and, hey you're a P.I., maybe that'd be the kind of case you'd have, right?*

I think I'd managed to stall for a while, but then some old guy—the aforementioned Richard, obviously—wandered up, inserted himself into the one-sided conversation and announced that he was taking it upon himself to establish a foundation for the young lad and his family. "They've been through so much, you know," he'd said from underneath a salt-and-pepper toothbrush mustache.

My thoughts after that point were as clear as scrambled eggs, which made sense, if what Hilda said was true.

"Hil—"

"I don't have time to get into this now, Rafferty. I was already going to be busy today, and that was before I had to start working damage control." I sucked in a breath, but she didn't let me get started. "Not now," she said. "I'll fix it. We'll talk later. Just promise me, you won't go and do anything stupid."

I nodded.

"See you tonight." She leaned up and kissed me on the cheek. "I do love you, you big lunk. Sometimes, I don't know why, but I do."

———

I loafed around the house after Hilda left. Thought about heading to the office then dropped that idea like a stolen piece of jewelry, after figuring I could lay around and do nothing just as easily here at home.

Normally didn't answer the phone at home, too many people trying to sell me stuff I didn't want or need, but I was at a loose end, so when it rang I thought, what the hell.

"Good morning," I announced cheerily. "And thank you for calling Acme Surveys. If I could take just ten minutes of your time and ask you a few simple questions—"

"Rafferty?" Ed's voice was wary. "Sounds like you. You finally decide to leave investigating to the professionals? You know they say that telephone sales can be a very rewarding car—"

"What do you want?"

"Not so chipper, huh?" I stayed quiet, didn't want to give him any satisfaction. "Okay then, thought you might like to know that we found the gun in the alley near where the Wright kid was hit."

"You said *the* gun. Not a gun."

Professionals, my ass. My instincts were as sharp as ever.

"That's right, I did. And why I waited a few days to call you. Only took us about twenty minutes to find the piece after you left here the other day. It had been dumped in a hurry, crudely enough that I was surprised it was still there and hadn't been picked up by someone else taking a shortcut through the … anyway, at that point we had *a* gun."

"And?"

"You giving me attitude, Rafferty? I don't have to be sharing this stuff, you know. I could hang up right now f'rinstance an—"

I sighed. "Give me the rest of it, Ed."

He paused. Made me wait.

"Ballistics spent the next two days working on it. Confirmed it this morning. The gun we found in the alley was used in the Columbus High shooting. Specifically, it was the gun used to kill the four vics in the hallway. Slugs pulled out of the bodies are a one hundred percent match."

I leaned back on the sofa.

"He did it, Rafferty. Bradley Wright did it. 'Course we'll have to match the prints on the gun to Bradley—there's a couple of nice partials, which should give us everything we need—but that ain't gonna be a problem. We have to wait until he wakes up to prosecute, but that's all just details."

Blew out a breath.

He wasn't going to get away with it.

He wouldn't be remembered as the unlucky kid who survived two tragedies on the same day.

Richard from last night could keep spending his money on mustache combs instead of establishing the Wright Family Foundation.

And I might be able to believe that, in the end, I did something to help.

"Rafferty?" Ed said. "Still there?"

"Yeah. I'm here."

"I'm not going to tell you that I owe you one. I'm still pissed that you didn't get in touch with us sooner, but ... this is gonna make a big difference. So ... thanks."

"Yeah. What happens now?"

I could hear him shaking his head. "Nuh uh. No chance.

This thing has to be locked down tighter than a drum, so I *can't* discuss what's going on behind the scenes. And that now extends to you too. You need to keep this under wraps until we make a formal statement. Got it?"

"What's the big deal? You've got this kid cold, said it yourself."

"Yeah, we do. But if you think that's all it takes, you've forgotten too much about policing."

I got it. One of the great luxuries of being a P.I. was not having to run the bureaucratic obstacle course with every suspect. Correctly identifying probable cause, obtaining the right warrant from the right judge, making sure the chain of evidence is unbroken and each step is documented and double-witnessed, processing the suspect correctly, and oops, you missed a step, back to the beginning, do not pass go, do not collect two hundred dollars, and by the way the perp now walks because of your fuck up.

It was easier for me. There's the guy. Did he do it? Yeah? Great, now I do what needs to be done. Simple, clean, and you can be in the bar by four.

"Okay, Ed. You can count on me. My thoughts are as a vault. My mouth is locked, and I've swallowed the key. I will not divulge any of the DPD's treasured secrets, no matter how bad the torture is. Unless they tickle me. I'm sorry, Ed, but I can't help it. Tickling is my Achilles' heel. Strangely enough, except for my heel, that's the only place that I'm not tickli—"

I wasn't sure how long ago Ed had hung up, but I expect it had been some time.

Mooched around the house a bit more. The eye was improving, but I lay on the couch with a bag of frozen peas on it just to make sure.

Lay there and thought more about Bradley Wright and the juggernaut of the justice system about to roll right over the top of him. Did he have any idea what was about to happen? His family? They were all in for a world of hurt once the DPD and the DA got up to full speed. Especially with the pressure coming from the Mayor's office.

Sat up and flicked on the TV, and I was swamped with the choices of *Donahue, Sally Jessy Raphael,* or *Geraldo.*

Remembered that's why I didn't watch more daytime television.

Decided to do something better with my time.

Showered, shaved, dressed, and headed downtown to clap eyes on Bradley Wright.

I wanted to see what he was like before Ed got hold of him.

9

wheeled into the parking area behind Parkland Memorial Hospital, only saw the pothole in the driveway at the very last second. Tensed and expected the steering wheel to cleave my thumb off at the knuckle, but the clown car just wallowed in and out of the pothole without the slightest complaint.

Maybe I should ask Peter to replace the shocks too, while he was elbows deep in the Mustang.

I parked, leaned against the fender for a few minutes with a pipe, looked up at the windows of the Dallas County Crime Lab in the adjacent building. Thought about the M.E. and his staff processing all the young bodies from Columbus, each begging to tell their story.

I was running down the steps, when something heavy hit me in the back. I fell down. My face scraped on the concrete. I wanted to get up and run again. I couldn't. I felt cold.

There was this enormous boom to my left. I looked around my locker door, and there was this kid with a gun. I turned to run and it felt like a heavy hammer slammed me in the back twice and I got pushed over onto the floor and I looked up and I could see the class-

room in front of me so I tried to crawl towards it and I was getting closer to it but at the same time it was getting farther away and then my fingers touched the door frame but it looked like they were at the end of a long tunnel and then the tunnel closed up and I couldn't see anything.

I was sitting there against the wall, thinking that my mom would be mad about all the blood on my dress. It was hard to breathe, and I could taste pennies in my mouth. Then this boy lifted a big black gun from under his overcoat and pointed it at me. He gave me a creepy smile and I saw a flash, then nothing.

The sun was trying to break up the clouds, doing a poor job of it. The usual clutch of people huddled outside the hospital's back entrance, enjoying the cold air and a few lungfuls of cigarette smoke before returning to oxygen tanks and beeping monitors.

A larger group milled together near the fence, and I'd have given good odds they were anything but a usual clutch. The painted banners, 'Get well soon, Bradley' and 'We love you, Bradley,' were a dead give-away of their status as hangers-on for one particular Parkland resident. Candles flickered, and flowers and stuffed toys abounded. It sounded like a small bunch of them were singing.

Michael, Row the Boat Ashore?

Good grief.

None of them had the first idea what had really happened Monday morning. How would they react when the truth finally came out? Would they be embarrassed that they supported a stone-cold killer who almost got away with it?

Found myself almost on my way over to let them in on a few home truths when I noticed a woman in a brown overcoat waving at me from the far side of the Bradley Wright Fan Club. She began to skirt the crowd, headed in my direction and I realized who it was. Gave her a head shake and a wave, bashed the dead ashes out on my boot heel, and headed for the front doors of the hospital.

———

Surgical ICU looked surprisingly innocent. The usual hustle and bustle of doctors and nurses keeping their charges alive but other than that it was relatively normal.

No cops on guard near any of the beds, no detectives huddled in the waiting room, comparing notes and planning their next investigative move.

Quiet. Ordinary.

Bradley Wright was anything but.

He lay on the bed, pin-cushioned with tubes and monitors. I didn't know what any of the machines could tell me about his condition, but the fact that the nursing staff weren't hovering over him or calling for a crash cart seemed to be positive signs for his continued existence.

That said, he was a long way from being the kid who had stood in the alleyway and yelled at me to shoot him.

He was alive and breathing, but there seemed to be no signs of life detectable by anything other than the cacophony of monitors surrounding him. And, based on the extent of bandages wrapped around his head, I figured he wouldn't be ready to make conversation for a long time.

A woman—red-haired and slim—sat by his bedside. She held his hand in both of hers, looked up at the visible portion of his face, and whispered to him while her thumb circled the back of his pale hand.

I leaned against the wall near the doorway and thought about what the hell I'd expected to achieve by coming here. Especially now that I knew the truth.

He was guilty. He might survive.

And after a couple of minutes of what passed for intro-spection, that was still all that I had.

So what?

Ed, Ricco, and everyone else who could get a ride on that train, were headed in Bradley's direction and they'd all make sure he got what he deserved. The DPD would have the weight and talents of the DA's office behind them and what-ever resistance Bradley and his family could dredge up at the time would be no match.

There wasn't a version of the coming story where I would play anything more than a forgotten chorus member. Like the kid in the school play who shouts, "Look! Here they come!" and then scampers off-stage so the main characters can deliver their lines, I'd already done my job. I gave Bradley to Ed and now he could take care of the rest.

"Oh, excuse me."

The harried man hadn't actually hit me with the large bag he was carrying into the ICU, but he apologized anyway. I tilted my head—*Don't worry about it*. He gave me a weak smile and walked to the unoccupied side of Bradley's bed. Reached across and gave the red-haired woman a rub on her shoulder. She looked up and gave him a tired smile.

He pulled up a chair and sat carefully, maneuvered the bag under the chair between his legs. Said something to the woman. She shook her head. He looked back at me and drib-bled another smile. I decided it wasn't a weak smile, just an extremely tired one.

We all waited.

Phones rang. Machines hissed and beeped. Nurses squeaked their way across the linoleum. Doctors looked at charts and made their pronouncements. Loved ones whis-pered, cooed, and sobbed.

I went looking for coffee.

———

I was seated in a bank of hard plastic chairs and sipping at coffee that was truly awful, when the harried man stepped into the hallway. He fed some change into the vending machine and waited for the paper cup to fill.

"You'll regret it," I said.

He turned to me. "I'm sorry?"

I lifted my cup. "Not sure how they get away with calling this coffee. Black, yes. Hot, yes. Liquid, yes. And yet, coffee it is not."

Confusion played over his face, then he seemed to come to the conclusion that I wasn't threatening him, just making social commentary. "We're not talking to reporters."

"Huh?"

He turned his back, fed another round of quarters into the machine. "I said, we're not talking to reporters."

I laughed. "You think I'm a reporter?"

He shrugged.

"A guy can't sit in an uncomfortable hospital seat drinking bad coffee without getting mistaken for a reporter? What's the world coming to?"

"Good question."

"You're Bradley Wright's dad."

Turned to face me. "How'd you figure?"

"Saw you in there. Near his bed."

"His uncle, actually. You sure you're not a reporter?"

"Sure as I can be." I stood. Held out my hand. "Rafferty."

"Ray. Ray Wright."

"How's he doing?"

"Uh, he's stable. That's about all we know at the moment." He gave another tired smile, looked like it might be the last one he had left, grabbed both cups of coffee from the dispenser. "I'd better get this back to Charlene. Good to meet you."

I saluted him with my cup and watched him disappear back toward his nephew. Sat on my duff, finished my so-called coffee.

All right, it was time to get the hell out of there and do… well, anything else.

As I stood to toss my cup in the trash, footsteps approached from behind and I turned to see the red-haired woman ten feet away, arms crossed against her chest, paper coffee cup still in hand.

"Mr. Rafferty?"

"Uh huh."

"I'm Charlene Wright." She uncrossed her arms, stuck out her hand, and stepped forward. "Bradley's mother. Raymond told me you were out here."

I'd only been planning to put eyes on Bradley, not get into a conversation with his mother but I thought, why not spend a bit of time chatting to the progenitor of evil. Since I had nothing else on for the afternoon.

I really needed to rethink using that as a guiding principal.

We shook. She had a firmer grip than I expected.

Five and half feet or so tall, a bit hippy but carried her weight well, and she looked like she took care of herself. Aerobics, Jazzercise, something similar. She wore her hair out which paired well with the understated makeup, and soft color on her nails.

Her dress and shoes weren't couture, but she wasn't picking through the bins at Goodwill.

Simple gold hoop earrings the only jewelry.

If I had to make a prediction, I'd have said working middle-class. A small three-bedroom ranch in, say, Lower Greenville.

"How's he doing?" I asked.

She let loose a big breath and rolled her head. Her neck cracked.

"He's alive, thankfully," she said. "Still in a coma, and I know that's what the doctors say is the safest thing right now, but I'd give almost anything to be able to talk to my boy again."

Before I knew what I was doing, I gestured, offering Charlene a seat. She took it with a small nod of thanks, and I eased back into a chair one over.

"It's so good of you to come down to check on Bradley. Especially with everything that must be going on at the moment. I can't even begin to imagine how you're coping with all this."

"Come again?"

"Well, I imagine it must be terrible down at the school right now, with so much to do, and probably not even any time for you to grieve."

"Huh?"

"You're one of Bradley's teachers, right? I don't remember seeing you at school, you sure don't look like a teacher, and now that I think about it, I can't remember Bradley ever mentioning a Mister Rafferty, but if you're not a teacher, then …"

She rose and, although looking equally as drained as Ray, her eyes flashed a look of determination that tiredness alone would not be capable of extinguishing. I'd seen that same look in Hilda's eyes from time to time, and the message was unmistakable—*Mamma Lion is here. Do not fuck with Mamma Lion.* "If you're another reporter," she hissed, "I already told your *colleagues*, I have nothing to say." She turned on her heel.

"Wait." I should have just let it go, but the word was out of my mouth before I knew it. She paused, turned, but didn't sit. "I'm not a reporter. Or a teacher. I'm a P.I."

"Oh, so you're *investigating* my son! It's not bad enough that he's lying in hospital in a *coma*, that you need to come sniffing around like ... like ..."

"No, nothing like that," I said. "I was in the vicinity when Bradley got h— when the accident happened."

Charlene shifted her weight. Raised one eyebrow. "That still doesn't tell me how you know Bradley."

"The cops interviewed me, after the accident, and I heard them mention his name."

"So? There's plenty of people who know Bradley's name, now that he's been in almost every paper. Just because he got hit by a ... by a ... by a bus."

That undid her and she slumped back into the seat, pulling out a tissue, pressing it to her eyes. I sat, let her do what she needed to do. Nothing I could offer anyway.

"What's his prognosis?" I tried.

She sniffed. "Like you care."

She was right. I didn't really care but, despite Bradley's actions, I wasn't unfeeling to her pain. Remembered watching my mother go through the anguish of losing a daughter, and I didn't expect the parent-child connection changed depth no matter what said child had done.

I mean, it was possible even that Hitler's mother loved him. In her own way.

Charlene dabbed at her eyes. Turned to me.

I said I wasn't unfeeling to her pain, not that she somehow got a free pass because of it. So I opened my mouth, ready to unload. Let her in on a few home truths about her son. What he'd done—what I'd watched him do—and the city-wide repercussions because of it. The dead kids, the broken families, the—

I don't know what made me stop. The way she looked at me—hopeful and oblivious—or the image of Ed in the back of my mind, knowing what he would say and do if I let slip things I shouldn't.

But I did stop, and that left me with nothing to say.

Her look of hope turned to one of confusion and I scrambled.

"I'm here on a completely different matter, Charlene. It's got nothing to do with Bradley."

"Really?"

"Really and truly."

She tried a smile and, in better times, it looked like it might have been a winner, but this one played on her lips for only a second and then fluttered away. "I can't tell you how much of a relief that is. It's just so hard right now. There's nothing I can do, not while he's still unconscious. But, I've heard that people in comas can tell what's going on around them, they can hear things, so I want to be with him as much as I can. I want him to know that he's not alone."

"Uh huh."

I'd started the afternoon just wanting to get eyes on the surviving school shooter, get some nod of confirmation that he wasn't going anywhere. That he wouldn't almost get away again. Now I found myself in conversation with mother of said shooter who, by first appearances anyway, was not at all who I would have been expecting.

Belligerent. Overbearing. Angry and aggressive. Chip on her shoulder.

I know that stereotypes are just that, and never a hundred percent accurate, but hell, they exist for a reason, and I would not have been surprised to find Bradley's mother—and those of the other two shooters, for that matter—to be easily fitted with one or all of these.

Not Charlene Wright.

She continued in her soft, almost sing-song voice.

"The doctors say they'll keep him in the coma for as long as they can, letting the swelling on his brain reduce as much as possible. They say it's the best way to avoid the potential for brain … for brain damage."

She teetered on the edge then and, just for few seconds, sobbed to herself. Fished another Kleenex out of her sleeve and blew her nose. She looked back towards the doorway to ICU. "Thanks so much for coming to check on Bradley. I'm sure he can feel the support he gets, somehow anyway, and the more people he has in his corner, the more likely it is that he'll pull through."

She forgot why I was there, reached across the empty chair between us and grabbed my hand between hers. Looked me in the eye.

"I mean it Mr. Rafferty. I thank you and I know Bradley does, too."

———

I headed back to the street when Charlene Wright turned back to "be with her boy". I perched my butt on the Pacer's fender, ignored the Bradley Wright Support Group, and fired up another pipe.

Just as I had it blazing away nicely, starting to settle my nerves and overpower the dead not-coffee taste in my mouth, a voice floated over my shoulder.

"Hey, Rafferty. Long time, no see. How ya doin'?"

I turned and smiled despite how I was feeling. "Monica. Yep. Been a while."

Monica Gallo was a reporter for the Dallas Morning News. Originally from New York, and so far keeping her hard-talking ways from being softened by the south, she'd made a name for herself by uncovering, and then reporting on, a scandal in the Mayor's office a year or so earlier. That it involved a highly placed politician, an underage prostitute, and drugs bought with public money made it front page material for nearly two weeks.

Not a bad effort given that at the time she was the arts and music reporter.

That little story gave her the cred she'd needed to demand a transfer to the crime desk, and we'd bumped into each other more than a few times when her stories and my cases crossed paths.

Five foot two, bright red lips, dangling earrings, and wrapped in a brown overcoat, Monica still looked like she should be covering gallery openings and who the latest new bands were, rather than dealing with the same elements of society that littered my path.

"What are you doing here, Monica? This isn't exactly the crime beat."

"Nup. But my editor wants to keep the Columbus High story as close to the front page as possible and the Wilson and McKinley families have gone to ground. I can't get nothin' outta them right now."

"Ain't no hill for a high stepper like you."

She flashed me a bunch of teeth. "Nup. I'll get something in the end but, in the meantime, Bradley Wright's the best I got. Besides, still beats the hell out of writing *another* story about a West Dallas shooting gallery."

"Uh huh." Couldn't fault the logic on that thinking.

"And maybe there's something more interesting here, anyway."

"What might that be, pray tell?"

"Well, for one, what the hell is Dallas's finest P.I. doing

here? Visiting some no-name high schooler injured in an accident? No offense, Rafferty, but that sort of sentimental bullshit
don't sound like you."

"Thanks, Monica. It's good to see you've finally recognized my professional standing within the community." She
gave me a wink. "But, given the responsibility that such
stature carries, is it really too much to think that I might just
be concerned for the kid?"

"Yep."

"Ouch. That hurts."

"What can I say, Rafferty? You might not like it, but I'll
never lie to ya. Now, whaddya got for me?"

I looked over her head to where the Bradley gang were
now running cheers. "One, Two, Three - WE LOVE YOU
BRADLEY, GET BETTER SOON!" Thought about the kid they
were cheering for. About the twenty innocent people killed,
the sixteen trying to rebuild their lives, and the countless
others who wouldn't ever be the same again.

Thought about Ed. *"Keep your mouth shut, Rafferty."*

Thought about Monday morning, when I should have
been basking in a mid-morning nap, but instead was standing
on a roof watching a bunch of innocent kids get slaughtered.

"C'mon, Rafferty. You know I can smell it on ya."

I looked down at Monica.

"Off the record, right?"

She nodded. Once.

"I mean way, way off."

Monica smiled like a hyena who'd just laid eyes on a
wounded wildebeest, and I thought maybe I should just keep
my mouth shut.

Shoulda, coulda, woulda.

10

Monday morning again.

Maybe I could get this one right.

It looked promising for a while: coffee, the paper, warm sun on my back, then the phone rang and downhill we went.

I grabbed the receiver. "Rafferty."

"Are you sure you know what you're doing?"

"Hey, Hil. I've been using a pocketknife to clean my fingernails for nearly forty years, so thanks for your concern but I'm fairly certain I know what I'm doing. It's not really that hard."

"I meant the story in the paper." I could picture her frown. "Monica Gallo?"

"Oh, that."

Monica's story splashed its way across the front page of the *Dallas Morning News* laying on my desk, casting new light on the movements of a certain teenager who survived the Columbus High shooting, only to get clobbered by a public transit vehicle later in the day.

She'd kept my name out of it, but that particular wrinkle

hadn't stopped Monica from picking up the threads of the story and running with it. The bold headlines told a very different story to that of the previous week's reporting.

WHAT WAS COLUMBUS HIGH STUDENT RUNNING FROM?

She'd gone further than asking big leading questions, getting her hands on the attendance registers and an unnamed source in the DPD to verify that Bradley Wright was not confirmed at school before the shooting. It didn't take a lot of column inches to draw the parallel between the two deceased shooters whose names also hadn't been marked off in class.

But, unlike the other gun-toting kids, Bradley's body wasn't located in the school grounds after the shooting either, and the story that fact told screamed louder than any headline.

EYEWITNESS SEES BUS VICTIM WITH GUN AT SCHOOL.

Monica reported the scenes that I'd seen from the rooftop accurately enough. The writing had a breathless, 'Can you believe this is happening?!' tone which I thought was beneath her and detracted from the quality of her investigative work, but I wasn't the city editor, so who cared.

"Yes, that. You gave her Bradley Wright's name, didn't you?"

None of this was new information. It had taken a little while the previous week to explain to Hilda that I'd witnessed more than just the massacre the previous Monday. Had, in fact, identified Bradley Wright as one of the three shooters and then been instrumental in making sure he was standing in the middle of the street when the 10:17 to Shreveport came through.

She was sympathetic as ever and did her best to make me feel as though none of it was my fault.

It helped. A little.

"You're pretty good at detective work, you know that? Got a gut feel for it. I pick up a couple more cases and you could come on full-time."

She sighed. I returned serve.

"I watched him do it, Hil. I stood there, and I watched him wander around the school with a gun during the massacre. Plus, the cops have proved that the gun he dumped in the alleyway killed four of the vics."

Another sigh.

"Tell me, babe, what else should I have done? He did it. Ed's gonna get him. Monica's story doesn't change that. All it does is let people know that he's not the innocent little boy who just happened to be in the wrong place at the wrong time."

"But—"

"But nothing, Hil. He deserves everything that's coming his way."

"I'm not going to debate that with you. But I don't see why you have to be the one stirring the pot. Just let Ed and the cops do whatever they're going to do and read about it after the fact."

"Ah, yes, but what a boring life it would be without a little pot stirring."

"I guess ..." Hilda's voice got faint. "What? Okay. I'll be right there." She came back to the phone. "I've got to go, hon. David's just arrived and I'm still trying to smooth things out with him after ... Anyway, I'll call you later."

And she was gone.

Turned back to the paper to pick up the rest of Monica's story.

DPD HAD ADVANCE WARNING OF SHOOTING.

Monica's unnamed source in the department had done more than just tell her who was marked in class and who wasn't. The story was pretty much the same as Ed had told me—a desk clerk received a call from a concerned neighbor and discounted it rather than passing it on. Coming hard on the heels of the inquiries from the TV reporters, and with more veracity than a hastily hurled question on a doorstep press conference, this would cause Ed a whole bunch of grief.

I grabbed at the phone as soon as it jangled, and the receiver only barely cleared the cradle before my favorite lieutenant was letting me have it with both barrels.

"The fuck do you think you're doing, Rafferty?" I assume he didn't want me to answer, because I didn't have time to draw breath before he was off and running again. "I can't believe I was stupid enough to think you actually understood how sensitive this thing is and that you'd stick to your word. I won't be making that goddam mistake again, that's the goddamn truth. Just what the hell goes on in that brain of yours? Do you have any idea—any at all—how much grief your little chat with that reporter is going to cause me?"

It sounded like he was finished.

"Did someone get out of bed on the wrong side this morning, Ed?"

And he was off again.

I let him rail while I poured another cup of coffee, leaned back in the chair, and hoisted my feet onto the desk.

When all I could hear was heavy breathing, I gave it a couple more seconds to be sure then tried again.

"Why decide to pick on me? Anyone could have given Monica that story."

"Don't even try, Rafferty. I'm not that stupid."

He was right; I changed tack.

"Fair enough. But where's the harm, Ed? So the city knows the kid isn't the bright and shining light of innocence they thought he was. Big deal."

"I'll give you 'big deal', Rafferty. Now that you've opened your trap and the news is out in the open, it's gonna be twice as hard for us to do what we need to do. I've got daily briefings with the mayor and I have to waste my time dealing with press conferences and reporters; all of which I wouldn't have to be doing if I could be building our case nice and quietly. In the way that I remember specifically telling you I wanted it."

I drew breath, but he rolled on.

"Second, the boy's parents will no doubt be working their way through potential lawyers, if they haven't already retained someone, which is guaranteed to slow me down even further once they get involved and start to gum up the works."

I tried again. Nope, not this time either.

"And lastly. But by no means least, the heat that is coming down about that call from the neighbor is … is … well, fuck it, you wouldn't understand any—"

"Ed," I said before he'd finished. "For what it's worth, that wasn't me. I don't know where Monica got that from, but I'd be looking around your own department before you start kicking my ass about that one."

"Yeah, I know."

Now that Ed had got it off his chest, he sounded resigned, defeated even.

"Cheer up, Ed. It's a slam dunk. The kid did it. You've got the gun. No matter what gets thrown at you, you're holding all the cards. I imagine you'll have officers on hand ready to arrest the kid soon as he sets foot outside the hospital."

"Already done."

"What?"

"Uh huh. You tipped our hand with that story, Rafferty. I just got back from the hospital where we arrested Bradley Wright. His mother didn't seem too pleased about it, in case you were worried."

"He's come out of the coma?" I asked.

"Nope. Still completely out of it. You know, Rafferty, I thought I'd already seen it all, but this is the first time I've ever had to arrest someone who was unconscious. And supervise him being moved into a secure room. All while the hospital staff told me how much this might set back his recovery and his mother took turns calling me names, some of which I hadn't heard before. So thanks for adding that to the list of things I can say that I've done. I owe you one."

"The DA's going to prosecute? While he's still out of it?"

"Nope, that's not an option. Still, she's gonna convene a Grand Jury. The kid don't need to be awake for that."

"So you've got everything in hand, Ed. Continue to be of stout heart my valiant crime-fighter! Thou will vanquish thy foe with one mighty sw—"

"Sometimes I don't know why I even speak to you. Most times, actually." Ed disconnected the call, more gently than he started it, so I felt like I'd done some good for the morning.

Time for a nap.

———

Hilda was naked, and I was too, and the bedhead was knocking against the wall making a helluva noise when I finally woke up.

The knocking was actually coming from the office door and I bet myself when it opened, I would be disappointed to find the reason not nearly as enticing as the dream.

"Come in," I gurgled.

It sounded more like *Cwwm unn*. How can someone's mouth taste that bad?

The door swung inwards and Charlene Wright walked in with a young man I didn't recognize.

She dredged up a short smile from somewhere, headed for the nearest visitor chair, and didn't even flinch at the layer of dust on it before sitting down and looking me square in the eye. Another attempted smile. She looked exhausted.

The guy in the three-piece suit and tie pin remained standing behind Charlene and hit me with a one-two punch of designer dimples and a thousand bucks of teeth whitening.

I blinked the sleep out of my eyes and tried to get my brain to engage first gear.

Charlene began to open her mouth, and I wondered what she would lead with after our meeting in the hospital hallway. She didn't get that far.

"Mr. Rafferty," the suit said. "Paul Eindhoven, Attorney at Law. I believe you've met my client, Charlene Wright."

I nodded once. "In passing, counselor. It's not like we've had fondue parties."

He frowned, shook his head, then reignited his zinger of a smile and continued.

"Well, undoubtedly you know her son, Bradley Wright. The Columbus High School student who was struck by the bus last week."

It wasn't a question, so I didn't answer.

"What you may not be aware of is that Bradley has now been placed under arrest by the DPD, on suspicion of murder in connection with the shooting that took place at Columbus High."

If this guy kept talking in statements, I might never get a chance to speak. Sounded fine to me. Then he went and ruined it.

"Charlene needs your help and wants to engage your services— "

"Okaaay." I had no idea where this was going. Judging by the look on Charlene's face, she knew the direction we were headed, and was eagerly anticipating a successful arrival at our destination.

"… for the purposes of investigation and protection."

Decided to speed things so we could get this over with and I could get back to my nap.

"Paul," I said. "I know lawyers get paid by the minute but we're on my time here. Cut to the chase."

Charlene looked like she was ready to jump in, but Paul grabbed another smile and tilted his head. "Well, since that outrageous and slanderous story in the paper this morning, the mood surrounding Bradley's plight has changed. Charlene was close to being physically assaulted by a crowd as she left the hospital this morning, and when she returned to her hous—"

"No dice."

"—to her house …" Charlene's eyes widened about the same time that Paul's brain caught up with what I was saying. "What? Mr. Rafferty, you need to understan—"

"Paul. I already understand plenty. I get why both she and the boy need protection. Why do you think the cops have him squirreled away in the hospital? And I do protection work. Sometimes. In this case however, I won't. Not after what Bradley did."

"How did you know …?" Charlene started, and then changed tack. "I thought you were on Bradley's side."

Paul talked right over the top of her. "That's what you need to investigate."

There it was. Not sure why I didn't see it coming earlier.

"Not a chance in hell," I said, working hard to keep my

voice level as I put the pieces together. I turned my attention to Charlene. "Forget your son. He's gone."

"You don't understand," Paul tried. "Charlene needs you to find out—"

"The cops are all over it, Paul. There's nothing to investigate."

"Yes, Mr. Rafferty, there is." Charlene shored herself up and weighed in, and although she kept her voice level, I could see the mother lioness stalking underneath the surface. "Bradley didn't do what the newspapers say he did. When the police arrested him this morning, they told me to get a lawyer. I did that. Then I thought I could do something even better. You're an investigator, right? You can prove Bradley is innocent."

I sighed. This story was old enough to be a classic. Every parent wants to think their children incapable of such horror but, as Cowboy says, "wanting sumpin don't make it so."

"Charlene." I took a breath. "What I didn't tell you the other day, is that I saw him on the day of the shooting. I watched your son walk around the schoolyard of Columbus High, with the other shooters, while carrying the gun that killed four people. If he ever wakes up, he's toast."

Paul narrowed his eyes. Charlene shuddered, clenched her jaw and took a breath. "You must have seen wrong. Bradley would never—"

"Whoah. You walk in to my office, ask me for help and then call me a liar?"

"I'm not calling you anything," she said, without breaking eye contact. "I know what you must think, Mr. Rafferty."

I was about to correct her of that misguided notion but she headed me off before I could get started.

"Let me guess, you figure Bradley is a bad kid who did this terrible thing and, as his mother, I simply don't want to believe it. In fact, I'm probably to blame. I'm either a religious fundamentalist or devil worshipper. I used to beat Bradley, burn him with cigarettes, lock him in closets. That explains, of course, why he was moody and withdrawn his whole life. He was obviously a time bomb waiting to explode, but I didn't see any of the signs. Perhaps I missed them, perhaps I didn't care, all I know is that Bradley wouldn't hurt a fly. I'm as shocked as anyone." She paused for breath, held my eyes. "Do I have that more or less right?"

"A little heavy-handed with the living-room psychoanalysis," I said. "Otherwise, you're on the money."

"That's not how things were," she said. "I know you expect me to say that, but it's the truth." I took a breath, she continued. "Bradley wasn't perfect. Neither was I, as a parent." She sniffed and slid a Kleenex out of her sleeve. "No-one is. But not being perfect doesn't mean you suddenly snap and start killing people."

"Who knows what it is that makes people do stupid and crazy things," I said. "I've been doing this for a helluva lot of years and I've still got no idea why anyone would do something like this."

Charlene glared at me but remained silent. She'd said her piece.

Paul said, "Don't you want to find out?"

"Nope."

Okay, maybe that wasn't entirely true. Part of me did want to know what the hell went on at the schoolyard that day, and the moths in my wallet could do with something to eat before the ASPCA came around to take me away for moth abuse, but it was another Monday and I'd be damned if I didn't finish this one better than last week, so none of the other stuff mattered right then.

Paul took another swing at it. "This is what you do, Mr.

Rafferty. Bradley is innocent and the evidence is out there. It just needs someone like you to find it."

I stared at him. "Not gonna happen."

"So there's nothing we can do," Paul said, "to convince you to take the case?"

"First of all, it's not a case, it's a last-ditch rearguard action with no possibility of success," I said. "And second, even if there was a chance to find some mysterious *evidence*, I can't think of what you could possibly offer to make it worth my while. Unless you happen to be carrying the deed to a 45-foot sailboat with my name on it in that fancy briefcase of yours."

Paul shook his head. "Wha—"

"Forget it. No, there's nothing you can do."

Paul eyed me for a few more seconds, reached down and picked up his briefcase. "Charlene." She stood and followed him to the door, watching me all the way with a face like thunder.

Their footsteps echoed in the stairway as I sat and thought about the morning so far. Yeah, things had been rough with Ed, but we'd work things out. Besides, I'm not sure what I'd do if Ed wasn't having a crack at me from time to time. Good to know that he helped keep me sharp.

And I was glad to see the back of Bradley and the whole Columbus High mess. I'd watch from the sidelines as the victims got justice and Bradley what he deserved, along with the rest of the city.

Not sure what my next case would be or where it would come from. It'd be handy if it was sooner rather than later, in light of my current fiscal situation, but I couldn't do anything about that at the moment.

So I went and had lunch.

11

t was three days later while I was sitting in the office, coffeed and smoked out, already done with the paper, and almost at the point where I was considering doing something about the cobwebs and the dust, when they came and tried again.

A curt knock, and I didn't even get a chance to answer before the door swung open and Paul Eindhoven ushered Charlene Wright through to assume the same position as seventy-two hours earlier.

"Paul. Charlene," I said. "Did you get lost on the way out? I should have mentioned that you turn *left* at the bottom of the stairs to get to the street. I hope you haven't spent the last few days in the furnace room."

Paul was still in the act of placing his briefcase on the floor when that percolated through his brain, and he gave me a tight-lipped glare. He nodded at Charlene.

"Mr. Rafferty," she said. "We ... I ... I'm here to ask you to reconsider taking on my case. Bradley's case."

"And why exactly do you think this conversation will be any different from the one we had on Friday?"

"I ... I don't know." She flicked a glance at Paul. "Paul thought ... I thought ...."

Paul decided she wasn't doing it right. "We're hoping to appeal to your better nature."

I couldn't help it. I laughed. Loud.

Charlene gave a start and Paul returned to his glaring approach while I ran myself down. "Boy howdy, you really didn't do your homework on me, Paul. Thanks. I needed that. One of the funniest things I've heard in a long time."

"Hmmph. Nevertheless," he said, "Bradley needs your help. He—"

"He needs a good neurosurgeon, not a P.I."

"—he did not do what the media are accusing him of, and he needs a good investigator to uncover the truth and clear his name."

"Why?"

"Why what?"

"Why does he need that? I've got good odds on him not coming out of the coma, so what's the point?"

"The truth, Mr. Rafferty."

"Oh. The truth. Well, why didn't you say so in the first place? Of course I'll do it."

Charlene beamed and I felt like an ass. "Really?"

"No."

Hope, confusion and fear swirled on Charlene's face. She sniffed and fished a Kleenex out from the sleeve of her blouse. That was the third time I'd seen her do that, which made me wonder why women use their clothing as a storage space, when they also carry big-ass purses. Surely there'd be room for a Kleenex or two.

So much for my pettifogging, Charlene had shored herself up again and was talking.

"Paul and I talked after our last meeting and he thought it

might change your mind if you spent a little bit of time getting to know me. See who I am, and just maybe find out more about Bradley. I didn't think it would make a difference and it looks like I was right. In all the times we've met, you haven't asked a single question about my son." She took a breath. "I told you this would be a waste of time, Paul. Mr. Rafferty probably doesn't care for anyone except himself. We should just go."

Paul didn't move, but his eyes narrowed ever so slightly.

I wasn't about to be guilt-tripped into a case, never mind that this was a non-case. I saw the kid with a gun. Point A. Other kids were dead and injured. Point B. I didn't need any help drawing the line of shortest distance between those two.

But, just to be thorough—because it seemed like the professional thing to do—I took a breath and thought about the options in front of me.

I could rant and rave again about all the dead kids and tell them both to get their asses out of my office and not show up here again. That approach had bonus points for being quick.

I could lie; sympathize with them, and say I was too busy to take on new cases. They'd see through that one pretty quick, I figured.

Running a distant third—and I mean dust-cloud-over-the-horizon-distant—was pulling out a fresh legal pad and getting them to cough up a retainer. I couldn't see what good that would do for anyone.

Although it had bonus points for being the fiscally responsible option.

I bypassed all of those and led with the truth.

I did, however, make a mental note to start culling such ridiculous behavior before it got me into trouble.

"Charlene. Despite what you think, I'm not unfeeling to your situation. I can guess that it's a difficult time." She forgave the understatement and nodded. "But the fact is your son, with his gun-toting friends, killed or injured thirty-six innocent people. That's a bunch of other families who feel as bad as you do right now."

Her breath hitched and she extracted another Kleenex.

"Add to that the thousands of other people hurting because of what the boys did. Have you been past the school? The road is almost closed because of the flowers and tributes and vigil—"

"Stop it," Paul said. "Just stop. Really? Taunting? I'd have thought—"

"Grow up, Paul. I'm only highlighting the repercussions of what her son and his friends did. Even though it's patently obvious to everyone but you two."

"But Bradley didn't—" Charlene said.

"Yes, he did. I watched him—"

"Listen to me, Mr. Rafferty! Bradley didn't know those other kids."

That denial was new information, but that didn't mean it carried more weight. "And you know that for an absolute fact, do you?" I said. "You know everything that your son did? Saw every move that he made?" She didn't break eye contact. Neither did I. "If that's the case, then you would have been standing there, watching him running around the school with a fucking gun. Like I had to!"

I'm not sure when I'd got to my feet, only knew that I was standing about the same time I noticed my palm stinging from slapping it on the desk.

Paul had taken a half step to get between me and Charlene. She stood before he could get all the way there, head held high. "Leave it, Paul. I don't know why we bothered to come back. He's not going to change his mind."

"Took you long enough."

Charlene made it to the door before Paul moved again. She looked back at me. "Well, we ... I'm not ready to give up. Bradley needs someone willing to fight for him. And if you won't, I'll find someone who will."

Round two of the pissed-off-non-client-exit-sequence.

This time though, Charlene hit me with a look of pity, not anger.

That was worse.

———

I'd take a whole month worth of pitying looks from Charlene Wright over the telephone call I got from Peter McLeod twenty minutes later.

"It's going to be *how much?*"

"Turns out that engine my buddy had was hot," Peter said, "and not just from the firebomb you unnerstand. Heh."

"That's not my problem, Peter."

"Well then, what you 'spect me to do, Rafferty? I'm jus' tryin' to help you out, gosh darn it. Spent three hours on the phone yesterday—time I don't got to waste—finding another motor for ya, and I know I ain't gonna get paid for that time. I did track one down, but it's gotta come all the way from Georgia. Was another'n in Mobile, but I don' trust the guy, he'd tell me it's perfect then it'd get here and I'd find it's got a twisted crankshaft and then we're both up shit creek."

That was the most words I'd heard Peter say in one conversation for a lot of years. While I did trust his judgment, my bank balance hated his commitment to doing things right.

"Tell me again, Peter. Slowly this time, and I'll make sure I'm sitting down."

"Well, it ain't done, the motor ain't even here yet, but with the extra cost of this one and the shipping, I figger closer to two grand than I firs' told ya. Plus tax, a'course."

"Of course," I parroted. Shit and damn. That's not money I had laying around, not even close.

"You want me to tell the guy in Georgia not to bother, come 'round and pick up your car?"

No, but then neither did I want to be on the hook to Peter for another two thousand bucks. It's just a car, I told myself, but it was handy for driving over things and not caring too much while I went about it.

"Hells bells, Peter, I really don't have an option here. No, go ahead and get it done. But. Nothing fancy, I just need it workable, no more."

"I know, I know. Boy, you make deadbeats look like the last of the big spenders, you know that?"

"It's a gift. And speaking of gifts …."

Peter let loose a big sigh. "Shoot Rafferty, I'd love to let you put it on the tab but … Aw hell, now you got me stuck between a rock and a hard place. I don' wanna say no since it's you but it's alreddy too high and I can't afford to carry it forever."

"It's not forever, Peter. I paid you three hundred last month."

"It was only two hundred, Rafferty. And it was two months ago. And it was nowhere near making a dent in what you owe me."

"Huh."

"You know, I appreciate the work you done for me and the family over the years, Rafferty, but I gotta look after meself, too."

Sounded like neither of us had anything more to say.

Peter sighed again.

"Tell you what I'll do, Rafferty. I'll get the motor in, and I'll do the work, so it's all ready for ya, but I'm gonna have to keep the car till you can pay. I'll carry the rest you got owing, but I'm gonna need this job paid for."

"Fuck, Peter. I can't be without a car, and I sure as shit don't have the money laying around. I'd pay you if I did."

"I know, I know you would, and I'm not gonna leave you without a car. I'll keep the 'Stang till you can pay for it, and you can use the Pacer in the meantime."

"The Barnum & Bailey clown-mobile?"

"Best I can do."

I knew Peter was doing me a favor, but I still didn't have to fucking like it.

"Okay, Peter. I get it."

"And don't worry, I'm not gonna sell your car out from under you. Wouldn't do that to someone with such fine taste in vehicles. You know, I was only thinking the other day I couldn't recall why I took your business in the first place."

"The way I remember, it was after I tracked down that guy who had stopped returning your calls for him to pay his overdue bills. You were so overcome, you practically begged me to work on the Mustang."

"Hmmm. That don't sound exactly right, but you did do a good job, I'll give you that. Now get the hell back to work so you can pay me. I'll call ya when it's done."

Peter rang off, and I looked around the office for some of that work he spoke of.

Must have been hiding. I never did find it.

———

But at least I got interrupted while I was searching with a call from my landlady, Mrs. Jorgenson. She took time out of her busy day to tell me that my latest rent check had bounced. Wasn't that thoughtful?

———

Hilda called not long after that.

Looked like it was turning in to a red-letter day for Southwestern Bell.

"Hi, Ugly."

"You sound bright. I assume good news with Steve?"

She harrumphed at me, but there wasn't any oomph behind it. "His name's David, silly. And yes, good news. In the end he came back up to my price. I shouldn't have been worried, he just likes the game, that's all."

"That's great."

I heard the smile drop from her face.

"What's wrong, big guy?"

"Wrong? Nothing. What makes you think something's wrong?"

"Don't even try, Rafferty. I know you too well. Is it the shooting?"

"No not that."

"Ah hah, I was right, though. You're moping about something."

"*Au contraire, ma cherie.* I've never moped in my life and I'm not about to start now. I wouldn't even know how to start."

"Sure you do. You just won't admit it to yourself. So tell me what's wrong."

"It's not that anything's wrong. It's just that …."

And I relayed my cheery afternoon phonecalls to Hilda, found myself sounding far too whiny while I did, and so found a way to feel even worse about the day so far.

"Is that all?" Hilda laughed. "This is just about money? Rafferty, with what David paid me today, I can give you whatever you nee—"

"It'll be fine. I'll work it out," I said.

"There's no need to get all huffy and defensive, babe. Let me loan you the money so you can get your car back."

"I said it'll be fine."

"Okay then."

"Thank you."

"You're welcome."

For the second time that day, I was stuck for words on a phonecall. What the fuck was happening?

"Rafferty, I'm about to head home and leave Ramon to shut up the shop. If you wanted to get your head out of your ass and drop by, that is."

I did, want to drop by that was, but had very little idea how to commence the cranial extraction Hilda suggested.

———

I oozed the Pacer to a stop on Hilda's driveway just as her garage door was closing.

By the time I got to the porch, carrying a six-pack of Samuel Adams and a chilled chardonnay, Hilda was waiting at the open front door for me.

She held the door with one hand while she finger-combed her black curls with the other. Gave me a smile that asked a whole series of questions, none of which I had answers to.

"Beware the stranger bearing gifts," she said. "Don't I remember that from somewhere?"

"Maybe." I shrugged. "Beware too long though and I'll sit out here and drink all this by myself."

"Sure you will. You hate white wine."

"Not enough to stop me making a point."

"I'd better let you inside, then."

"I thought we'd save that for later, babe, but if you want to skip the foreplay and go right to the main event, I'll play along."

"You wish, Ugly."

"Yeah."

We kissed, but it was awkward while I was still carrying the booze, so I walked to the kitchen. Hilda slapped me on the ass as I squeezed past. I dropped everything on the counter, turned and pulled her close.

The kiss was better this time and I lifted her off the ground to nuzzle her neck and lose myself in that delicious area where her neck flowed into her shoulder and picked up the delicate sweep of her clavicle. She clasped her hands behind my neck, hooked her stockinged feet behind my knees and let her head sag back, eyes closed.

I kissed, nuzzled, and nibbled. She sighed and I wanted the world to stop.

"Tough day, big guy?" she whispered.

"Shhhh." My lips fluttered against her skin.

"Mmmmmm."

Despite my yearnings, I placed Hilda back on the floor, kept my hands around her waist. She looked up.

"What's wrong?" she asked.

"The wine'll be getting warm," I said.

"Uh huh."

"It seems more macho to say that than to admit I was gaining significant momentum towards that main event of which we spoke."

Hilda laughed, placed a hand on my chest. "I love you, Rafferty."

"You too, babe." I kissed her forehead and went to pour the drinks.

————

We sat on the love seat near the fire. Not that it was burning—too warm for that—but the hearth and mantle and stacked logs made a nice focal point. I was sitting at an angle, with my right foot hanging off the far end, while Hilda sat between my legs and leaned back against my chest.

I sipped beer and listened to Hilda swallow her wine.

She had a loud swallow which belied her physical presence, and I thought about her multitude of wonderful contradictions.

She had a formal, soiree-ready smile which would have been *de rigueur* at a Swiss finishing school, but if she ever got laughing hard enough, she would snort. This, in turn, would get her laughing even harder, and lead to more snorting. She'd been known to keep this cycle up for several minutes once she got going.

Dressed in a serious business outfit, she could hold court with the well-to-do while she talked antiques in words they understood. Later the same day, she could peel off that business outfit, and run me ragged in the bedroom using language the same well-to-do would definitely not admit to understanding.

And, not that I was an expert in the matter, but I'd bet my oldest blackjack that she'd forgotten more about antiques than most people would ever know. Despite that wealth of knowledge, I'd watched her speak with clients who didn't have a clue what they were talking about—those members of the 'like to hear my own voice' club—and seen her weave the right information into the conversation without making the over-confident and uninformed client ever feel wrong.

I was one of the few people lucky enough to see these different facets of her. I reminded myself yet again to never take it for granted.

"… hear that the DA has called for a Grand Jury?"

I kissed the back of her head and didn't reply.

She knew me well enough to not repeat the question and we sat in silence for a few more minutes. I found my thoughts and answered.

"Yeah, I saw that, too. Gonna be the quickest Grand Jury in history."

"Oh, I don't know."

"Trust me on this. There're enough people in this city who want to see the kid fry for what he did. Won't take long at all before DA Hernandez gets the go-ahead to prosecute."

"Maybe you're right. Monica's latest piece about the protestors all over the family's home was scary to read. I feel for the boy's mother."

"That was the other half of my day. Having to head off Charlene Wright and her lawyer, hell-bent on wasting my day with incessant pleas to help her son."

"What's she like?"

"Who? The kid's mom?" Hilda nodded. "Not what I expected, that's for certain."

"How?"

"I figured her to be aggressive, belligerent even. You've seen some of the things written about the parents of those other two asswipes." She nodded. "I was expecting much the same from her. Not even close. She's strong, I can tell that, but reflective, measured. Rational. Not the least bit a reflection of her son."

Hilda wiggled around to stare at me.

"What?" I said after she didn't follow the stare with words.

"How would you know what her son was like?"

"Huh?"

"You said you expected her to be a reflection of her son." I raised my eyebrows. "How do you know who her son was, Rafferty? You didn't say more than half a dozen words to him, then chased him in front of a bus. You couldn't possibly know what her son was like as a person."

I needed to move so I stood up, avoided Hilda's outstretched hand, and faced the fireplace.

"Honey," she said. "I'm sorry. I know you didn't mean for him to get hit. That's not what I meant."

I drank. Heard Hilda get off the love seat and come stand behind me. Felt her arms slide around my waist and her head nestle against my back.

"You think I'm upset because he got hit by a bus?" I said to the mantle.

"Uh huh."

"Because he's in a coma and it's not clear whether he'll pull through?"

"Umm, yeah?"

"Not even close."

"What?"

I turned around, held Hilda by the shoulders, and looked her in the eye. "Boy, you missed that one, babe. I'm not upset. I am pissed off that he's in a coma, but only because that means that Ed and the DA can't get up to full speed in prosecuting him yet."

Hilda's eyes were moist.

"I watched him, Hil. I stood there and watched the three of them stalk around the schoolyard with guns. I watched while kids died, and I couldn't do a damn thing about it. I will never get those images out of my head. I'm pissed off that the other two assholes took the coward's way out and I'm pissed off that Bradley Wright is not wearing an orange jumpsuit right now and sitting on a concrete bench waiting for a jury to tell him he has to take the long walk."

I wanted to wipe away the tears in Hilda's eyes, but I was too wrung out, afraid of trying too hard to erase the pain, rubbing too roughly.

"I'm pissed off that because I let him get away we all—the whole fucking city—have to wait to see what happens, when if I'd just been able to keep a hold of ... of him ... then we ... we could ... could ... and I'm also mad as hell that I don't have any other work to do while I sit on my hands and wait."

I was breathing heavily by this time.

"But I am not—not the slightest bit—disappointed or upset that he tried to headbutt a Greyhound bus and lost that particular contest!"

I stalked to the kitchen, slammed my empty bottle down on the counter, wrenched open the fridge and knocked the top off another beer, drinking half of it while leaning against the bench. I could feel my pulse and stuffed my left hand in my pocket to stop it trembling.

Hilda backed her way to the couch and sat.

Fear glimmered behind her eyes and I was reminded again just how much of an imbalance our relationship could be. She was a strong woman, one of the strongest I'd ever met, but if I ever lost control of the rage inside she could be in a world of hurt real fast and I'd be no better than any one of thousands of wife-beating men across the country.

Or an angry schoolkid with a rifle.

I upended my beer and placed the bottle down next to its brethren. The glass made the barest sound as it kissed the countertop. Looked up at Hilda.

"I'm sorry, hon. This thing must have me more riled up than I know."

She nodded. Leaned against the back of the couch and studied me.

"It'll be better once the DA can get moving," I said. "We'll all start getting some satisfaction, rather than being left in limbo with nothing to do other than wait. Bring on the Grand Jury, I say."

She nodded again. "If you think that's what it'll take."

I grabbed wine from the fridge and refilled Hilda's glass, snagging another beer as I put the bottle back. She watched me carefully throughout the whole process, still wary.

I risked it and sat on the couch.

Hilda's voice was low. "You do know that it's not your fault Bradley's in a coma. Don't you?"

I shrugged. It really didn't matter, and there wasn't any point going through that again.

Hilda continued. "I guess I just don't understand what it is about the shooting that has you so much on edge. Is it one of those arcane male honor codes again?"

Thought about that while I swallowed. If being pissed off about failing to save innocent kids from dying stupidly—wastefully—was an honor code, then I'd be happy to cop to that. But.

"That's not it," I said. "It feels like I've fucked this one up. Without actually doing anything. Very unlike me, I know." Hilda smiled and I saw the sun break through the colors in her eyes. "I couldn't save any of the kids on the day of the shooting. I was close enough to watch them die, but not close enough to protect any of them." The smile dropped and the tears came again. "And now, Bradley Wright can't pay for what he did, because I couldn't keep hold of his skinny ass on the day."

I drank beer for punctuation.

"Oh my god, Rafferty," Hilda said. "You feel responsible for them. Oh, honey." She shuffled along the couch, wrapped her arms around me and whispered into my neck. "You're not responsible for any of this. Not one little thing."

"Hmm," I said. "Never thought of it like that."

She leaned back, looked me in the eye, and punched me in the arm. My beer almost spilled. It's lucky I'm so strong.

"Bullshit," Hilda said. "You're thinking of it exactly like that. But, it's true. You're not responsible for any of it; what those boys did, or the kids who got hurt. You did what you could on the day and that's enough. You told Ed about Bradley and that made a difference. What's going to happen now will happen anyway, no matter what you did or didn't do."

"Hell of a pep talk, babe. Would have been perfect for your typical desk jockey who spends all day worrying about everything. I, on the other hand, am—"

"A big ol' softie who won't admit it. That's what you are."

I started to bristle, then she leaned forward and her tongue did things in my ear that made me forget what I was bristling about.

"Take me to bed, Ugly."

"You said I was a big ol' softie."

She slid her hand down my chest, over my belt buckle and did warm, wonderful things in my lap. Her lips found my ear again and she whispered, "Maybe not that much of a softie, after all."

12

t took the Grand Jury exactly thirty-seven minutes late on a Friday afternoon to give District Attorney Maria Hernandez the indictment she wanted.

So said Monica's latest report in the *Dallas Morning News*, so it must have been true.

Details aside, Bradley Wright had been indicted to stand trial for the murder of four people on the day of the Columbus High School shooting—Rebecca Gibbons, student, age 16; Steven Erwin, student, age 17; Riley Inglis, student, age 13; Catherine York, teacher's aide, age 34—being an accessory before the fact for the other fourteen victims, and a slew of other offences.

It was finally happening. Bradley was going to get everything he deserved. All he needed to do was wake up first.

It looked like I wasn't the only one pleased with the latest turn of events. Continuing from Monica's latest front page— *KID KILLER INDICTED*—a series of interviews spilled over nearly a dozen pages where Bradley's schoolmates left nothing to the imagination in describing the troubled youth:

'Weird kid. Always by himself. Quiet. Like a time-bomb waiting to go off.'

'Bradley Wright? Yeah, I knew him. Not very well, you know. He didn't seem to talk to many other kids. No, I didn't have any idea that he would do something like this, but then you really never know about someone else, you know?'

'What? No, I didn't ever see him hanging around with Randy or Kevin, but I avoided those two like the plague, and I didn't have any classes with the three of them so I wouldn't really know.'

'Brad was such an idiot. Like he couldn't even stand to be called Brad. Always insisted that his name was Bradley. Like there was one time where I called him Brad when we were working together on a project and he got really mad and yelled at me that he wanted to be called Bradley, not Brad, and how would I like it if he started calling me Penny instead of Penelope. Cause that's my real name, Penelope, but like I don't mind it if I get called Penny. In fact, it sounds kind of nice. Kind of perky. Like Bunny or Cindy. Like it's not such a big deal. So I really don't know what Brad's problem was.'

'We had a few classes together. Nope, never had any problems with him. He was always real quiet, though. Seemed to be by himself a lot. Nope, didn't see it coming at all.'

The phone rang, jerking me away from the collected mutterings of the next generation of people to run our country. I was glad for the interruption.

"You've reached the offices of Holmes and Watson Esquires. Purveyors of the world's finest opium and ponderers of the world's most quizzical riddl—"

"Rafferty?" a female voice said.

"This is he."

A chuckle. "I figured it hadda be ya. No-one else coulda come up with a line like that."

"Hey, Monica. Actually, just been reading your latest piece. So, Maria Hernandez is locked and loaded by the looks of it."

"Yup. Just gotta wait until the Wright kid wakes up. He's gonna be in a world of hurt, won't know which way is up."

"He has it coming."

"Not for me to say. I don't make the news, just tell the stories as they happen. Anyway, I'm callin' 'cause I wanted to say thanks for the heads-up on Bradley. You gave me a jump start on everyone else in town, not to mention a huge boost with my editor. So, thanks."

I waited for a few seconds in case Monica wanted to add anything else. Like, 'So, as a token of my thanks, I'm gonna have a cashier's check for five grand sent over to you this afternoon.'

Crickets.

I couldn't remember who it was that said no good deed goes unpunished, but it probably didn't matter. Whoever they were they sure seemed prescient.

"No problems, Monica. Always happy to help out."

"Huh? Oh yeah, thought you'd dropped out there. Anyway, my editor's gonna keep kicking my ass to keep this story rolling, so you hear anythin' else, you let me know, okay?"

I promised I would, though I couldn't think at all what that might be now that the case was firmly in the hands of the DA's office, and I hung up the phone.

Grabbed a fresh cup of coffee and turned back to the paper.

The father of one of the dead shooters was in jail after running over a reporter on his front lawn. Looked like the reporter would be okay once the broken bones healed. A lawsuit was being considered.

Imani Laweles was still newsworthy, taking up column inches with a spread less about the tragedy on the day and more about her family and how they spent their time when she wasn't being shot at.

Turns out that Imani was a foster child. The article didn't go into detail about her background, but I assume it had been worse than the three siblings she now shared a mother and father with. Photos with the article showed the family on the rear terrace of a two-story pile in the Park Cities. The six of them looked close, with arms around each other and smiles all around. Except Imani. She looked haunted.

I was about to turn to some work—checking what else the paper had to offer—when there was a knock at the door.

Aha! A client. Or a bill collector possibly, but I could at least attempt to be optimistic.

It turned out to be Paul Eindhoven, which was a disappointment all the way around.

He stepped in, sat, and waited.

I leaned back and put my feet on the desk. "Why me, Paul?"

"I hear you're the best."

"Where'd you hear that?"

"I asked around."

"Not very far, obviously."

"You'd be surprised. I also spoke to that Sergeant at DPD. What's his name? Rocco?"

"Ricco."

"That's him. Anyway, he says, and I'm quoting here, 'Rafferty is the biggest pain in the ass you'll ever find ...'" Paul paused and smiled. "'... but if you need help, he'll do you right.'"

"I should probably send him a thank you note," I said. "But, there's got to be someone else."

"Ricco told me about the job you did with that missing girl. What you went through to get her back to her family."

I waited. Here it came.

"Bradley deserves the same."

"Kimberly had been drugged, kidnapped, and held hostage in the desert by a religious nutcase. She didn't shoot anyone."

"I don't believe Bradley did either."

"That's all well and good, Paul, but let me ask ..." I looked him in the eye. "Would you use that defense in court?"

"Of course not."

"So why do you think it'll work with me?"

"Because, the other thing I hear about you is that you keep an open mind. That's exactly what Bradley needs right now."

"An open mind? Me? The man who thinks that Colt hasn't improved the design of the handgun in more than seventy-five years?"

"Joke all you like, but Ricco also told me how you were the only one who believed Kimberly was in trouble. Everyone else wrote her off as a runaway. You didn't. You went and found her."

I didn't want to think about the shit-storm that happened in Lincoln, so I sipped coffee and tried to ignore Paul. He didn't play his side of the scene well.

"You keep saying that Bradley did this."

I smiled and spread my hands wide.

"Okay," he said, "show me evidence of that and I'll walk away."

"Are you deaf? Or stupid? Have you already forgotten that I saw him? With a gun. Or did you miss every single one of the papers last week? Not counting Bradley and his rifle-toting friends, twenty dead. Sixteen injured. Which part of—"

"No," he said. "Evidence. Not statistics. Show me hard

evidence that a single person was injured or killed by anything Bradley did."

Interesting. I'd never had anyone ask me to prove them wrong before.

"So all I need to do is to dig around, confirm what is obvious to everyone, and you'll lay off?"

"That's it."

I swiveled the chair a little further left to take the pressure off my right ankle. "I don't work for free. No matter how easy the job is."

Paul reached inside his suit jacket and pulled out a calf-skin wallet. Leaned forward and counted bills out onto the desk. "Will five hundred be enough to start?"

"You're not going to let this drop, are you?"

He let the dimples and teeth hit high beam, tapped the pile of bills and raised an eyebrow.

If this thing wasn't going to leave me alone the least it could do was help me get the Mustang back. Shook my head. "One thousand," I said, figuring that he could afford double my retainer. I sure as hell deserved it, and if it was too rich for his blood, that suited me fine too.

"One thousand dollars it is then, Mr. Rafferty."

Damn.

Paul laid another five hundreds and a business card on top of the stack. "Consider yourself engaged to find hard evidence connecting Bradley Wright to the deaths and injuries from the Columbus High School shooting."

"No guarantees, Paul. I keep the money no matter what I find."

"Understood."

I looked at the money sitting on the desk. Didn't get out of the chair, didn't even take my feet off the desk as Paul stood and stopped in the doorway. "Goodbye, Mr. Rafferty. I look forward to hearing from you next week."

I stayed sitting a while longer, watching the stack of bills like they might spontaneously combust. Maybe if I ignored the cash, it would go away and take this stupid case with it.

On the other hand ...

Finally, I put down my coffee, reached for the fridge and pulled out a Shiner Bock, swept the cash into my top desk drawer, and tried to figure the downsides to this deal.

By the time I had finished the beer, I hadn't come up with any.

The school had been knee-deep with evidence, which would all be cataloged by the investigating teams and being put into neat piles for the DA to use in their evisceration of Bradley Wright. I'd talk to Ed in the next day or so, pick over my choice of collected items to show Paul, and that would be that.

Easiest money I'd ever make.

13

'd expected Mrs. Jorgenson to be a little happier now that I was once again fully paid up for my rent, but it turned out the dour frown she wore seemed to be permanent.

Paid a couple of other bills too, with the receptionist at my answering service reciting me a tired "Thanks for your custom, Mr. Rafferty. Please be more prompt with future payments," as I headed back out the door.

Fuck 'em. I wasn't going to let them spoil the rest of my day.

I still had a couple of hundreds in my wallet and I headed downtown to see if I could get lucky with Hilda.

Turns out, I couldn't.

McKinney was jammed and it took me longer than I'd hoped to get the car squared away in a lot a couple of blocks down and over, then hoof it back to *GARDNER'S ANTIQUES*.

The bell on the front door was still tinkling when Hilda's head salesman, Ramon, glided into view.

"Ahh, it's you," he said, lips clenched.

"Always good to see you too, Ramon."

"Yes, well, Hilda's not here. She's *working*."

Ramon never missed a chance to let me know his impression of my enterprises. "A half-witted quest to save the world" had been his most recent assessment.

I didn't have to stand still and take an insult like that from him.

I had hundreds of people ready and waiting for that honor.

"You know when she'll be back?"

Ramon smiled and shrugged, made the gesture look elegant, and left me with no doubt that he knew and wasn't telling.

"When she comes back, let her know that I dropped by and I'll see her at my place tonight."

Ramon inclined his head. "Certainly."

I was confident that he would remember my message verbatim and be precise in his non-delivery of it upon Hilda's return.

But, I also knew when I was beat so I headed back out to the street. Presumably, Ramon went back to polishing Edwardian sideboards or to brush up on his rich-folk speak. Repeat after me: Investment Opportunity, Increasing Value into the Future, Can you put a Price on Status, etc., etc.

I busied myself with more important things and went to lunch.

The chatter at Rush Diner, a Reuben, a mess of potato chips, and a Miller's Genuine Draft did the job nicely to start the afternoon off right. Lisa was working her usual routine behind the counter and I sat there for a change.

"Haven't seen ya'll for a while, Rafferty," she said, in the middle of making coffee, a sandwich, and change, all at the same time. "Y'all come back now, y'hear," she called to the back of a departing customer without breaking stride.

"Uh huh," I said.

I'd long become accustomed to talking to the back of Lisa's head. It wasn't that she was rude; she was doing so many things at once that she was always in the middle of all of them. Didn't matter, she could carry on a conversation at the same time.

"You hear 'bout that shooting over at Columbus?" she said.

"Yeah."

I didn't want to talk about it.

But not talking wasn't an option when Lisa was involved.

"What an awful thang," she said as she breezed past with two plates for the couple in the nearest booth. "Not fair that the kids who did it should get off. Gets me madder'n a wet hen!"

In the past, we'd talked about some of the cases I'd been involved in, just passing the time of day. Lisa had shown no more than a fleeting interest, no strong feelings one way or the other.

She stopped in front of me on her way back to the coffee machine, took a big swallow from a glass of water and stood with her hands flat on the counter. "I keep thinking 'bout those poor kids. Should have been just another day at school, having fun with their friends, and complainin' about teachers and homework." Tears welled in her eyes and she ran a finger along her lower lids. "But instead, they're murdered—frightened and screaming—by three punk-ass shits."

"You didn't have kids there, did you?" I'd never heard Lisa talk about children, or even being married for that matter, but had the feeling we were skirting hallowed ground.

"No." She sniffed. "I don't have kids ... but my best friend's daughter went to school there." I whistled out a breath as she continued. "She was one of the lucky ones, but been waking with nightmares each night since. Won't leave the house. Too scared to even go into the backyard. It's getting to the family, too. My friend and her husband are startin' to argue. And that ain't like them."

Lisa looked over my shoulder and nodded, grabbed a napkin from the dispenser and wiped her eyes again. "Just a minute, honey," she called to a man at the far end of the counter. Walked to the coffee machine and tuned up.

"I don't mind telling you." Lisa played her coffee concerto as she spoke. "Watching my friend bawl her eyes out, feelin' helpless 'cause there's nothing she can do to protect her daughter is one of the saddest things I've ever seen. I don't like to wish bad on anyone, Rafferty, you know that, but if someone was to offer me the chance to kill those two again, I'd git her done. And that one still in the hospital? All I can say is that I can't wait for the DA to get through with him. Just what he deserves."

Lisa finished her coffee-making and bussed it to the booth. I finished my Reuben, upended my beer, and felt like I had an itch I couldn't scratch. Fished a few bills out to leave on the counter.

"See ya, Leese," I said from the door.

"Don't be a stranger, Rafferty, y'hear?"

———

Maybe I'd been wrong about Ramon. Hilda turned up at my place earlier than usual, found me sitting in the back yard with a beer. She prepared a couple of grazing plates, joined me with wine, and we watched the sun go down while sipping, nibbling, and holding hands like teenagers.

Paul butted his way into my thoughts now and then, but I managed to push him to the back without too much effort. There was plenty of time to get done what I'd been dragooned into. The DA's office, and Ed for that matter, would be swimming in evidence, so two days would be plenty for me to get what I needed.

The evening came and went, and it was a while later when Hilda and I fell asleep naked, sweaty, and wonderfully exhausted nestled together like two spoons.

It was a great afternoon.

———

Woke up in the middle of the night, the streetlight at the corner of Palm Lane brightening the gaps around the edges of the curtains.

Bedside clock glowed a red 2:37am.

I could hear the dull drone of late-night traffic a block away on Mockingbird, and the distant bark of an insomniac dog.

Hilda burbled away in her sleep, bed warm beside me.

Nothing out of the ordinary. All right with the world.

Rolled over and waited to drop back off to sleep.

Ninety minutes later gave up and rolled on to my back. Scratched my whiskers.

Thought about what I'd got myself into with the All-Singing, All-Dancing, Let's Rescue Bradley Wright Mercy Mission.

Charlene was so convinced of her son's innocence that she was prepared to blow the better part of a thousand bucks on a wild-goose chase.

"Find hard evidence connecting Bradley Wright to the deaths and injuries from the Columbus High School shooting." That's what Paul had said. Even after hearing me repeatedly say that I watched the Wright kid stalk around the schoolyard with a gun.

The gun later proved to have killed three students and a teacher's aide in the Columbus hallways. Hallways which, I'm sure, had plenty of doors that were less open and shut than this case.

What was she hoping for with this stunt?

Why the half-witted quest to save her son? Did Charlene not understand just how much trouble he was in? I'd seen healthy doses of naiveté before, but this had to be a new high.

I wasn't unsympathetic.

When things fell apart for Dad after Mom and Kate died, I didn't want to believe it at first. Buried my head in the sand, and work, and ignored the locker-room whispers and glances.

Even once the whole shit-show came to a head and they forced him into an 'early retirement,' I had trouble admitting the truth. Only a drunken heart-to-heart convinced me otherwise. It hurt like hell to watch his pride wither and see him withdraw into himself over the next few years but by that time, I could no longer avoid what was patently obvious.

At some point, Charlene Wright would have to do the same.

She'd have to carry on living with the knowledge and acceptance that her son committed an act that she couldn't fathom. That, or fall apart completely.

But that wasn't my call.

I would do what I'd been paid for: deliver the evidence of her son's actions at her feet, and whatever happened after that was up to her.

Thought I could see the edges of the window brightening a little more as I promised myself I'd get that train moving later in the morning. I rolled over, pulled Hilda close, and went back to sleep.

14

H it the office in the morning with a renewed sense of purpose. A couple of hours and I could have this thing wrapped up, send Paul and Charlene on their miserable ways and put my feet up for the rest of the week.

Started with the easy stuff.

Drank coffee while I re-read all the papers from the last two weeks since the shooting, on the off chance there were a couple of threads I could pull on.

Hey, I said it was the easy stuff, not a high-percentage play.

But it wasn't completely fruitless. I did finish the task with a new appreciation for Monica's ability to write thousands of words, rehashing the same points over and over, making it appear as though each paragraph was *Oh-My-God-Will-You-Look-At-This* breaking news, while actually saying nothing new.

It also netted me my first look at the crowd of protestors on Charlene's front yard. A handful of carefully framed and dramatic close-up shots of angrily righteous (or righteously angry?) people holding home-made signs and making their voices heard at something out of frame. Didn't look like there were more than about half a dozen total, so I couldn't see what Paul and Charlene were so worked up about.

While the coffeepot perked again, I dialed DPD. Ed was in a meeting so I waited while the switchboard found, and then connected me with Ricco.

"What the hell do you want?" Ricco said.

"Good morning, Ricco. Might I say that your phone manner needs work. Have you been taking lessons from Ed? Myself, I've found some of the Dale Carnegie techniques quite worthwhil—"

"Worthwhile? This from the man who dropped a huge turd in our lap just to get in good with a fucking reporter? Uh huh."

"You still have a stick up your ass about that?"

"Just be thankful you're not talkin' to Ed at the moment. He's off licking the Chief's boots and kissing the Mayor's ass trying to keep his job. No thanks to you."

"Hey, it wasn't me that fucked up taking a simple phone call. It also wasn't me who gave that little piece of information to the press. You need to spend a little more time looking over your own shoulders."

"Yeah, but you putting Bradley Wright's name out there hasn't exactly helped the situation neither."

"What do you want me to do about it? It's moot anyway. The DA's got the indictment, and with all the evidence you've got, once the kid wakes up, he'll go down faster than a two-dollar hooker. Speaking of—"

"Two-dollar hookers?" Ricco cackled. "You that hard up, Rafferty? I could put you in touch with a coupla guys from Vice, you need a street corner. Me, I'd rather sun-bake nude at Three Mile Island than get within fifty yards some of those girls. But ..."

"Droll, Ricco. And quite frankly beneath you. I—"

"Just like you want Slutbag Susie underneath you, I get it." And he careered off into a laughing wheeze.

"Evidence. For your information, I was talking about evidence."

The laughing disappeared and the auditory scowl returned.

"What about it?"

"What do you have connecting Bradley Wright to the shootings?"

"Like I got time to do nothing better than shoot the shit with you, Rafferty." I waited. Ricco sighed. "What's the matter? His prints all over the gun that killed four not enough for you? It was more'n enough for Hanging Hernandez and the Grand Jury."

"I know about the ... Wait a minute, did you say *Hanging Hernandez*? So that's where I've been going wrong. I need a kick-ass nickname to strike fear into the hearts of my enemies."

"Yuck, yuck."

"People call her that to her face?"

"'Course not, don't be stupid, but she makes people use her last name, and she's got a better record on killin' than Jesse James."

"Rides that death penalty hard, does she?"

"Uh huh, and she's good. I'm pretty sure she ain't ever lost a murder case, not even as a prosecutor, but I do know for a fact she ain't never had a death penalty request turned down."

"Not looking good for Bradley."

"Nup." The chuckle was back.

"What else can you give me on Bradley?"

"Aside from the fact that the kid is officially fucked, nuthin'."

"C'mon, Ricco, you've got to have more than that. You've had teams working on this for two weeks now."

"No chance, Rafferty. Ed let me know what it was worth for me to let anything slide to you and I like being a cop more than I like unemployment. Why the hell you care, anyway?"

I told Ricco about the case I now had and then wished I hadn't.

"You talked the Wright broad in to givin' you money to prove the same thing as Hernandez?"

"It seems so."

"How the fuck you get so lucky to fall in to shit like that I'll never know. Meanwhile, the rest of us have to work for living."

I couldn't be bothered correcting him of his misconceptions on the pleasures and intricacies of the P.I. game. Besides, while I still had him on the phone ....

"I can't sit and chat all day, Rafferty. I know it's not the same for people like you with their wealthy patrons, but—"

"There's gotta be something you can give me." My voice sounded wheedley in my head and I didn't like it.

"No there isn't. Later."

So Ricco was a bust, but at least I confirmed that I was probably better keeping my distance from Ed for a little while yet.

Stood up and looked out the window, between buildings and over to the Columbus High schoolyard. No kids playing, no kids running in terror.

Still and silent.

With school out, not for the summer but for the foreseeable future, would there be anything to find if I was to head down there?

Maybe, but I doubted it. Anything that hadn't been processed and cataloged by now, that had been left at the scene all this time, if it had any relevance, it'd be guarded by cops. Especially now that the investigation was very much in the public eye.

Turned to the next arrow in my quiver—without getting out of the office, that was—and called the Office of the District Attorney.

Didn't get to speak to Hanging Hernandez, not even close. In fact, the associate I did speak to, who couldn't have been any more than twenty-four, twenty-five tops, gave me much the same response as Ricco.

She didn't take as long or make as many references to cut-price streetwalkers. But she did give me a healthy mix of incredulity and derision when I explained what I wanted.

By the time she'd hung up abruptly, I had already decided I was finished with the phone for the morning.

Locked the door and went to lunch.

————

Trust me on this, not all hot dogs are good.

So I put on the coffeepot and fired up a pipe to get rid of the aftertaste before I snagged the phone and dialed my service.

Eight calls.

What the hell?

Hilda, saying that she'd see me at her place tonight. No means the worst news I'd ever heard.

The next seven?

Paul Eindhoven. I sighed when the girl at my service mentioned his name, thinking it was a bit early to start chasing results, drew that breath back as she read the rest of the messages.

They all differed in detail, but the theme was the same.

"Wrights in danger. Need help."

I rolled the chair out from under the desk and put my feet up while I dialed. I had the receiver wedged into my shoulder and watched clouds gather outside my window.

"Paul Eindhoven, Attorney at Law," said a cool female voice.

"Get me Paul."

"And may I ask who's calling?"

I hate it when secretaries pull that routine.

"Yeah, sweet cheeks, the name's Sonny Crockett. I'm a pretty big thing on TV. *Miami Vice*? Maybe you've seen me." No response. "Well, I've contracted a horrible case of bunions from my character wearing shoes without socks and I think I've got a big case against the studio for permanent metatarsal disfigurement."

"Hmmph. Let me see if he's in."

A few minutes and a couple of clicks and pops later, Paul was on the line.

"Who is this?"

"Rafferty."

"Where have you been?"

I shook my head.

"Paul. You asked for results and, for the next two days, I'm still on your retainer. I don't owe you or your clients jack right now."

"It's no longer a matter of whether you will protect Charlene at her home. You must act now," Paul said. "And regarding payment, she is prepared to pay for your time in helping with her personal security."

"That's table stakes, Paul. Don't make it sound like she's

doing me a favor," I said, but I wasn't disinterested. The long-range forecast was still for a whole lot of nothing on the financial horizon.

Still, I stayed quiet and let Paul come to me. It would do him good.

"She needs help, Rafferty. After the cops finished the initial search of the house, a crowd of protestors began to camp out on the front yard and they're starting to cause damage. To date, it's just been some graffiti and tearing up the front yard, but it's only a matter of time. Charlene can't afford to lose her house."

"I saw the pictures in the paper. It doesn't look that bad. Just tell her to get out there with a gun. Her son was pretty handy with that approach."

Paul ignored the bait.

"She's not at home."

"Well she sure as hell isn't vacationing in Acapulco. Not with Bradley still in hospital."

Paul sighed. "When it became obvious the crowd on their front lawn wasn't going away, she thought she might as well get out of the house and hide for a while."

"And where is she hiding?"

"She and Ray are in a no-tell motel on Harry Hines Boulevard. The manager won't give them up, but there's no additional security. If a reporter could track them there, then ..."

"I can't babysit and investigate. If I do this, I'll have to bring in outside help. That goes on the bill."

"Okay."

"And it'll cost you double, and split my forces, if I'm trying to watch two separate locations. Better to move them home."

"I told her it was a bad idea in the first place."

"Even if we can get Charlene home, that's going to be two

fifty a day for me, plus expenses, for an unspecified time-frame. That'll add up quick. Can she handle that?"

"We'll review in a couple of weeks if things haven't settled down, but I expect you'll have found proof of Bradley's non-involvement by then."

"Counselor, let me make this clear: I'm not a charity. No pay, no work. I will walk away from all of this—investigation, babysitting, the works—when the money runs out. Got that?"

I could hear Paul purse his lips. As if he wouldn't do the same damn thing.

"Understood."

"All right then. Gimme the room number and name of the motel?"

I knew it. I'd even used it before. He was right about the manager—the guy was old school, wouldn't roll over for anyone—and the privacy was okay, but security? Motels were built to get people in, not keep them out.

"I'll call Charlene and convince her that she needs to go home," Paul said. "What time will you get over there?"

"Not so fast. I've got other things to do. I'll get to her in the next couple days."

Paul wasn't happy. There wasn't much he could do about it.

I wasn't lying when I told Paul I had things to do. Now that the Wright house was empty, it gave me the perfect opportunity to break in, ahem, investigate.

I wasn't sure exactly what I'd find in a house already picked apart by the police, but it did fit with one of my more oft-used approaches—it seemed like a good idea at the time.

It certainly couldn't make things worse.

Uh huh.

15

Turned out I was wrong about where Charlene lived.

The address I got from Paul was a lot lower than Lower Greenville, closer to the city and jammed in between Main and the E. R. L. Thornton Freeway.

I parked down the road from the smallish two-story frame house and sat in the car.

The group on the Wright's front lawn was larger than I expected, three or four times the half-dozen that I proclaimed. They sat, stood, and walked back and forth on the front lawn in front of parked cars. Tent shelters had been erected and lawn chairs scattered. A series of signs had been planted curbside: Pictures of Bradley Wright from recent newspaper articles blown up and emblazoned with the words *KID KILLER!!* and *MURDERERS WILL BE JUDGED AND BURN IN HELL*, and other epithets.

Two news vans leaned against the curb on the opposite side of the road. I couldn't see any spiderish tripods with cameras or toothy reporters, so probably a skeleton crew left behind to get extra footage in the event the killer's parent decided returning home was a good idea.

The house and gardens looked old and worn but neat, like a woman past her prime fooling no-one but herself with the judicious application of makeup and hair dye. The front lawn nearest the curb wasn't faring well, what with being torn up by the repeated movement of the crowd.

The front door looked secure and the windows unbroken for the moment. A couple of black paint starbursts punctuated the garage door and a MURDERER!! graffito in blood red stained the wall under the front porch. A jumble of boxes, plastic bags and stuff which I couldn't define as being thrown away or stored jammed the space between the garage wall and the near fence.

I wasn't going to learn any more by sitting there, so I decided to 'git amongst 'em,' as Cowboy would say. Thumbed open the glove compartment, wondered why the Colt .45 wasn't there, and spent too long working out that it was still in the Mustang. At McLeod's.

Goddamn.

I got out, locked the car, and started a pipe as I leaned against the front fender. Once it was going, I strolled down the street, just another passer-by taking in the sights.

"What's going on?" I asked a middle-aged woman wearing a screaming-eagle baseball cap. She leaned against an older model Ford station wagon adorned with two bumper stickers: GUNS DON'T KILL PEOPLE, I DO. and HONK IF YOU LOVE JESUS.

Catchy.

"You haven't heard?" She twisted to look at me, without moving her sizable butt from the support offered by Henry's finest sheet metal. "One of those school shooters lived here."

"You mean the Columbus High thing?" I played dumb. Hilda often said it wasn't much of a stretch.

"Uh huh. God exacted his retribution when he struck the

boy down for his heinous acts. He'll get dragged before the Almighty Lord soon enough to answer for what he done. The mom and some guy hid in a taxi as they ran away like the cowards that they are, but we're staying here to remind them that the Everlasting Fire of Righteousness is Coming."

I kid you not. She said that.

It was all I could do not to laugh.

We were joined by a middle-aged, clean shaven, guy carrying thirty pounds more than he should have been. Conservatively dressed, didn't look that smart, and seemed blissfully unaware of the fact.

"Everything all good, Ruthie?" he asked.

"Uh huh," she said. "Just this guy here asking about what's going on."

"You got a problem, mister? We got every right to be here, you know. It's a free country."

"Oh, I know it," I said.

When I decided not to follow that with further information, he moved from defending his rights to glaring at me.

I turned and said to the woman, "No sign of the mom?"

She smiled, showing a lot of teeth and gums. "Not yet. It don't matter. We'll be here whenever she decides to slink back in shame."

"Uh huh," I said.

Looked over the rest of the assembled multitude and figured I'd get much the same story from each of them. There was an impressive range of ages—from a pimple-faced boy who should have been in his elementary school classroom to someone's grandmother sitting in her bright green lawn chair knitting the beginnings of an American flag—and they sent a unified, unspoken message. Lots of patriotic sweatshirts and hats, a few hip-holstered pistols, and more than one bible being thumped.

While I could spend the rest of the day and amuse myself by collecting a series of outrageous viewpoints and religious quotes, that wouldn't get me any closer to extracting info from the interior of the house.

I nodded at Ruthie and the other guy, circled back to the Pacer, bashed my pipe out on my boot heel, got in, and drove around the block to another chunk of suburbia. Quiet this time of day; householders away at work, shopping or such. I cruised down the street until I estimated I was behind the Wright house. I kept going for another hundred yards and parked under a big shade tree.

Cursed myself for not having disposable gloves—also left behind in the Mustang—and resigned myself to being careful. Grabbed the clipboard from the front seat and did the 'lock up and stroll' routine again.

I glimpsed the roof of the Wright house beyond another downtrodden two-story home in the middle of the block. I stopped, looked down the path beside the house, pretended to consult my clipboard. I looked up, down again, then stepped off the sidewalk with purpose and walked between the house and the side fence. The locked gate halfway down the lot was out of sight from the street and I had no problems hopping it.

I landed in a crouch and waited. I didn't want to be surprised by dogs, actual meter readers, or the lady of the house sunbathing nude, though I wouldn't have complained about the latter.

Silence.

I walked to the rear of the house, checking windows and readying excuses on the way.

Followed the fence line to the corner of the backyard and hoisted myself up to peer over it. I was looking into the back-yard of the house next door to the Wright's. I crossed to the other corner of the yard, looked over my shoulder once, then heaved myself over the fence. Hidden from the curbside gaggle of the righteous and vocal, I scanned the Wright's backyard as I crossed to the back door.

Like the front of the house, everything was tidy but held an air of general aging. Not unloved or abandoned, more just a 'doing the best with what we've got' feel. The house needed painting but the lawn had been cut recently. Badly. Thin grass patches, baked dry by the recent weather, lay like liver spots.

A basketball hoop rusted out of its bracket above a square of concrete. A swingset and slide in the far corner looked ignored, and liable to disintegrate on the slightest touch.

The wooden screen door flapped a corner of loose flywire as it creaked open, and I held it with my hip while working my magic on the door lock. Took a few minutes, but the black art of lock picking has always been kind to me, and the lock finally popped. I wiped the doorknob with a handkerchief and stepped inside.

Stood still in the kitchen and listened. I had no reason, especially after the fine recon work done by Ruthie, to think there was anyone in the house but it pays to play all the angles. An empty house has a particular feel and it didn't take long for me to be convinced I was alone.

Okay, I was here now. What I was looking for?

Proof.

Of what? Bradley's innocence? Guilt? Evidence of a torture dungeon where Charlene had turned her son into a stone-cold killer? That was a long way down the list of possibilities but it never hurt to keep an open mind.

Still, I figured even the cops would have recognized the significance of something so obvious in their sweep, so anything I might find was likely to be a tad more subtle than blood-encrusted chains hanging from the ceiling. And, speaking of things that should have been obvious, it didn't look like the cops had been through the house at all.

Crime scene investigation is not like TV and film producers would have us believe. Cops—for the most part—are respectful, so they wouldn't have trashed the place during their time here, but I still expected to see some detritus left behind. Maybe not upturned drawers and holes in the walls, but at least some remnants of the team dusting for finger-prints, personal items not yet returned to their correct places, a track of muddy boot prints on the floor, that kind of thing.

The kitchen showed none of these. The fittings and surfaces were old and well-used. Water stained the sink underneath the dripping faucet and the Formica counters were chipped in places. But for all that, there wasn't a speck of dust anywhere, and a comprehensive organizational system in place, including labelled plastic containers in the shelves and fridge. Dry and empty dishwasher, clean dish-towel folded and hanging over the oven door handle, and a fresh garbage bag in the trashcan. Windows had been washed. The frames needed paint.

The kitchen had two doors—not counting the one to the backyard—which opened into a garage and a laundry respec-tively. Just like everything I'd seen about the house so far, a place for everything and everything in its place.

Mid-size station wagon, parked straight in the middle of the garage, hanging tennis ball resting against the windshield. Small bench, a space for your basic D-I-Y problems, nothing serious. Some cheap and nasty tools hung on pegboards above an empty workbench. A few small paint cans stacked underneath. Boy's bike hanging from the ceiling, tires soft and chrome freckled with rust.

The laundry also a picture of domestic efficiency. Washer and dryer in one corner, hanging rails above a sink. Cupboard with half-full laundry basket at the bottom and a black void above. Laundry chute from the second story, I guessed.

Stepped into the hallway, scuffed hardwood floor with a blood-red carpet runner stretching towards the front door, between dented and chipped skirting boards. Dining room to the right, to judge by the corner of the dark brown table, with wide windows that would have overlooked the street had the curtains been open.

Still, the low murmur of the protestors on the front lawn encouraged me to keep away from the front windows. I hugged the left-hand side of the hallway, alongside the stairs. With wavy yellow glass in the front door and sidelights, I'd be dead unlucky to be seen through them but I crouched anyway as I rounded the foot of the stairs. Living room opposite the dining, with comfortable, mismatched furniture, all inexpensive and worn.

Time to check out the boudoir.

I crept up the first half of the stairs, until I was sure I wouldn't cast a silhouette on the front door glass, then worked back to full height by the time I got to the second floor. A carpeted hallway ran at right angles to the stairs, and judging from the light spill, all the upstairs rooms had been left with open doors.

Main bedroom on the left. Bed made, pillows fluffed, no underwear or laundry laying around. I had a fleeting, time-capsule inspired thought about the whole place being a hotel, or a museum.

The other end of the hallway had three rooms opening off it: a small office and what looked like a guest bedroom facing the street and a teenage boy's bedroom overlooking the backyard.

The guest room was plain and boring, as they most always are. Single bed jutting out from one wall, a three-drawer side table with lamp, and a smattering of framed prints on the wall. Mostly desert landscapes. Scuffed leather suitcase lay on the floor, lid open, Ray's clothes inside. The bed had been slept in recently but, like the rest of the house I'd seen, it was made, and the rest of the room was neat and tidy.

The office had a bookshelf at one end, and a few more desert prints on the walls. The bookshelves had a wide range of titles, thriller fiction to money management guides, and no discernible organizational system. A comfortable-looking wingback chair angled in a corner alongside a floor lamp. Small desk on the other wall, with a stack of envelopes, and a corkboard above with what looked like bills and reminders fixed with brightly-colored plastic pins. A metal three-drawer filing cabinet butted up against the desk and tantalizingly held all sorts of imagined clues, but I didn't want to be seen through the window to the front yard mob, so I put that on the back burner and moved on to Bradley's room.

With the privacy of only the empty backyard visible through the window, I stepped inside.

Bradley's room was larger than the other two rooms at this end of the house. Points to Mom for letting the teenager have his way. Or was it a matter of a belligerent kid demanding the best and getting angry—perhaps violent—when he didn't get what he wanted?

Double bed underneath the window, made and neat, simple dark blue blankets and matching sheets. A skateboard peeked out from underneath, alongside several pairs of sneakers.

Cheap student desk which made a pigeon pair with the one in the office. Probably bought on a two-for-one special. School binders aligned across the back edge of the desk: *Geography, Mathematics, English, Biology,* and so forth. Shiny, dust-free square in the middle of the desk. I assumed a computer confiscated by the cops had sat there 'til two weeks ago.

Mid-size stereo system on the floor, with a stack of records in the cabinet underneath.

Bookshelves in here too, again with a mix of titles. I guessed most of the non-fiction to be school textbooks, but *South* and *The Oregon Trail* were more likely to be a personal interest. Non-fiction aside, this kid was a serious reader. I didn't take the time to read all of the spines, but I could see a whole section of science fiction—Isaac Asimov, Ursula K Le Guin, Arthur C Clarke—what looked like the whole collection of Tolkien, and a bunch of Greek classics. A gap at one end of the bottom shelf held testament to whatever it was that had been there, but gave me nothing as to what that might've been.

Three white mice scampered about in a glass-walled enclosure on top of one of the lower bookshelves. One ran endlessly on a wheel, while the other two dashed laps from end to end like their lives depended on it.

Maybe they did.

Two-door closet, clothes folded and hung neatly. Nothing out of place, and all a damn sight neater than I remember my teenage room being.

I guess every teenager's room has posters on the wall and Bradley's room didn't disappoint. A mix of singer and band posters and sports. Not that I recognized any of them right off the bat, but most of the posters had names helpfully attached. Bon Jovi, Poison, Whitesnake, and someone called Cyndi Lauper who looked like she was having trouble seeing out from underneath all the eye makeup. Didn't know anything about their music, but it looked like big hair was a necessity. Especially for the guys.

A couple posters of kids doing their best to ignore the laws of gravity, launching out of swimming pools and off ramps on skateboards and BMX bikes, and the obligatory Texas shrine to the Cowboys and Rangers.

Realized that I'd been hoping to find a definitive story about Bradley when I first set foot in the house, particularly where the anger that led him to picking up a gun and shooting four people had stemmed from, but so far the only phrase screaming in my head was 'typical teenager.'

So I tossed his room.

Without gloves, I took it slow and careful, setting everything back the way it was and wiping down anything I touched. Didn't need the hassle of Mom calling the cops, the cops calling me, and … well, it was just easier for things to look like I hadn't been there.

Fat lot of good it did me.

I give the cops a lot of credit for their investigation. They do a good job, but they would have been looking for the obvious. Guns and ammo, ranting diatribes on the computer, that kind of thing.

But I'm a lot sneakier than most cops, so I figured I'd have no trouble finding the not-so-obvious key: diary hidden in an A/C duct. Manifesto tucked behind a loose baseboard. Polaroids of murdered animals secreted in a hollowed-out bedpost. Something.

Nope.

After a good hour, I'd confirmed that the details of the room reflected the surface impressions. Bradley was a kid who worked hard enough at school to get by but no more—a couple of his report cards I found in his desk drawers used that exact phrase—had healthy, and pretty tame, interests in sports and music, and exhibited no signs of anger or rage anywhere.

And I'd looked.

I'd found the empty hiding space under the loose floor-board. Thought it smelled like pot down there, but it was musty and hard to tell for sure.

Also found a couple of dog-eared copies of *Penthouse* magazine on the top shelf of his closet. And the record single wedged between two LPs under the stereo. Some band called Bad English, more of the big hair, with a song called *When I see You Smile*. Hand-written across the mostly blank back of the record sleeve was a note that said, *Love U 4 Ever Bradley! B. xxx*, surrounded by a big heart. In glittery pink pen.

So Bradley maybe smoked the occasional joint, probably whacked off from time to time, and had, or used to have, a girlfriend.

Big fucking deal.

Once I made sure everything was back in its place and the room looked the same as when I walked in, I sat on the floor in the middle of Bradley's room, surrounded by the bits and pieces that made up his life and tried to think. The back of my scalp prickled and the whole goddamn situation was starting to feel wrong.

Neither the house, nor Bradley's bedroom, fit my expected mold of Bradley as the pissed-off killer taking out retribution on the rest of the school. Everything I'd seen indicated that he was the typical, and very ordinary, teenager. Like his mother had said, I couldn't find any indication that he knew the other two shooters, much less spent any time with them. There was no sign that he had weapons, ammo, another duffel bag, a penchant for violent imagery, or had written anything that might indicate he was gearing up to murder three of his class-mates and a teacher.

And that didn't make sense.

Because that's what happened.

No wonder his mother didn't want to believe what her

son did—there wasn't a single warning sign to be seen anywhere. The girlfriend might know more, probably did, but trying to track her down from a single initial? Without spending interminable amounts of time talking to teenagers who might have known them both. *'Like, I was so like, jealous of Bradley and B ... (Barbara, Betty, Bathilda?) They were so in love, you know.'*

Like, ugh.

I'd think again about it all later, but for the moment, I wasn't going to have an epiphany sitting around in that tired, empty house. Thought about the office filing cabinet again but didn't figure I could pull that off without at least one of the front yard crowd seeing me.

So I decided to get out of there and head home, to a beer and Hilda.

I checked the bathroom on the way back down the hall, more of the same. Clean, ordered. Towels folded and hung. Floor rug laying without wrinkles on stained and cracked linoleum. One toothbrush standing in a glass by the sink, which confused me for a minute until I realized the master bedroom must have a closet and master bath tucked around the corner and out of my sightline from the hallway.

The final door in the hallway opened to reveal a closet. The usual familial stuff tucked away; taped and labelled boxes on the floor and up high, crisp folded linens on the middle shelves complete with shelf labels. Boring.

I crept back down the stairs, went back to the kitchen. Double-checked the staircase, laundry and garage to make sure I hadn't missed a door to a basement or other hidey-hole. Nope, I hadn't.

And I was done.

I pulled the rear door closed, making sure it locked, and let the screen door swing shut with a soft thump. I stepped off the porch and was three strides closer to the back fence when a voice behind me said, "Freeze!"

I halted mid-step and turned towards the voice, which turned out to belong to a DPD officer about the same age as my Mustang. "Hey pal! You deaf? I said *freeze!*"

His canned dialogue would have been easy to ignore.

But the service weapons he and his partner—standing ten feet to the side—had triangulated upon the body that Hilda loved and craved caused me some discontent. I stopped moving, held my hands away from all my pockets and took them up on their generous offer to inspect the lawn from a very close distance.

16

At the cop shop, I was marched down the corridor by my elbows and treated to all the charm and hospitality the Dallas constabulary had to share.

It's a good thing they weren't trying to wedge their way into the tourist accommodation market.

This auspicious occasion would mark my debut in the Grand DPD Arrest Stage Show and Musical. I'd played the role to critical acclaim in rural East Texas, but this would be my first time under the bright lights of the big city.

After processing, they let me sit in holding and I wondered how long it would take for the news of my capture to filter up to Ed. Then I wondered how long he would wait before letting me in on his innermost thoughts. I had no expectations it would be any time soon, so I sat in the corner farthest from the drunks, silently blessed the guys in Processing who let me keep my pipe and tobacco pouch, and smoked the time away.

There was a decent progression in and out of the cell: bail bondsmen, and women in house-dresses springing their charges for more truncated time on the outside, a revolving carousel of drunks, and a nervous junkie who twitched his way around the cell asking each of us if we could see the lizard men. Two of the drunks agreed with him.

I did my best to ignore the hell out of them all.

Two pipes and a short nap later, I stood at the bars and tried to get one of the uniforms interested in bringing me a cup of coffee. None of them shared my enthusiasm for the idea.

Since I had nothing better to do, I sat on the hard bench and thought about the different facades of Bradley Wright.

To his mother he was a typical teenager with acceptable grades and pictures of the latest bands and football players on his walls.

His school friends saw him as the quiet kid, aloof, which could mean anything. And nothing.

I watched a desperate killer with a handgun stalk the rec-area of Columbus High.

A skinny kid in a Deep Ellum alleyway terrified about the idea of being taken to the cops and desperate to stop me doing so.

Begging me to shoot him because that couldn't hurt any worse, whatever the hell that meant.

And finally, as an unmoving shape beneath sheets and blankets, being kept alive by medical technology and whatever human survival instinct lurked in his deepest recesses.

Would we see another side to Bradley Wright? Would he join us back in the land of the conscious and tell us what really happened in the schoolyard that Monday morning?

Until that happened, I'd have to make do with what I already knew, and what I could find out. Which, to date, hadn't been all that enlightening.

The longer I sat there, too, the more I thought I might have trouble with Ed this time. Normally, I could find a way to square things and convince him we're on the same side. The lockpicks could be a problem, unless I could improvise a few good lines when my curtain call came.

And then it did.

"Rafferty!" A bored cop with a shaved head and a thick neck yelled through the bars.

"Yo." I stood and swept an arm at my fellow inmates. "I believe my flight is being called, gentlemen. It's been a peach of a time."

The junkie tried to walk out with me, mumbling about going to see the 'main lizard man.' He received a stiff arm in the shoulder for his troubles and sat down hard on the concrete floor.

"Lead on, my good man," I said to the back of the cop as he turned from locking the door.

"Ed said you were a dickhead," he replied without turning.

"If you're gonna be like that, you don't get to hear my re-telling of *Rime of the Ancient Mariner* as we journey onwards."

He grunted and we walked. Down hallways and up stairs, and soon we were standing outside the glass-paneled door of my favorite lieutenant.

The cop knocked.

"Yeah," Ed growled from inside. "Oh, damn," he said as the cop opened the door. Looked up from the paper he was reading, headline screaming *DPD SAT ON MERCY CALL ABOUT SHOOTING*. "As if I needed more cheering up from you today. Get your ass in here and sit down." Ed jerked his chin at the thick-necked cop. He closed the door, I sat and hoisted up a smile for Ed.

I tried for a mix of a contrite whoops-I-messed-up-this-time-but-it's-no-biggie and a deflecting I'm-sure-you've-got-

better-things-to-do-so-I'll-be-going-now. Difficult combination that one, to get it just right.

I didn't.

"Jesus Christ, Rafferty. Every time I think I got through to
you, like you might have listened for a change … every time,
bar fucking none, it comes back to bite me in the ass. Do you
have any clue how much shit you're shoveling my way?" He
rubbed his face. His jowls wobbled. Earlier than usual, I
recognized the rhetoric and opted out of engaging.

I tried again with the smile.

"Knock that stupid shit off," he said. "Whatever it is you
think you're doing. That's the same damn face my grandkid
gives when she's about to fill her diaper."

"What can I say? Maybe you should get her to a doctor.
Could be serious."

"I'll give you serious. You fucked up this time. Neighbor
kid saw you jump the fence and break into that house. Called
it in. You're gone."

He stared at me for a few beats, then continued. "Only
reason you're not still in holding waiting for a judge is that
I've still got some pull around here, and I wanted to hear your
bullshit story for myself, even though I'll cop hell from the
Chief."

"I didn't break in. That house belongs to—"

"Bradley Wright's mother. I'm not stupid, Rafferty, but
that never seems to occur to you, does it?"

"I was going to say 'my client,' Ed, but I'm so glad that
you used the mighty resources of the DPD to save me an elab-
orate expl—"

"Your client?!" Ed exploded. "Whose fucking side are
you on?"

I had no idea what he was talking about, so I raised an
eyebrow and waited for him to carry on.

"You're working for Missus Wright? Did you think that you might like to fill me in on that little detail at some stage? Because, oh I don't know, it might be important in the City's case against her son." Ed glared at me across the desk.

"What's the big deal? You and I both know that anything I dig up is only going to help your case."

"The big deal, smart-ass, is that you're playing both sides of the street. You're a material witness to Bradley's movements between the schoolyard and the bus accident. You were the last person to talk to the kid while he was still *compos mentis*, and you're the guy who told us where to look for the gun." Ed took a couple of deep breaths and shook his head. "You really think you're going to be able to testify on all that, now that you're working for the kid's mom? Christ, Hernandez is going to shit a brick when she hears about this."

"Relax," I said, trying to take my own advice, though the back of neck was beginning to crawl. "She won't need anything from me. You guys must have everything you need to prove the case."

"You better pray that we do. If this thing falls apart because of you fucking things up, I will make goddamned sure that I take you down with me."

Ed and I had been friends for a lot of years, too many to remember, and we'd been through the wars. We'd both held each other's careers, and lives, in our hands at one point or another, and I'd have always said that, other than Cowboy, there's no-one else I'd want covering my back. But the look he shot me then left me in no doubt that he meant every syllable of what he was saying.

"C'mon, Ed. You've had half the department working on this for more than two weeks. You must be chest deep in all matter of evidence to throw at the kid. And, having seen the inside of the house, there wasn't anything left, so you got it all, I assume."

"Yeah, good point. Let's get back to that. B & Es gonna look pretty good on your rap sheet." Ed's mouth came up to almost level so I knew he was happy about something at least.

I always did feel a certain pride in being able to spread good cheer.

"I didn't break in," I said. Ed rolled his eyes. "I was investigating. In fact, you might think—" I pulled up short once I saw his lips droop back towards the floor. I don't mind poking the bear from time to time but needed to remember that sometimes the bear bites back. And today's bear was already in a nasty mood.

"Didn't break in? Uh huh. Why sneak in and out of the back door? If you ain't got nothing to hide, that is?"

"Did the first graders in blue serge not tell you about the lynch mob out front, Ed? Heavens, I was fearful for my well-being if they were to misconstrue my intentions."

"Uh huh," Ed said again. "How'd you gain access? If you weren't breaking and entering, that is."

"A key. When I met with Charlene Wright, told her I wanted to look through the house. She gave me a spare."

"Where is it?"

I shrugged. "With my wallet and other stuff, I guess. I hope Processing didn't lose it."

"Interesting you mention that Rafferty, because there was an item within your 'other stuff' which caught my eye." Ed reached behind a pile of papers and held up the little leather case I keep my lockpicks in.

"Care to explain why these tools of burglary were on your person, Rafferty?"

"Found those in the house. After I used the key to let myself in, of course."

"Uh huh." When Ed found a line he liked, he committed to it.

"Yep."

"And they ended up in your pocket, because ..."

"Hell, Ed. I felt sorry for the family. They've been through a lot and I thought—"

"There's your mistake, Rafferty: thinking too much. I'd advise against it." He leaned back in his chair, blew out a breath and rubbed his upper lip. "Rafferty, you're fulla crap. I know you broke into that house. I know these are, or rather *were*, your lockpicks. And you're already in the system on this one, so I'm willing to throw you back in holding because I'm too busy and tired right now to straighten it out for you."

"But ..."

"But, what? You thought there was something else I was going to say. Nope." Ed leaned back and looked at me for about three weeks longer than was comfortable.

And I thought I was the master of the awkward silence.

He blew out a breath, reached into a drawer, removed a paper bag and threw it at me. I caught it one-handed and dumped it in my lap.

"There's the rest of your stuff. I don't want to see you again until this thing is over. Clear?"

"Sure, Ed." Now that it looked like I was going to be headed home instead of back downstairs I decided to take a chance. "Hey, before I go ..."

He closed his eyes. "What?"

"Tell me you have everything you need on Bradley." Hoped that I hadn't been too generous in my expectations of DPD.

Ed opened his eyes, looked at me, hoisted both elbows onto his desk. Brown elbow patches on a brown suit coat.

"Not as much as we'd like."

"What?"

He sighed. "Found a little bit of weed in his room, but that's nothing. The techs are breaking his computer down as we speak, and I'm hoping we'll find out he's also the goddamned Unabomber."

"Shit."

"Shit is right. Now are you starting to get it?" He sighed. "We've got the gun, and his prints on it, so that's a lock. It might be enough, but I doubt it."

"So Hernandez might call me to testify."

"After hiring yourself out to the mother of the accused? You'd better hope it doesn't come to that."

I should have seen that coming. Kicked myself for being too eager to take the money.

"So quit fucking around, wasting my time, and getting in my way. You want to do something useful, get outta here and find something that proves the little shit did it."

Halfway out the door I turned back. "Thanks Ed."

He didn't look up from his paperwork. "Close the door."

17

I was in the office and sipping coffee the next morning as an alternative to twiddling my thumbs. Cleaning up and dusting had also been possibles, but not as worthwhile. A small spot of firearm husbandry always brightened my day, but I hadn't fired the .38 since its last clean …

Hence, coffee.

Doing a good job of it, too.

Until the door banged open without warning and a tall Hispanic woman in a camel-brown power suit stepped through and headed for my desk. She was followed by a three-piece-suited guy who blinked owlishy behind round glasses.

"Mr. Rafferty," the woman said. "District Attorney Hernandez." She stuck out a hand and waited for me to stand and return the handshake. My god she was strong.

I sat again, leaned back and waved in the direction of one of the visitor's chairs.

"We won't be that long. I'm here because of a disturbing phonecall I received last night from Lieutenant Edmund Durkee of Dallas Police Department."

Uh huh, I thought.

"Go on," I said.

"He informs me that you are working for the mother of the student who's been indicted on four counts of murder from the Columbus High School shooting."

That wasn't a question, so I didn't respond.

"I assume that information is correct?"

That seemed to qualify as a question.

"Yes. I'm also chasing down an informant who swears Hauptmann had nothing to do with the Lindbergh kidnapping, but I don't imagine you want to talk about that."

Owl-Eyes flicked Maria a glance. She ignored us both. "Mr. Rafferty, I'm going to ask once, and only once, to terminate your contract with the Wright family and cease all associated work."

"You should know, counselor, that I very rarely do what I'm told, but let's play along for a while. As I understand it, Charlene Wright is currently not accused of a crime. She's a private citizen, free to come and go, with a need of my services. In addition, I'm a small businessman just trying to make my dreams come true here in the land of the free and the home of the brave. What possible reason would I have to turn away work?"

"Maybe I didn't make myself clear, Mr. Rafferty. This is not a request."

"A threat?" I said.

"Call it what you like, your connection with Charlene Wright represents a risk to the case we are building against Bradley Wright and I will not have this case compromised."

"Or what?"

"Excuse me?"

"I said, 'or what?' As in, I have to lay off this case, *or what*?"

"Or I will use whatever measures I have at my disposal to protect the city's case."

"So I'll sleep with the fishes, is that it? Concrete boots?"

"Don't be so melodramatic."

"If you're going to appeal to my better nature, you should have phoned ahead, and I could have told you not to waste your time."

"I'm not sure what the DPD lets you get away with, but my office will not be as forgiving." I raised my eyebrows. Hernandez almost sighed and I had to stop myself from licking my finger and chalking an invisible scoreboard. "I'll have you so deep in court orders that you'll be too busy meeting with your attorney to do anything other than breathe."

I tried to look bored.

"And, if that's still not enough for you to see sense, I really think that I might start to become worried about your safety."

"Here it comes."

"I'm not sure what you're trying to imply, Mr. Rafferty, but I could possibly be so concerned that I would find it of critical importance to have you identified as a protected witness and jailed until the case comes to trial. For your own safety, of course."

"Of course," I said, trying to make it sound like I didn't care.

"And with Master Wright in his current condition, who knows how long that could be? I was reading an article the other day about a woman who regained consciousness twenty-eight years after a car accident first put her into a coma. Fascinating, simply fascinating."

I knew when I was beat, but I'd be damned if I was going to admit it out loud. Hernandez was classy enough to know that, and went up about twelve notches in my estimation.

She moved to the door. Owl Eyes opened it for her, and she turned to me before stepping into the hallway. "I suggest you think about it, Mr. Rafferty. Hard."

The door was barely closed before I'd grabbed the phone receiver and nearly ripped the dial off as I rang Paul's office.

"It's Rafferty. Get Paul for me," I growled to whoever answered the phone before they could even wish me a good morning.

"Mr. Rafferty," Paul said. "I assume you've got some news fo—"

"Can it, Paul. You fucked me on this one, didn't you?"

"I don't have the faintest idea what you're talking about."

"Browbeating me into taking on Charlene as a client."

"Surely you don't mean that. You're a grown man who makes his own decisions. Obviously. I really don't think I could make you do anything you didn't want to do." I could almost hear Paul's dimples and dazzling teeth buzzing through the phone line.

"We're not in court now, you're not fooling anyone. You knew that if I took on Charlene's case it would almost certainly exclude me as a witness from any upcoming trial. Or that it would at least throw enough shit in the game to make it easier to discredit whatever I had to say about Bradley. Didn't you?"

He chuckled. "Of course I did. And, to be honest, I'm a little surprised that it took you this long to twig to it."

I didn't want to admit that I hadn't really thought it would be a problem. That I'd figured the cops had such a watertight case that my puttering around on the edges wouldn't make a difference. I was also pissed for letting myself get stuck in this situation.

But I wasn't going to admit that to Paul.

"What do you know that I don't?"

"What are you getting at?"

"You know that I saw Bradley in the schoolyard with a gun."

"You've made that abundantly clear, yes."

"And I can safely assume that you know I followed him from the school to Deep Ellum, where he got hit by the bus?"

"Monica Gallo's not the only one with contacts inside the DPD."

Damn, his chuckle was infuriating.

"So what do you know about what really went on? What's so incriminating that I needed to be sidelined from any trial? It can't be anything that sees him acquitted, because you'd be touting that all over the city, so I'm guessing you know something that proves Bradley did it.

"And you didn't want me telling a courtroom about watching him and his buddies shoot up the school. So, what is it, Paul? He leave a note? Ranting and raving and telling you why he did it?"

"You've got an overactive imagination."

"Maybe it's Charlene. Got the hots for Mom? Gonna use whatever tricks you can to get little killer Bradley off, so that the thankful mother can truly show you just how grateful she is. Maybe a quickie in the courthouse bathrooms after a not guilty verd—"

"Fuck off, Rafferty."

"Did I strike a nerve, counselor?"

"For Christ's sake, Rafferty. To quote your good self, 'I don't owe you jack shit.' So get off your high horse, swallow your pride, and do your job. You say that you're a good P.I. Prove it. If you're so damn good, find that evidence."

And then the prick hung up on me.

Ranting at lawyers did have its upsides, but I had to be

honest; it wasn't going to extricate me from under this stupid case, even if it did feel good in the moment.

Nope, the only way was forward now.

I grabbed the phone again.

"Yo, boss-man," Cowboy drawled down the line.

I shifted the phone to my other shoulder and started to pack my pipe.

"Hey, Cowboy. You and Mimi doin' awright?"

Damn, I was doing it already.

Every time I called Cowboy, I promised myself I wouldn't fall into his country-boy speech patterns. And yet, every time, I did. The slow, almost lazy, way he spoke was hypnotic, I reckoned.

Goddamn, even my thoughts were doing it.

I jerked myself back to the moment.

"… good, for a coupla country folk. Y'all know how it is."

"Yeah." I focused. I wouldn't be outwitted this time. "You interested in some work?"

"Mebbe," he said. "Whatcha got?"

"Protection for a woman and her brother. At their home."

"Fine." *Fahn*. "The Mob after them, they informants, or what?"

"Uh, just flying the flag to make sure a bunch of front yard protestors don't get ideas."

"Protestors? Hells bells, Rafferty." *Hayells-bayells*. "You gone and got yoreself mixed up with god-botherers again? What is it 'bout you and god-botherers? I ain't never seen a man—"

"They're not god-botherers, Cowboy," I said. "Well, maybe some of them are … anyway, it doesn't matter. Besides, it's not me. I don't go looking for them."

"If'n you say so. Alls I know is I've seen more religious

loonies while working with you than anywhere else in my li—"

"You interested or not?"

"Shore," he said. "Think it needs Meems, too?"

"I'm not sure what it needs, yet. We'll see how things pan out. Mimi can come up later if we need her."

"Thass no problem. She migh' need a coupla days' notice so's she can get Adam over to her sister's, but I'm shore it'd be fahn."

"Okay. Tomorrow morning?"

"Yep. Your place?"

"Yeah."

"Need transport? I can boost a truck."

"Nah, bring your own wheels this time. I want to stay clean with DPD."

"Hmmph. Protestors. Actin' legal. I purely am worried about you goin' soft, boss-man."

"Take a number."

I would have liked to keep shooting the shit with Cowboy, but it was time to get moving.

I needed a beer.

18

Seven a.m. Thursday, Cowboy's truck squeaked to a stop in my driveway, the big whip antenna swaying back and forth.

I was sitting on the front porch filling my system with the requisite caffeine and nicotine to start the day right.

"Howdy, boss-man," Cowboy drawled from the truck. "What happened to the pony?" He nodded at the Pacer sitting serenely by the curb.

I shrugged. "I accidentally put it in the dryer and it shrunk."

"Ah yuh. Well, we need to chase us any jaywalkers in Highland Park, you'll be set and ready."

"Yuk, yuk." I shook my head. "You want coffee?"

"Naw," he said. "Let's git 'er done."

"Yeah." As Cowboy wheeled back out into the street, I bashed my pipe out into the flowerbed, locked the house, and slipped into the Pacer. It started on the first twist of the key and I found I could live with that. I pulled out and started leading the way to the Wrights.

About halfway to the motel I started thinking about what

we were doing and began looking for a tail. There was almost zero chance that anyone who wanted to get to Charlene would try it through me. Not that I thought I was that good; I just couldn't see a way anyone could figure I was involved, though after Paul's comments a day earlier, I'd started to get a new appreciation for just how effective the Dallas grapevine was.

Couldn't see any vehicles that looked like they may have been following us, but made a couple of loops around various blocks in case. Pulled over and rummaged in the glove box while Cowboy drove past, in case a car had locked onto him. After I didn't see anything to be worried about, I retook the lead and Cowboy dropped farther back, giving more space for anyone to show themselves.

No-one did. I found it strangely disappointing; I wanted something, anything, to happen, but in the absence of that at least it felt good to be in motion.

Pulled into the motel parking lot and reversed as close to the room as possible. Watched Cowboy park on the other side of Harry Hines Boulevard with a clear view in both direc-tions. He'd be ready to high-tail it into the parking lot if I needed help, or to remove anyone who tried to chase us as we left. Again, I figured it low odds that any of the sign-waving populace from the Charlene's front yard were going to cause us major troubles but, like the Boy Scouts say, it never hurt to be prepared.

And carrying weapons.

Ray was ready to go, but it took Charlene twenty minutes to get organized. She was lethargic, absentminded.

Finally, she was ready and they squeezed into the back seat of the Pacer while I stood near the front fender, the .38 in my right hand and out of sight. Cowboy's head swiveled with the morning traffic. All was quiet.

No trouble on the drive to the Wright house, contentment starting to overtake my disappointment, but I wasn't ready for it to take root. This wouldn't be like coming home after a quick shopping run to Piggly Wiggly.

"Pull that blanket up over both of you," I said over my shoulder, "and whatever you do, keep your heads down."

"What are you going to do?" Ray asked.

"Need to check out the house, make sure those folks on your front yard haven't been helping themselves to your liquor cabinet. You two are gonna stay in the car until I come back and get you. Understood?"

"Yep." Nothing from Charlene, but in the rearview mirror I saw her pulling the blanket up over her head. At least she was listening.

Turned the corner, gunning it—such as was possible—as we approached the property line to arrive with some element of surprise, lurching to a stop on the driveway an inch and a half shy of the garage door.

I was out, stepping toward the porch, watching the protestors gather their collective courage and moving to intercept me. I showed them the .38 and they slowed.

They didn't stop, however, so I angled away from the house to meet them in the middle of the lawn.

"There she is!" shouted a skinny guy in the second row, pointing over my shoulder, at about the same time I heard the car door squeak open.

Turned in time to see Charlene wriggling her way out of the back seat with Ray trying to grab her arm. "Charlene. No!" I yelled, causing her to turn away from the car and stare at me—and presumably the crowd behind—with wide eyes.

We all held that scene for a couple of breaths, then she flicked her head toward the front door and I knew it was too late. I shouted at Ray. "For god's sake, catch her and don't let her get in the house. I'm coming."

He was having trouble getting past the stupid fold-down seat and out of the car, but the part of my back between the shoulder blades started itching, so I ignored him, turned around, stepped back and brought up the .38.

The crowd hadn't started to press forward yet, but it wouldn't take much and, once they did, I wasn't sure I'd be able to get them stopped again.

"Okay, hold it right there, everybody."

Took a cautious step backwards, feeling for the lawn.

"We are all going to calm down right now. Got it?"

Heard Charlene's sandals slapping on the concrete path. Listened for Ray's heavier steps. He was out and running. Couldn't be far behind her. I just needed to keep these turkeys under control until the three of us could meet on the porch, and we could at least sweep the house together.

Wasn't a great plan, but it was all I had.

Swung the gun back and forth on the crowd, shouted over my shoulder. "Do not let her get in the house. You hear me, Ray?"

Took another step backwards.

"Uhh, Rafferty ..."

"I don't want to hear it, Ray. Just do not let her get inside the house."

"Uhh ..."

Two or three steps more and I'd be on the path, then I could move sideways to the base of the porch stairs and this would almost be over.

And then a voice I didn't recognize growled, "I've been waiting all week for this."

———

I pivoted, bringing the gun up as I did, trying to work out what to aim at and whether I should be turning my back on the people I'd just been pointing a gun at.

Ray was about halfway along the path from the driveway, looking at me, then at the bottom of the porch steps where his sister was being held by a bearded man with wild eyes.

His arm draped over her left shoulder, across her chest, palm resting against her ribs under her right breast. It could have been a lover's embrace.

The Smith & Wesson he pressed to her right temple said different.

Charlene blinked staccato at me and Ray continued his head-swiveling approach to the situation.

"Easy there, buddy," I said. I ticked the .38 up a notch, focused it on the end of his bulbous nose to make sure he could hear me.

"Don't fucking tell me to take it easy, man! You have any idea what her kid did? Do you?"

I felt like the contestant on a game show where any answer I gave would be wrong. Instead of answering, I settled my feet a bit firmer on the driveway, gripped the pistol a little tighter and shut the hell up.

"He killed my angel! That's what he did! He took her away, and he won't be around to pay for what he done." Beard pushed the S&W's muzzle harder into Charlene's temple. She tried to tilt her head away from the pressure. He tensed his arm, holding her in position. "So don't tell me to ... Take. It. Easy."

My mouth was dry. Ray was still doing his tennis-spectator impersonation in my peripheral vision. What worried me more was what the folks on the front lawn behind me were up to. I didn't think they could conjure up a backbone between them, but all it would take is one weekend warrior with a twitch in his trigger finger and this could turn to shit real quick.

I heard one of the news van doors creak open and a few raised voices. Just what we needed: Live coverage from our team on the scene.

"Why'n't you tell me why I shouldn blow Momma's head off right now. Huh?" Beard said. Charlene closed her eyes and started to slump. I wasn't sure if Beard would notice the extra weight, but I didn't want anything to rattle him further right now.

So I started talking.

"What's that gonna solve?" I said. "It won't bring your girl back. You know that." Christ, I hated this shit. "It's not gonna help anything. You kill her, I kill you. More dead people. That's all."

That's all? As lines go, that one sucked like an industrial vacuum cleaner. No wonder I hadn't gone into hostage nego-tiation when I was on the force. *Do you feel lucky?* That's more my style. Still, this turkey didn't deserve to die. He was having a shitty day and needed to take it out on someone else.

But it wasn't gonna be my client.

"So what? I don't care anymore, man," Beard said. "She was my everything. My whole world."

I couldn't stop myself from asking. "What's her name? Your girl."

"Her name *was* Rebecca, man." His eyes flashed and I knew I'd fucked it up. "And she's never coming back. Because of what her son did. And now she—"

I didn't hear any more, I'd started to move by then. Knew he was gonna do it, the only hope I had was to get moving towards him and draw his fire before he put a bullet through Charlene's brain.

I got two steps, Beard started to move his gun arm toward

me, I wished I'd put the bullet-proof vest on this morning but I hadn't thought there'd be a need for it and could I get a shot past Charlene without hitting her and there wasn't a lot of Beard to aim at and now that I was running my aim would be off and what if my first shot missed and I wished I had the Colt instead of this pissy little .38 and ... and then Cowboy stepped lightly out from behind the corner of the house and placed the muzzle of his shotgun at the base of Beard's neck.

"When the boss-man tells you to take it easy, pardner, best you take his advice."

———

After we got Beard disarmed and Charlene and Ray inside, I started a pipe to shut my nerves up. I stood on the porch and glared at the protestors now reassembled on their patch near the curb. All the cameras were out now and there was lots of focus towards the house, trying to get a shot through the foliage of Beard who sat, legs crossed, with his hands behind him, cable-tied to a porch post. His head was down and other than the drips of tears landing on his lap, he might have been taking a nap.

Cowboy eased against the porch railing beside me.

"Missus Wright's layin' down," he said. "She found some Valium, so I 'spect she'll be out for a while." I nodded. "What we gonna do with him?" He jerked his chin at Beard.

I wasn't ready to deal with that yet. I was still coming down from either being shot or shooting a man who'd done nothing more than been gripped by a tragedy he had no control over.

I wasn't sure which was worse. Continuing to think about both didn't seem to have a lot going for it either.

"He's not going anywhere for a while," I said. "May as

well do something useful. Move your truck into the driveway and unload. We'll swap cars around later."

"Shore."

I leaned on the railing. Watched the protestors and camera guys watch Cowboy as he humped his stuff into the house. No reason at all for him to take his guns out of their cases before carrying them across the yard, but the effect on the assembled multitude was fun to watch.

If only they'd seen the toys he left in their bags.

On the third trip back to the truck, I said. "Hey. Thanks."

"What the heck for? Woulda bin here las' week if'n I'd known it were gonna be this much fun."

19

The sun had set but the sky glowed clear in the west.

Charlene was still sleeping, and I think Ray was inspecting the bottom of a Scotch glass when Cowboy and I had a little heart to heart with the would-be retributor.

His name was Gibbons, Frank Gibbons, and he wasn't a bad guy. He had a fair right to be pissed off with the world after being told his daughter was one of the first killed, in the hallway slaughterhouse.

Still, motivations aside, anyone who holds a gun on me or my clients has some explaining to do.

Cowboy slashed him free from the cable ties and the three of us sat on lawn chairs I'd found in the yard shed. If we'd had beers and a grill going it could have been Memorial Day weekend and we would have been jawing about who we liked in tomorrow's game.

Instead, Cowboy and I had Frank backed into a corner of the porch. I tapped Frank's S&W against my thigh, in case he suffered any sudden memory loss about what was going on. Cowboy sat a couple of feet behind my left shoulder and grinned as he sharpened his hunting knife on a leather strop.

Frank's eyes were really interested in that knife.

"Now then, Frank," I said. "I've got a problem here. Maybe you can help." Frank's eyes flicked to me for a second, then back to Cowboy's handiwork.

"Yoo hoo ... Frankie." I snapped my fingers in front of his eyes and he flinched. "Over here." Looked back at me. "That's better," I said. "You should know it displeases me greatly when someone ignores me while I'm talking." I had his attention now and his eyes trembled as he stopped himself from looking toward Cowboy. The hiss of the blade on leather was captivating, I had to give him that.

"What are we gonna do with you, Frankie, old boy?" He blinked and his head shook. "My colleague here thinks we should take you on a little one-way ride out to Lake Ray Hubbard." That got his attention. I shrugged to show him that I didn't care one way or the other.

"Whaaa ...?"

"You said it yourself. You don't care. Be a bunch easier if it all came to an end, wouldn't it? Might even be doing you a favor."

Frank shook his head so quickly I thought it might come spinning off. "Noooo," he started.

"Of course, there's also the matter of you holding a gun to the head of a friend of mine, not to mention looking a bunch like you were gonna shoot me, too. Gotta be honest, acting like that doesn't make me want to keep you on my Christmas card list."

His mouth opened and closed several times.

"Something you want to say there Frankie?" I said. "'Cause now would be a good time." I leaned back in the chair and disinterestedly thumbed the hammer on the pistol.

Wondered if I was overdoing it but Frank took it right to heart.

"I ... I ... I'm sorry," he blurted. "I didn't want to hurt anyone. Really, I didn't. It just hurts so ..." He reached up— Cowboy's knife ministrations stopping in time—to press his thumb and forefinger against his eyes. His nails were dirty and ragged. "So much." He lowered his head.

"If we let you go," I said, "you gonna try this shit again?"

"Nope," he said, shaking his head. "No way."

"Okay." I blew out a breath. "I don't care what you do: get drunk, get laid, get in your car and drive to Alaska, whatever, but we ..." I flicked my thumb between me and Cowboy. "will be here, waiting, and if either of us sees your ugly mug again, we will shoot first and ask questions later. Got that?"

He looked up at me, half as large as when he was holding the gun and my client.

"Yes," he whispered.

"What? I didn't catch that."

He sat up and exhaled a big breath. "Yeah. I got it."

"Okay then. Piss off."

I stood and moved my chair to let him through. He stood, crossed to the stairs, and started down. Two steps from the bottom he paused a couple of seconds, shook his head, jammed his hands in his pockets and headed across the lawn. The crowd swirled around him and he ignored them all, walked down the street. Two reporters and camera crew bustled out of the news vans and surrounded him, jabbing microphones and fill lights at him as he walked. The caravan continued like that for forty yards, until he stopped at an old Pontiac, pushed one of the camera guys out of the way so he could get in, and drove away.

We watched the taillights disappear around the corner at the end of block.

Rafferty's Rule Forty: Any day you can end without getting shot is a good one.

The last vestiges of penumbra leaked out of the sky and we went inside.

———

With our interrupted arrival at Casa Wright and no chance to grab supplies, there wasn't much in the way of food in the house so Cowboy went out to pick up burgers and beer. I sat on the porch with the light on, my feet on the railing and the shotgun across my lap while the curbside gathering eyed me eyeing them. I wasn't ready to let go of the thought there might be another Frank Gibbons in their midst.

They were a weird mob. Their outrage was palpable, and righteous indignation followed every step but no-one had yet made a move toward the backyard. Wasn't sure whether that was a conscious decision to honor the sacred private space of a homeowner, or an understandable fear that Cowboy might be waiting back there with a Bowie knife.

Probably a split decision.

Ray came outside, handed me a glass swirling with two fingers of amber liquid and pulled up the other lawn chair.

"Thought you might want that."

I took a bite of the scotch; not bad, and I tipped my glass to him.

"I guess things like that happen pretty often in your line of work," he said.

"Actually, not as often as you'd think," I replied. "But don't tell anyone, I'll have to lower my rates."

He forced a short smile in the gloom.

"Um, your partner ..."

"Uh huh."

"Has anyone ever told him how much he looks like—"

"James Coburn?"

"Yeah."

"Best you don't mention that to him."

It was true that Cowboy looked like Coburn. A lot. Especially from his role in *The Magnificent Seven*. They were both lean and rawboned, forthright, and shared a similar proclivity towards a limited lexicon. Cowboy always claimed it bugged the hell out of him, but the longer I'd known him, the less certain I was. He didn't complain as much as he used to about signing autographs.

"Leaving doppelgängers aside for the moment," I said, "tell me about your sister and nephew. I'm not getting closer to disproving his guilt. Or proving it either, for that matter. The place where I'm getting bogged down is that I've only got impressions, but I still don't know anything about him."

Ray picked at a loose thread on the knee of his jeans.

"What do you want to know?"

"Let's start with the obvious. Did he do this?"

I hadn't finished asking the question before Ray started shaking his head. "Nope. No way."

"Convince me."

"Um, well—"

Ray's attempted defense of Bradley was interrupted by the squeak of timber and a voice from my left.

"Sir, what do you have to say about the tragedy that almost occurred here today?"

I got up and met the reporter at the top of the steps. He kept firing questions at me while I made myself large and began stepping down from the porch.

I backed him down the stairs—he didn't fall, dammit, but I saw his camera guy twist an ankle—and when I had enough space on the garden path, I reached for a coiled hose. Before I could turn the faucet on, the duo had begun to retreat across the lawn, the camera guy protecting his equipment and the on-air talent his suit, I imagined.

Stood there a while longer, glaring at the fearless news crew shuffling their way back to the comfort of their truck, and eyeballing the rest of the crowd.

Since Frank's attempted bravado earlier in the day, I felt like the energy on the front lawn had been pulled just a little tighter. Like the way a sail sheet will start humming when the wind fills the canvas.

The tension in the system is obvious and even magnificent, as long as that power remains contained. If the sheet or any of the rigging ever lets go, then all hell breaks loose and people get hurt.

I hoped we weren't heading towards a similar catastrophe on this boring suburban front lawn.

Stumped my way back up the steps and pulled the lawn chair back under my butt.

"So, Ray, I think you were about to deliver an impassioned defense of your nephew when we were rudely interrupted."

"It's been hard since Bradley's father lef—"

"That's not a terribly good start. My mind leaps immediately to the idea of an angry young man, missing out on a male role model, and pissed off at his mom and the world for making his life too hard. It's easy to see how that combination could lead to—"

"You didn't let me finish, Mr. Rafferty."

I shut up and let him finish.

"It's been hard since my ex-brother-in-law left, but that's mainly been the financial stress on Charlene. She had to go back to work after being a stay-at-home Mom for nearly ten years and that was difficult for her to do. She tended bar for a while, worked at Safeway, a few other things, long hours wherever she could get them, until she got the pharmacy job."

I raised my eyebrows. I'm all for gathering backstory when it comes to working out the players in a case, but I was concerned about falling asleep before we got to the good stuff.

"But for all that, they—both Charlene and Bradley—have never been happier or more settled. It's been a really great move for them to come up to Dallas."

"Where were they before they came to Dallas?"

"Galveston. We both grew up down there and I, well, I guess I never moved away. Never saw a reason to. But once that prick had left Charlene and Bradley high and dry, I encouraged her to make a new start of it."

"Big deal to move a kid away from family," I said.

"I guess so, but she asked my opinion, and I agreed that starting over somewhere that didn't hold so many bad memories was the best thing to do. She could always move back if it didn't work out."

"When was that?"

"Nearly four years ago. Everything had been going great until ... well, you know."

"That still doesn't give me anything about why Bradley didn't shoot anyone, Ray." He flinched twice on the words 'shoot anyone,' as though I was pulling the trigger right in front of him. "Could he have still been pissed off at his dad, trying to get back at him? Hell, could he have hated Dallas so much that he would do almost anything to get away?" I didn't really believe any of that, there'd been no evidence I'd seen so far to back up that idea, but I was starting to feel like I was getting to the point where I was glad there weren't straws on the side table for me to grasp at.

"No. No," Ray said. "That's what I'm trying to say. Things

were so much better for them both here than they were in Galveston."

"How so?"

"Okay. Bradley's always been a sensitive kid. Kept to himself mostly. Loved—loves!—music, books, art. Could spend the weekend holed up in his room reading about Middle Earth, or the great explorers." Ray smiled at a memory.

"So he's going to be the next Renaissance man. So what?"

"You don't understand. His father, Clint, was the complete opposite. Never read a book in his life and was proud of the fact. Boasted about it to anyone and everyone. A hunter, a drinker, a wife-beater, and an all-around waste of oxygen. He was always trying to toughen Bradley up, 'make him into a man.' Take him hunting, make him fight, drink beer—at nine years old for heaven's sake!—and do whatever he could to make Bradley more like himself."

"Maybe some of that finally rubbed off."

"Nope. Bradley hated every bit of it."

My eyebrows bounced up again.

"I swear," Ray said. "The number of times a hunting or fishing trip would end with Bradley crying in the car on the way home and Clint yelling at him to stop being a 'fucking sissy and harden up,' well I can't even count that high."

"What was that about?"

"The very first time, just the sound of the shotgun sent Bradley into a panic. He screamed and screamed and screamed, like he was in pain just hearing the noise. Wouldn't stop. Carried on for half an hour like that, until Clint yelled at him for scaring all the ducks away and slapped him across the face.

"Later on, Bradley would put on a brave face and even got to the point where he could shoot a gun. Tears would be streaming down his face, but he wouldn't make a sound." I watched Ray's eyes well up. "He told me once that he didn't want his dad to be angry, but he always missed on purpose whenever he had to shoot at something. He just couldn't bring himself to hurt a defenseless animal. Even though he knew that Clint would yell at him for being such a 'piss-weak Momma's boy' and would more than likely hit him, too."

Ray sniffed, reached into his back pocket for a handkerchief to wipe his eyes and blow his nose.

"So when Clint finally said he couldn't take no more and walked out on them, I don't think anyone was happier than Bradley. See, Charlene knew who Bradley was—is!—and just let him be. He's a good kid, Mr. Rafferty, the last four years of his life have been the best so far and I'm as lost as anyone as to how he's involved in all this. I mean, I think he's even got a girlfriend."

"I figured. I found a note in his room. From 'B'. Any idea who that is?"

"Nope. I was only guessing about it because when we spoke on the phone, 'bout three weeks ago, I asked him if he had a girlfriend yet. You know, just an uncle teasing his nephew, but he wouldn't answer. The rest of the conversation, he was happy, really happy. I could hear it in his voice."

We sat in silence.

"So tell me, Mr. Rafferty. You tell me why he would do what the police and the papers say he did."

Racked my brain, but right then, I had nothing.

Yet.

———

None of the front yard assembly had tried storming the house by the time Cowboy got back so we decamped from the porch, and the three of us—Cowboy, Ray and I—sat around the kitchen table and ate.

Ray put his burger down, wiped his hands on a napkin and said, "Gotta say, I feel sorry for Frank." I raised my eyebrows, and he continued. "I don't know him or his daughter, obviously, but what a hell of a thing to go through."

Strange words about a man who had held a gun to his sister's head a few hours earlier. I was about to pick up that thread and run with it when I heard soft footfalls on the stairs. I turned and Ray got up as Charlene padded into the kitchen with sleep-tousled hair and red eyes. He gave her a sad smile, which she didn't return, then pulled out a chair for her.

"I smell food?" she asked.

I motioned towards the paper sack.

"Don't know what you're partial to," Cowboy said. "There's burgers, fries, and onion rings in there."

Charlene unwrapped a burger and took a bite. Chewed methodically, mechanically. No pleasure, or even recognition that she was eating. Just instinct to keep the body alive.

I wanted to interrogate her, find the missing piece, get a better picture of this kid that I knew so damn little about. I also knew how my nerves were still faring after the day we'd had and I couldn't imagine hers were any better, nor did she even seem to recognize that the rest of us were even at the table, so I didn't.

Cowboy? He sat there, munching his burger like it was that Memorial Day weekend I would have preferred.

"You all right to bunk down here tonight?" I asked him. "I hadn't planned on staying, but after today ..."

"Shore," he said. "I'll jes' do a scout around 'fore you leave. Get an idea of the killin' zones, but we won't have trouble tonight. Folks out by the curb got a good look as I brang the guns in from the truck. They'd be dumber than a box of hammers to try sumpin."

I nodded. "Call me at home if anything happens."

"Ah yuh."

We finished eating in silence, thinking about the day, what tomorrow might bring, and hoping like hell it was a damn sight better.

Well, I was. I had no idea what the other three were thinking.

20

The next morning looked a lot better.

Hilda flew out of the house with a piece of toast and coffee, headed for an early meeting with a potential buyer for a French ivory-handled mustache comb. Or something.

Sat on the back porch with coffee and a pipe drifting blue smoke into the morning sky. The air was still, and the smoke drifted a little left, then right, not dissipating.

Like this case.

The basic facts had been the same since day one but, no matter what I did, I couldn't grab hold of it; whatever I squeezed slipped through my fingers to hover in the air in front of me again.

Nothing I'd been able to gather so far proved or disproved Bradley's innocence or guilt. I'd seen him with the gun, seen him fire off a shot, but hadn't seen whether that shot hit anyone. If what Ray said the previous evening was correct, and there was no reason to think that it wasn't, then Bradley had to be innocent.

C'mon Rafferty, you've got to stay objective about this. Let the facts lead you; don't impose a result.

Good advice, and a path I was usually apt to follow. I had a problem this time. My gut was starting to tell me different.

I had nothing—nothing at all—to base Bradley's innocence on, and truth be told, if I had to give a decision based on the facts I had to hand, he was guilty. Every day of the week.

But that was feeling less and less right.

I walked back inside, for more coffee. While it perked, I grabbed the phone to check in with Cowboy before realizing I hadn't made a note of the Wright home number. He'd have to handle things a while longer without me; I needed to start making progress on this thing before I drove myself mad, or Charlene's house got torched.

I wondered which might happen first.

That day's edition of the *Dallas Morning News* wasn't committing itself to finding a resolution either.

SUBURBAN SHOOTING AVERTED. MYSTERY MAN SAVES THE DAY.

A wildly wordy article got two of the basic facts correct about my dance with Frank Gibbons on the Wright front lawn, and then gave up caring. A couple of blurry photos of Cowboy—never with a clear shot of his face, how did he do that?—accompanied a large one of me, scowling at the camera from the Wright's porch.

There wasn't anything newsworthy in the body of the article, but the paper did its best cross-promotion and highlighted the latest report of the school shooting by Monica Gallo on page twenty-four. Now that the city's raw grief had begun to wither, Monica and her editor thought it was time to throw on some fertilizer and get watering.

And so she had a sprawling, eight-page article rehashing

and detailing exactly what happened that fateful Monday morning at Columbus High.

There were maps of the school, with graphics identifying the calculated movement of the shooters, the panicked fleeing students, and specific highlights where the luck finally ran out for too many kids.

Grabs from interviews where various kids described their horror at not knowing whether they would make it home that day, where they hid while it was all going down, and their relief at being led out of the school to safety by the police.

A couple of the excerpts spent a little too much time on the graphic scene of the bloodied hallway. I'd seen a lot of sick shit in my time, and here I was trying to forget the image of that space I'd seen on the day. I wondered how the kids would cope with it as they grew up.

Imani was there again, retelling her story, still amazed that she made it out alive.

I don't know what was different this time, whether there was something in this version of her words, or the way I was reading them, but I finally started to look at the scene that Imani, and other students, had described so many times since the day of the shooting. Maybe it was that I'd spent all my time staying focused on what I'd seen, that I hadn't looked at it from another point of view.

Whatever, for the first time, I saw it.

Really saw it. It came down over my eyes like a projector screen and I could spin the entire scene around with a thought.

I could see the angles. The buildings, the students, the escape paths. The details of who was where, doing what, and with whom.

I didn't yet know why but, for the first time, I realized that Imani was lying her teenaged head off.

———

"Gallo."

"Monica. Rafferty."

"Hey, Rafferty. Good to hear from ya. I'm pretty busy at the moment. Can I get back to ya?"

"Just a quick one, Monica. Who's the cop who gave you the inside info from Columbus High?"

Pause. "Nice try, Rafferty, but hey, ya know I can't reveal my sources. Whatcha looking for?"

I wasn't ready to tell Monica exactly what I was thinking. The last time I was up front with her, Ed felt it was his duty to rip me a new asshole. And while I could cope with Ed's ranting, I thought that if I could cut the DPD a break, it might be the right thing to do.

"Just chasing down a few things. They might not go anywhere, but I need to cross them off the list."

Monica had a nose for a story, and I tried to give it enough aroma that she could smell it through the phone line.

"C'mon, Rafferty. You've got something, I can tell."

"You know how it is, Monica. There are times even I can't tell you what's going on. Like your sources."

She waited so long that I thought I'd blown it.

"Tell me what you're after."

"I don't know, Monica." I wiggled the bait. "It might be pretty sensitive."

She rushed at that. "You need me then," she said. "If it's that big a deal, I can protect you."

"Like you did with the story about Bradley Wright."

"Fuck you. I never mentioned your name."

"That's true. I apologize."

"Fuhgeddaboutit."

I couldn't help it, I smiled. I loved it when the old NY Monica came through loud and clear.

"I don't know. I'm not sure I can tell you what this is all about just yet."

"What about this? I can talk to my guy. If he's willing to give me the info you want, and I should stress that he might not be, but if he is, I can pass it on to ya."

"What's it gonna cost me?"

"You gotta give it to me so I can keep this story rolling."

"No chance, Monica. It's not worth that."

"Don't you think the public has a right to know the truth?" While I agreed with that sentiment, I thought it was a long bow to draw that everything in the media was automatically the truth, given some of the things I'd seen and heard.

But I needed her onside, so I stood up for the freedom of information.

"'Course they do. But I don't have all the facts yet. And I'd hate for you or your paper to get caught up in a story that turns out to be different than what it looks like."

"You leave that to me, Rafferty. We've got lawyers to cover that."

"Ummm ...."

Pause. Sigh. "Okay, an exclusive then. I do this for you, I get first chance to write the story."

That I could live with.

"Done. You got a paper and pen?"

"I'm a fucking reporter, Rafferty. Whaddya think?"

"Fair enough."

I listed all the documents I wanted from her contact, which was a lot more than I was actually interested in, but I needed to bury the important needle in the middle of a bigger haystack, in case Monica went digging. She'd find it eventually, but I wanted to buy myself some time at least.

Said she'd get back to me in a few hours and we'd set up a place to meet for the handover. Sounded good to me.

So good that I went and had a nap.

———

Later, at the dining room table, I separated out the majority of the pages from the manila envelope Monica had handed to me in a grubby little alley in West Dallas. Good grief, this wasn't Watergate and I wasn't Deep Throat, but she picked the location and I didn't want to tarnish whatever images she had of clandestine meets and backroom deals.

The other documents might be useful later, but I concentrated on the ones I really wanted. It took me about two hours to get my answer and when Hilda got home from work, I asked her to double-check me.

"Seven kids," she said as I stood in the kitchen with a beer. "Yep, from what I can tell, you read it right. Seven kids that weren't marked off in class at the time of the shooting." She looked up from the dining room table.

"Don't forget the other three—Bradley Wright and the other two shooters—but yeah, seven kids unaccounted for at school when it all went down."

"Thanks." She took a sip from the glass of wine I handed her. "So, what does that mean?"

"I imagine there's innocent explanations for most of them. Kids sick at home and Mom forgot to let the school know. Maybe one, or a couple, running late and hadn't made it to school yet. Whatever the reasons, I'm sure the cops have already eliminated anyone who wasn't at school on the day, to make sure there weren't unaccounted students on the school grounds after the shooting."

"That makes sense."

"What I'm more interested in is why Imani Laweles was *at* school, but not marked off in class."

"The girl from the paper?"

"Uh huh." I finished my beer and put the bottle on the countertop. "She's made a big song and dance about being rescued on the day of the shooting. From her classroom. But she wasn't there. Why would she lie about that?"

"I can't tell you that, Ugly. But you want to know what I can?"

Hilda smiled up at me and my heart melted. She had this ability to catch me at odd moments and shatter me into a billion pieces. Whether it was the light, the flecks of color in her eyes, or the way her mouth twisted up slightly more on the left-hand side, I wasn't sure, but whatever it was, she had it in spades.

"What's that, babe?" I said.

"I'm starving. Let's eat."

21

We got one of the last tables at the Indonesian place, started with more wine and beer, and pored over the menu. Now that we were here, my stomach decided it wanted to play, and roared to life. We settled on *rijstaffel* to share, and the beaming waiter bowed and scurried away to the kitchen.

"How did the sale of that underarm hair curler go? Did you get a good price?"

Hilda took my hand across the table. "It was an antique mustache comb," she said, "and you knew that, silly."

"Guilty."

"Yes, I did get a good price, and the buyer was happy to add it to his collection. I might even be able to find some more pieces for him in the next few months. But, speaking of guilty, big guy, what's this I see in the paper about you nearly getting shot yesterday?" Her voice was light, and her touch soft, but her eyes let me know in no uncertain terms that she was anything but relaxed about what had transpired on the Wright's lawn the previous day.

"It was nothing. A minor misunderstanding if you will.

Some redneck mistook Charlene's front yard for the local wrestling camp, that's all."

Hilda's eyes flashed. "How can you be so cavalier about it? You almost got shot."

"But I didn't." I shrugged. "Not sure what else there is so say. The worst part is that the paper didn't get my good side in the photo. I told them to make sure they shot me from the left, but they never listen."

Hilda poked her tongue out at me. "Are the natives getting restless? The protestors, I mean."

I pulled my hand away. For some reason, I think better when I can use my hands. Italian blood from way back where, maybe. Hilda took the opportunity to sit back, fished a cigarette out of her packet and lit up. I reached for my pipe.

"They've been camped out on a stranger's front yard for nearly a week now. They're tired, probably hungry, and uncomfortable, and with Bradley still in hospital, there's no outlet for their anger. I think restless is a fair word for it."

"So they just decided that they could attack the boy's mother?"

"It was only one of them, not the whole bunch ..." I had an image of the whole crowd storming the house, mob mentality taking over, Cowboy and I trying to hold them off, but being overwhelmed by sheer numbers. Maybe getting Mimi up here wouldn't be a bad idea.

"Rafferty?"

"Sorry, hun, just updating a mental to-do list. Nah, Frank was just one guy, and probably closer to the shooting than most of the crowd out there." I relayed the story of his daughter, killed in the hallway. Hilda teared up almost immediately.

"Oh, Rafferty. The poor man."

"Hey. Just a minute ago it was, 'Poor Rafferty. You almost got shot.' What happened to that?"

"But you didn't get shot, right? You said so yourself."

"Touchè."

"And how's Bradley's mother doing? Happy to be back home?"

I thought of Charlene sitting at the table when I left the previous night, cocooned in her own little world as she pushed food toward her stomach. "Not necessarily happy per se, but relieved, I think."

"That's good. So where's the case at? Any new evidence on Bradley?"

"Nothing specific either way at the moment."

The food arrived, we piled plates high, and I made sure another round of drinks was on the way.

"Whatcha gonna do about the girl?" Hilda said around a mouthful of *gado-gado*.

"Imani?" She nodded. "We'll have a little chat and, like the super sleuth that I am, I'll glean exactly what went on from a combination of her physical tells, the heightened smell of pheromones, and the minute—but obvious—modulations in her speech patterns. From there it will be a simple job to make the case for or against Bradley."

"Really?"

"Of course not. I just hope I can understand what she's saying. The youth of today …"

"Rafferty, are you becoming a curmudgeon?"

"I sincerely hope so."

We shut up and ate then. The rijstaffel was excellent and, despite the literal translation being 'rice-table', only one of the dishes was actually rice.

Hilda and I ate and sipped and held hands like silly teenagers.

Dinner was done—I was stuffed full—and I forced myself

to not order another beer. "I'm bushed, hon. You ready to head home?"

Hilda swallowed the rest of her wine. "Ready to go anywhere with you, Ugly. Especially home."

I waved for the check, paid with plastic, and we walked down the cool sidewalk hand in hand. Happy and contented for the most part, but I couldn't stop myself thinking about Imani Laweles, why she would be lying about what happened on the day, and who else might be doing the same.

I was so lost in thought that I didn't immediately register the two guys sitting at a high bench in the window of the bar that we walked past. Didn't realize that I had seen the flash of recognition on one's face, saw him slap his buddy on the shoulder, or that they got up from their table.

Those realizations all coalesced and hit me about twenty seconds later, as I heard the front door of the bar bang open and the blast of music and laughter follow us down the street. The Pacer, and the Colt in the glovebox—shit, no, that was still in the Mustang. Well, the car was in a lot two blocks over, but I didn't want to hurry and scare Hilda, it might be nothing.

It wasn't.

We were halfway down the block and under a streetlight, when the voice came.

"Hey! Hey you!"

I stopped walking and turned to put Hilda behind me and next to the light pole.

"Rafferty?" she breathed.

"It's okay, babe. Probably a couple of Jehovah's Witnesses who've been missing me at home."

The two guys stepped into the fringe of light. Middle-aged, clean shaven, both carrying more pounds than they should, and didn't look all that smart.

"Hey you!" the dark-haired guy said again.

I replied. "Lucky I heard you. I usually only respond to 'Mr. Caulfield.' 'Holden' is also acceptable, though I prefer 'Oh Captain, my Captain.'"

"What the fuck?" the buddy said.

Dark Hair took up the dialog. "We don't care who you are, Caulfield ..."

Like I said, not that smart.

"... you're that dickhead looking after that killer's mom."

"Rafferty?" Hilda whispered and clutched at my arm.

"I believe you have me confused with someone else," I said, "though I'm sure this other fellow is also handsome, and physically impressive, with a rapier-like wit."

"Not gonna be so impressive when we whup the shit out of you."

"As I already said ..." I didn't break eye contact with the would-be rumblers while I reached around and pried Hilda's hand off my arm, squeezed her fingers twice and let them drop. "... I think you're looking for someone else."

"We're looking for you, asshole," Buddy said.

"Not so tough without a gun, are you?" Dark Hair finished.

About what I figured. A couple of forthright watch-people from the Wright front lawn. The crowd had grown so much I hadn't been able to keep track of all the faces.

"Oh, I'm plenty tough enough, with or without a weapon. Don't worry your pretty little heads about that. But, like I've explained previously, I *really* think you're looking for someone else."

Buddy decided that rhetoric had gone far enough and the time had come to take action. He stepped forward, thrusting out his right arm. I don't think it was a punch, probably just a stabbed finger in the air at me.

He didn't get that far.

I sidestepped in time with his move, shielding Hilda as I did, grabbed his wrist, jerked down and stepped into him. Grabbed his shoulder with my left hand and before Buddy, or Dark Hair for that matter, knew what was happening, I had him spun around, his arm twisted behind his back and I was levering his hand upwards. Shuffled us both sideways, keeping our little dance routine between Dark Hair and Hilda. I could hear her little gasps, forced myself not to concentrate on them.

"Okay guys," I said. "Here's how it shapes up. I have no idea what the hell you thought you'd accomplish with this stunt. I've got no beef with you. And you only think you have one with me."

I watched Dark Hair's eyes. He was squinting questions at Buddy and I could see his hands clenching in my peripheral vision. I levered Buddy's wrist and arm a little higher, put more pressure on his shoulder. He struggled, shook, I stayed with him and pushed up further. He gave a little shake of his head. Dark Hair relaxed a touch, held his ground.

"Don't waste your time, guys," I said. "It makes you look stupid, and you don't know when and what I'll be carrying. F'rinstance, I could reach inside my jacket right now, grab my .38 and pop you both right here." I kept the pressure on with my right hand, stepped into Buddy, while shuffling my left hand inside my pocket.

That was enough. Dark Hair took a step backwards and Buddy slumped. I went with him a little. No point dislocating the guys shoulder for no reason.

"Are we clear, guys?"

"Yeah, yeah," Dark Hair said.

"Good." I pushed Buddy away and made sure I was still shielding Hilda while he collided with his friend. They got their collective feet underneath them and stood again on the edge of the light circle. Buddy massaged his shoulder with his left hand, while Dark Hair glared at me.

"Knock yourselves out with your protesting, guys. I don't care. Sing your songs, write your witty signs, whatever gets your juices flowing. But ..." I pulled out my pipe, went through the theatrics of lighting and tamping.

"... if you come at me or my clients again, all bets are off. Got it?"

They nodded, looked like they wanted to speak, couldn't think of what they might say, turned and headed down the street. They stopped several times down the block to look back, and I kept watching until they were back inside the bar.

Hilda grabbed my arm again. "Oh my god, Rafferty."

I put an arm around her shoulder and pulled her close. "Beats bad after-dinner coffee, don't it?"

"How can you make jokes? Those men wanted to beat us up." She shivered. I rubbed her arm, turned her around and we started walking toward the car again.

"Not that it makes much difference, but I think they only wanted to beat me up. Poor, misguided fools."

"I know that's supposed to make me feel better, Rafferty. It doesn't."

"I know." Wondered whether it was weird that I felt better than I had all day. Yeah, it was weird, but what the hell.

"They weren't interested in hurting you," I said. "Hell, they weren't even that interested in hurting me. They're just pissed off and want to get rid of that anger." I leaned down and kissed the top of her head.

"Is that why you didn't hurt them?" Hilda tucked her head into my chest, and we kept walking.

"Oh, he'll be feeling that shoulder for the next few days."

"You know that I mean."

"Yeah, I do, and I think you give me too much credit, babe," I said. "If I think like that, it's after the fact. During, I'm not thinking much at all. I'm focused on eliminating threats and protecting what I need to protect." I squeezed her. "If that comes across as a deep assessment of the circumstances and the delivery of a thoroughly analyzed moral and ethical response, so be it."

I stopped and turned her to face me. She looked up at me, eyes glistening, and I fell in love again for about the thousandth time. I held her shoulders and leaned in close. Whispered.

"Don't tell anyone. It'll ruin my reputation as a hard-ass."

Hilda laughed, a caw that ricocheted off the nearby buildings. She snorted then and pulled me close, linked her hands behind my neck and buried her face in my chest.

"I love you, Rafferty."

"You too, babe."

We stood on that side-street and held each other close. I rubbed her back, felt her heartbeat slow and her breathing relax. I kissed her head and looked both ways down the street. There was no-one else there.

We hurried to the car and I watched everything, checking shadows and making sure that I kept myself between Hilda and blind corners. Driving home, Hilda rested her head on my shoulder, I patted her leg and vowed that I would get the truth from Imani Laweles tomorrow and this stupid case off my back.

22

Before I got to Imani though, I needed to check in with Cowboy, so I drove to the Wright house, parked a way down the street and watched the front yard crowd. It had swelled since two nights earlier—no doubt due to the Frank, Cowboy and Rafferty show on the late news —and the two network vans seemed to have procreated, giving birth to a couple of new arrivals.

Nothing screams ratings and human interest like footage of people almost being shot. Film at eleven.

I wasn't keen on running the gauntlet. Cowboy's truck was still parked, nose in, on the driveway and I knew by the time I stopped the Pacer, got out, locked up, and tried to make it to the porch, I'd be swamped with reporters and, on their heels, the fervent and righteous.

Maybe Cowboy was right. My cases did seem to include more than my fair share of god-botherers.

Hell with it, I couldn't wait out on the street forever.

I pulled the car up in the single driveway as close as I could get to the back of Cowboy's truck and found my instincts were still sharp. Before I had the park brake engaged and killed the motor, microphones and camera lenses were competing for turns to bump against the driver's side window.

I rolled the window down a half-inch, fired up the pipe and blew smoke at the gap and those behind the recording devices.

"What do you have to say about the near-tragedy on this front lawn the day before yesterday, sir?"

The reporter, with his serious voice and his serious look and his serious suit, shot questions at me while I sat and smoked. Thought about giving him the bird, decided that would give them footage they could use, so I did my best at boring him to death. Didn't acknowledge his questions, or his existence, and when my pipe was finished, I reached around to ferret in the pile of crap on the back seat for a John D. MacDonald novel I thought was back there.

Wondered for a few seconds why the back seat was so clean, then realized that the novel was in the Mustang. Along with the Colt. And the gloves. Goddamn. This constant not having the things I needed within reaching distance was starting to piss me off.

For the moment I was trapped in the car, within talking distance of the front porch, but it might as well have been the width of the Atlantic, given the predatory newshounds still tapping on the window.

Nap time.

When I woke up a while later—about forty-five minutes, actually—it had got awful quiet. The human tide had receded to the curb, so I checked twice to make sure no-one was interested, hopped out and hoofed it into the house.

———

"Our audience is growin', boss-man."

"Yeah," I said. "Another week and we'll have a big enough fan base to take this show on the road."

Cowboy and I sat in the living room, couldn't be bothered sitting out on the porch being pestered by reporters and the righteous. Ray made us coffee and then disappeared upstairs with his sister. She was brighter today but shooing away Frank Gibbons hadn't solved the main problem and I thought she'd looked more drawn than when we first met in the hospital. Low murmurs floated from the sitting room down the stairwell.

"Anything exciting happen last night?" I asked.

"Naw."

"Good."

Cowboy shrugged. "That's as may be, but it shore is borin'. After the excitement of the other day, I kinda 'spected a mite more."

My turn to shrug. "My guess is that the gang down there could maybe muster up a full backbone between them, but no-one wants to make the first move."

"I'd rather that than havin' to lie in my bunk and listen to 'em sing 'Onward Christian Soldiers' at three in the ay em."

Nothing to say to that. I shrugged again and sipped.

"What's the skinny on this kid, boss-man? He do what those folk say?"

"It sure looks like he did," I said, "but I'll be damned if I can find any hard facts to prove it."

"That never stopped folks believin' whatever they want to."

"True. I'm trying to make some progress and I've got a lead to pull on today, but I need your help." I outlined the phonecalls I wanted Cowboy to make, discounting the other six kids who weren't at school at the time of the shooting.

Yes, I was assuming that each of them would have innocent explanations for their absences but, in the case that they
didn't, Cowboy could handle it. I had a date with a lying
teenage girl.

"Good idea. Gimme sumpin to do. Here I'd bin startin' to
think 'bout shootin' someone jes' to break the monotony."

Sometimes the scariest part about Cowboy was my
inability to tell if he was joking.

"You think Mimi can come up?" I said instead of trying to
read his mind.

"Losin' faith in me, boss-man?"

"We can handle it for the moment, but if the crowd gets
much bigger, we're gonna want to be watching all the flanks,
especially while I'm out talking to people."

"Well, right there's your problem. Too much talking, not
enough action. You ask me, you'd get a lot further with someone's toe wedged 'tween a pair o' bolt-cutters."

"Christ, Cowboy. Did you have posters of Genghis Kahn
on your wall while you were growing up?"

"Naw. Babe Ruth."

"Really?"

"Swear to god."

I stood. "Let's get Mimi up here in the next couple of days.
Maybe she can bring your bat and glove with her."

"Har de har har. I'll call and get her movin'. Whatcha
gonna do now?"

"Gonna question one of the students and see why she's
lying about what she saw on the day."

"Got your bolt-cutters?"

"Of course not."

"Wimp."

———

Imani Laweles was taller than I expected from her pictures. She was also corn-rowed, bangled, with acne-scarred cheeks, and filled out her double denim outfit in a way that belied her sixteen years. But she was quietly spoken, polite enough—she called me sir—and lacked the sneering attitude I expected of a typical teenager.

She was also nervous as hell.

We were all seated in the sunroom of the family home. Outside I could see the flagstones and terrace from the newspaper shoot, stepping down to a good-sized lawn bordered by tall hedges.

Imani was centered on the floral couch between her foster-parents, Donald and Martha Beckett. Donald leaned forward, ready to come off the couch at me at the slightest provocation, and Martha thumbed her rosary beads like there was no tomorrow. They were both too preoccupied with me to notice their foster-daughter's constant foot-twitching and finger twisting.

"My daughter has been through this with the police, Mr. Rafferty. I don't see what good it will do." I imagined the phrase *basso profundo* was created just for him.

"Harassment, that's what it is," Martha interjected.

I raised my eyes to the crucifix on the wall behind the couch and fished my pipe out of my pocket as I weighed the options for my next line.

"I'll ask you kindly not to pollute my home with that foul stench," Donald said.

I thought about making something of it, then remembered why I was here—I can get distracted—and put my pipe away. I started softly.

"I'm clarifying a few details from some of the kid's statements. Just making sure everything adds up."

"What's to add up? Those two dead boys and that one still

in the hospital wreaked unspeakable acts on my girl and the rest of her school. When he wakes up, he'll pay for what he did."

Goddamn, if he could get the projection right, he'd do a hell of a version of *Ol' Man River*.

"Lordy," Martha said and crossed herself.

While they were making their pronouncements, they both missed the blink and shudder Imani gave at the phrase *'my girl'*. She twisted her fingers harder, turned one foot on its side and placed the other on top.

"My daughter hasn't slept right since that day. Terrible nightmares."

"Terrible," parroted Martha.

I blew out a breath and tried to relax. "I only have few questions." They squinted at me. "If you'll let me get through them, then you'll have me out of your house, I'll be able to smoke, and we'll all be a lot happier, I promise."

Martha declined to respond and started double-timing the rosary beads. Donald put his elbows on his knees, got one fist nestled in his other hand and tilted a nod at me. "Okay," he rumbled.

I chinned him a nod and leaned back in my chair. Opened up the space a little. Imani took the moment to tuck a Conversed foot up underneath her other leg and crossed her arms. Looked at her lap.

"Imani," I said, letting her name hang in the air until she looked up at me. "You were at school on the day of the shooting, right?"

"Mr. Raff—" he tried. I threw him a look that said, 'We've been through this, remember?' He chose to rub his fist and glare at me instead.

"Imani?"

Looked like she was trying to figure out how the question might be a trap but couldn't quite get there.

"Umm, yeah. I was." Glanced down and nodded to herself.

"Imani?" Donald rumbled.

"Sorry," she said. "Yes, sir. I was."

"Okay," I said. "That's great. You're doing fine." That earned me a shy smile. "And you escaped without injury?"

"Yes, sir." She grimaced for a second before finding the shy smile again.

I forced myself to stay relaxed.

It was harder than it sounds.

"How long have you been at Columbus High?"

She glanced at Donald then. He was too busy steel-eying me to catch the gesture.

"Almost a year now."

"You like going to school?"

"Yes sir." Pause. "I'm working hard. There's been a lot of time when I didn't go to school when I was younger ..." A glance to the side. "So I wasn't sure if I would like it so much, but I do. Well, I did, until the other day."

"Yeah. But it's got to be tough sometimes. I remember being a teenager and wanting to be anywhere other than in school. You must want to cut class sometime."

I didn't think Imani would admit to being out of class, not in front of her foster parents, but I threw it out there just to see her reaction.

Before we got to that point, Donald decided to join in. "There's two rules to living in my house, Mr. Rafferty. No drugs and perfect school attendance. Imani knows this. Right, child?"

"Yes, sir."

Okay, so that explained why she was cagy about not being in class on the day of the shooting, but it didn't answer the questions of exactly where she was.

Or why.

"Did you know any of the kids who were killed? Rebecca Gibbons, for example."

"Who?"

"The kids with the guns? You knew them?"

"No sir, not at all."

Probing exactly who she did and didn't know might be interesting, but there was another destination I had in mind. "It must have been scary to be in the middle of everything that was happening that day."

It wasn't a question, but Imani didn't seem to notice the technicality.

"Umm … yes it was, sir. It was really scary. I wasn't sure if I would make it back here. Back home."

Martha beamed but kept her thumbs working hard on the rosary beads.

"Can you tell me about it?"

"About what?"

"Just describe what you saw."

"Well …" She got started and, as I expected, gave me the exact same story that I, and everyone else in Dallas, had read in the papers. But I wasn't interested in what she had to say, I wanted to watch her say it.

Once she began, she transformed from the agitated teenager I introduced myself to, to a smooth, composed orator.

I'd been lied to. A lot. She wasn't the best I'd seen but she was pretty damn good.

And unless you were watching hard enough to notice the

slight foot tap and the constant eye flicks to the high left, you'd never know that she was making the whole thing up. Given how many times she must have told this story already, I wasn't surprised at how good she was.

"What about Bradley Wright?" I said, interrupting her in the middle of a particularly touching line about being led to safety and knowing that she would be re-united with her family.

"Umm … what? I mean, I'm sorry, sir?"

"Bradley Wright. The boy indicted to stand trial on murder charges."

The swallow she gave must have sounded like an explosion to her, but Mom and Dad were so busy watching me that they didn't notice.

"What about him?"

"How do you know him?"

"Umm, I don't really know him. I maybe saw him in the playground once or twice, but that's it."

"You saw him in the playground during the shooting?"

"Whaat? No. No. I didn't see him at all that day. I was in my classroom with everyone else. No, I meant I *had* seen him around the school. *Before* the day of the …"

"Okay," I said.

We all waited a few seconds. When they started shooting me questioning looks, I decided it was now or never.

"Imani, why are you lying to me?"

"Whaaa—" Imani started, before being drowned out by another "Lordy!" from Martha and Donald's "How dare you!" He was on his feet and stabbing a fat finger in my direction. I stayed on my butt, hoping that I could avoid getting spun off on a tangent. Or into a fist fight. We were about even in height but I bet he had forty pounds on me and I didn't want to have to pistol whip him in front of his family.

Bad form, thinking like that. Probably get me hurt one day.

"Imani, you know something else about what happened don't you?" I asked.

"No, no, no. I don't know nothin ...."

"That's enough, Mr. Rafferty."

I could barely hear Imani around Donald's bulk as he advanced, and as he got right up close, I stood in case he decided he wanted to take a swing at me.

I kept trying. "What is it, Imani? What happened on the day that you haven't told anyone about?"

Donald backed me up to the door into the living room. "Get out of my house now, Mr. Rafferty. Before I call the police." I hesitated a step, tried to bluff him, and he called over his shoulder. "Honey. Call 911. Tell them we have an intruder in our house and he's threatening our teenage daughter."

"Lordy!"

I patted the air. "Okay. Okay. I'm going."

He slammed the heavy door behind me, probably watched me through the peephole as I headed across the street to the car.

Sat on the hood and treated myself to a pipe. I was confident the attendance registers were correct, that Imani wasn't in school on the day, and her whole story was a smokescreen.

Why?

Just to lie to her parents about her school attendance? Maybe, but it didn't seem right. And the way she reacted to my question about Bradley and seeing him in the rec-area during the shooting, that was definitely a thread that needed unraveling.

By the time I finished my pipe and was heading home, I was pretty certain that not only did Imani know that Bradley was involved, she was protecting him. I didn't yet know from what or why, but I would.

Only a matter of time now.

23

I didn't come up with any brilliant ideas about Imani's involvement in the shooting for the rest of the weekend, and there wasn't anything exciting waiting for me at the office, so on Monday morning I rolled up to the cop shop. I thought it could be prudent to talk to someone who should know her a damn sight better than I did.

It wouldn't go well, but how was I to know?

Ed wasn't in his office—probably a good thing, given our last conversation—so I headed around the corner, and stuck my head into the Homicide report writing room.

Ricco was sitting next to a tiny desk near the window, looking over the shoulder of a fuzzy-cheeked officer banging away on a typewriter old enough to have seen Oswald's arrest details.

I made it all the way across the room before Ricco noticed me. He rolled his eyes in return, held up a finger. I nodded and walked to the coffee machine to wait for him.

Eight minutes later, he peacocked his way down the corridor, holding a mug that looked like it needed a forensics assessment, and re-filled it.

We both sipped and grimaced.

"Damn, this coffee is shit, Rafferty," Ricco said.

I shrugged. He was right.

"What's up?" Ricco said.

"Imani Laweles. What do you figure her for?"

"Who? Columbus High's Little Miss Popular?"

"Yeah, that's her. You interviewed her on the day. What's your impression?"

Ricco squinted at me, checked a wristwatch underneath a purple shirt sleeve. I assumed that he had a lemon suit coat that matched his pants strung over a chair somewhere.

"Why?" he asked. "What you got?"

"I asked you first. Seriously," I said, when I saw Ricco's look, "I'll tell you, but I'd rather hear your thoughts without you knowing what I'm looking for."

"That's fair." He nodded. "Uh, she was one of the kids rescued by the cops soon as the shooters were dead. Obviously, we didn't know about the Wright kid at that point."

"Uh huh."

"Well, she was shit-scared, lucky to be alive, and … shit, I don't know, Rafferty. You gotta give me something."

"Not yet. What did she say happened?"

Ricco ran me through her story. Another carbon copy of everything that had been reported over the past three weeks.

"And you believe her?" I asked.

"Any reason I shouldn't?" He grinned then dropped the smile. "Tell the truth, something about her did bug me, but I couldn't figure out what. So I did a little digging."

"And?"

"She's in the system."

"Do tell."

"Yup. Juvie stuff. Some shoplifting, and a coupla possession charges. Got the details from Houston PD."

"Go on."

"They all came from when she was living on the streets down there, after runnin' away from home. Prob'ly saved her life, though."

"Bad home life."

"Majorly fucked-up. Stepdad—no-one knows what happened to her real father—weightlifter and steroid junkie, ran around as an enforcer for one of the local crime mobs."

"The Mob?"

"Fuck, no. Nothing that organized. Just a bunch of local mouth-breathers running stolen car parts, drugs—speed and angel dust mainly—and a string of the scuzziest whorehouses in the city. These guys made the Dallas DeathStars look white-collar.

"Anyway, step-daddy liked to bring his work home with him. Usually he'd just wale away on Momma. Presumably the kids, too. 'Cept this particular night, he came home jacked up on some shit and butchered all five of them. When the cops finally busted down the door a day later, he was sitting in the kitchen with five heads lined up by size on the floor in front of him."

"Holy shit."

"Uh huh. She'd been there, Imani would have been the sixth. Nothin' surer."

"How'd she get to Dallas?"

"After her last possession bust, Social Work got involved. Helped get her clean, that's what it looks like, got her into a shelter. Spent eighteen months there before the family she's with now decided to foster her."

"Lucky for her."

"You know how rare it is for a fifteen-year old to get fostered? Like winning the fucking lottery. The sorta luck I don't got, I'll tell you that. Add to that the family wanted to take her and she's the luckiest girl in the country. She don't wanna be fucking that up."

"I guess so. Dad seems a little intense."

"Oh shit, Rafferty. You haven't been rattling that hornet's nest, have you?" Ricco obviously didn't believe my head shake. "Why you gotta go and make our jobs harder? Why?"

"What the hell are you talking about?"

"Her foster father is the Chief's brother-in-law."

"Chief who?"

"Chief of Police, numb-nuts. Whatever you do, just leave that one alone."

"Okay, okay. Calm down. Back to the girl. All you've given me so far are the facts." Ricco nodded. "What's your gut tell you?"

"Nuh huh. You gotta spill. What're you looking for?"

"Okay. I think she's hiding something."

"What?"

"If I knew what, I wouldn't be here with you trying to work it out, would I?"

"You gotta have something."

I blew out a breath. "She didn't see the hallway where the four bodies were. The one that she was supposedly walked through while being rescued."

"How the hell you know that?"

"Call it a hunch, gut, whatever, but I've read all the articles about her, and all the ones about the other kids, too. It's the way she talks about it. There's plenty of detail about the who and the how of what happened in the rec-area, but nothing about the hallway. You saw it ..." Ricco nodded. "You couldn't have walked through there and not seen what happened."

"Maybe she just didn't want to talk about it?"

"She's talked about every goddamn other thing. And when I asked her about Bradley Wright—"

"You talked to her? Oh fuck. Ed is going to have your ass. I don't wanna be around when that happ—"

With the perfect timing that only occurs in real life, there was a bellow from down the hallway.

"HE'S HERE?! WHERE?"

I didn't hear the response, but figured what would happen next, topped up my coffee cup and leaned against the wall.

Ed came around the corner at the closest thing he could get to a run.

"You!"

"Ah, Ricco," I said. "I believe your lieutenant wants a word."

Ricco smiled, folded himself against the wall and watched. Ed pounded the last ten feet to me, breathing heavily. I had an image of the cartoon bull blowing steam out of nostrils before getting ready to charge.

"What the hell do you think you're doing?" he said. "Are you deliberately trying to give me a stroke or get me fired? How stupid are you? Do you ever think about what you're doing?"

"Good morning, Ed," I said. "In answer to your questions; sometimes, almost never, with a white wine sauce, and forty-three point seven. You were talking a bit fast though, so I may have got those in the wrong order."

Ed's eyes widened, but his breathing had started to slow down, so I was less concerned that one of us might have to do CPR, which was good.

"I should have you arrested right now," he said.

"On what charge? Loitering, probably, but given half the cops here are doing less than I am, Holding's gonna be pretty full."

Ricco chuckled.

"Go do something useful, Sergeant. Like your job."

Ricco melted away.

"My office. Now!"

I was barely inside, before Ed slammed the door hard enough for the glass pane to rattle.

"Let me tell you about two of the phone calls I've had this morning," he said, weaving around the end of his desk and dropping himself into his desk chair. "From the Chief, and the DA themselves no less."

I raised my eyebrows. "You're better connected than I am, Ed. They almost never call me."

"Shut up."

I shut up.

"They both want you detained, and they'd be happy to see it take a long time for arraignment. A very long time."

I leaned forward in the visitor's chair and held both my hands out, wrists up, fingers curled into loose fists.

Ed glared at me for about six months.

"Stop that. You know I can't do that without cause. So do they. Even though god knows it might make my job easier." I sat back. He sighed and dry-rubbed his face. His jowls stuck at the job for a few seconds longer. "Fuck me, Rafferty. I don't know how you get so lucky."

"Skill. Daring. Years of clean living," I said.

Ed snorted, so I knew we were starting to make progress.

"You are getting dangerously close to stepping on toes that shouldn't be stepped on."

"Sometimes, people deserve to be walked over."

"Not these people." He looked at my face. "I mean it. And you should be goddamned thankful that they're both as honorable as they are, 'cause I've worked with plenty of others who'd think nothing of drumming up phony charges that would mean you wouldn't see your next birthday on the outside."

It was time for me to stop caging.

"Okay, Ed. Something about the Columbus High shooting stinks. I'm just trying to work out what it is."

Ed looked down at his lap, breathed in and out for a count of ten.

"If I pretend to listen, will you go away, stop bothering the people who make decisions on my continued employment, and leave this thing alone?"

"Never say never, Ed."

"Christ. I'm gonna regret this, I know it. Okay, give it to me in twenty-five words or less."

I was about to launch into my theory that Imani was lying to protect Bradley Wright but didn't know how to handle the distinct lack of proof or any logical reasoning.

Thankfully the phone rang.

"What?" Ed growled into the receiver.

Heard the low murmur though the phone and watched the line of Ed's mouth as it morphed from annoyed, through curious, blipped past amused, and alighted on confident. All while keeping his lips perfectly horizontal.

He hung up the phone, looked at me expectantly.

"Well, looks like we both win. I don't have to sit here and listen to you anymore. And you might get some of those answers you're looking for. Whenever I decide to tell you, of course."

"How's that?"

"That was the hospital. Bradley Wright just woke up."

———

I figured Ed would take some time to get rolling. After all, the kid was under police guard, so he wasn't going anywhere anytime soon.

Not the case for me. I needed to get to Bradley before the justice system descended upon him and stopped him from being able to tell me what I needed to know.

I don't think Ed fully believed my rushed agreement to staying off this case and out of his hair, but then he also wanted me out of his office, so I don't think he cared too much.

Called Paul Eindhoven from a payphone on the way to the car. Brought him up to speed and told him to do whatever he could to make sure that I could talk to Bradley for as long as possible.

There was more than one room with a cop standing duty outside, so it took me walking too damn many yards of the hallways to work out which door Bradley was behind. Wondered for a couple of moments what lay in the rooms behind the other cop sentries but didn't have time to dwell on it.

I camped around the corner, out of sight of the cop, while I waited for the doctors and nurses to exit Bradley's room, and thought about my next move. Magnum would have Rick and TC distract the guard while he slipped inside, Spenser would render the guards defenseless by hurling Thomas Hardy quotes at them, and Mike Hammer … well, Mike would probably just shoot someone.

This shit is a lot easier on TV.

The guy who'd drawn the short straw to be guarding a door in the hospital instead of being out on the streets knocking heads was young though, so I thought I might have a chance.

I came around the corner looking purposeful, flipped him

a quick glance at my license and said officiously, "DA's office. They wanted me here asap."

He didn't look convinced. "I wasn't told anyone was coming."

"You think you get copied in on all her correspondence? She wants to make sure that no-one, and I repeat her words, 'not a single living soul is to speak with Bradley Wright before I get there'. You want me to tell DA Hernandez I couldn't do my job 'cause you knew better?"

"I don't know."

I pulled out my notepad. "What's your full name? I want to make sure I spell it right when I report back to Hernandez."

That did it. The kid looked each way down the hallway and stepped aside.

I pulled the curtains across the inside window, dragged a chair up to the bedside and sat down next to Bradley.

It was the first time I'd seen him since he was lying in ICU and he didn't look a whole lot better. The network of tubes still snaked from under the sheets to the bank of bedside monitors. The bandages around his head seemed to have lessened, but the parts of scalp now on display were pasty-white bald, with dots of hair struggling to grow back. His face was so bruised it was almost impossible to tell what complexion he had been before being hit by the bus.

His eyes were open and glazed, but he looked like he was doing his best to bring them to heel.

"Who are you?" he croaked.

I'd focused so much on trying to beat everyone else here, that I hadn't thought about how I was going to play it with Bradley. In the end I didn't have to.

"Wait a min … I kno … know you." He closed his eyes and his breathing slowed. Just when I thought he was out of it, he came back. Cranked one eye open. "You're that guy …

from ... the alley. Chased me ... don't know what happened ... where am I?"

Any kid waking up from a three-week coma in an unfamiliar hospital deserved to be slowly, and calmly, introduced to the truth by a small group of loving family members.

Bad luck.

"No time for that now, Bradley. You're gonna have to listen. Fast. You've been indicted to stand trial on four counts of murder from the day of the shooting."

"Huh?"

"What is it between you and the two other shooters? Kevin and Randy."

"Wh ... Who?"

"How did it all go down?"

"Why are you here?"

"Your Mom hired me—"

"Mom? Is she here? Mom?"

"Shut up and listen." Decided on a different tack. "What's the story with Imani?"

"Who?"

"Imani Laweles. Why is she covering for you?"

"Don't know any ... named ... Imani."

"From school. She knows you."

"Uh huh."

Bradley closed his eyes again and his body sagged. The monitors continued to do whatever it was that they were doing, but no alarms went off, so I assumed that he just went back to sleep.

Sure enough, about a minute later, he started snoring.

Heard the door open behind me. "I told you," I growled over my shoulder, "the DA's office doesn't want anyone else in here. Got it?"

"Oh, I got the message, Mr. Rafferty," Maria Hernandez

said, "but it appears that you didn't. Officer, get him out of here."

I stood and turned, saw Maria flanked by Owl Eyes and the young cop, who didn't look so unsure of himself now. He crossed the room and moved to grab me with a come-along hold.

"No chance," I said, swung my arm out of his reach.

Unfortunately, on his final step toward me, the kid's shoes scuffed the linoleum and he lurched forward.

I barely grazed him on the side of the head, and with an open hand too, but in no time at all he had his gun out and I could barely decipher what he was yelling at me, but I think I heard Owl Eyes say "Assaulting an officer," Hernandez saying "Good-bye, Mr. Rafferty," and when all was said and done, for the second time on this goddamned case I found myself in a pair of handcuffs and being bundled into a blue and white.

24

Hilda drove and I stared out the window and mulled. She might have thought I was sulking, even said as much after we were away from DPD Headquarters, but she was wrong, I was mulling.

Definitely.

The guys at Processing had chuckled when the young cop prodded me inside, though I didn't see what was so goddamn funny. Four hours later in holding—*sans* pipe this time—I was ready to snap.

Judge Winslow had taken his own sweet time in getting to the courthouse for the bail hearing. Apparently, I had interrupted a black-tie gala at the country club and he was in no mood to rush. Or be reasonable, obviously, since ten grand as bail was ridiculous. But the prosecutor they rolled in from the DA's office made the whole incident sound like I'd bare-knuckled the life out of the young cop.

I didn't respond. Not much point, when Winslow brought up knowing my old man and clucked his tongue while sighing his disappointment over seeing the younger of the Rafferty cops 'headed down the same path to nowhere'.

So they dragged me back to holding and I managed to get a phone call to Hilda. I tried her place, but no luck, so I left a message apologizing for not seeing her and explaining the situation.

She showed up at 9:10 the next morning with a cashier's check and a worried frown. Three hours later, the check had been gobbled up by a cashier of very few words, but they left the frown for Hilda to take with her.

Generosity knows no bounds.

In all that time, I didn't see or hear from Ed or Ricco and it pissed me off.

Okay, so I'd told him that I'd lay off. Big deal. He can't have thought that I actually meant it. We knew each other better than that.

Hilda was talking.

"What?" I said.

"Are you still sulking about being arrested?"

"I'm not sulking, I'm mulling. Maybe a bit of brooding thrown in for good measure, but definitely no sulking."

"Whatever you say, Ugly, but it's hard to see a difference from here."

"Uh huh."

"So what're you *mulling* about?"

"Ed left me hanging."

"Can you blame him?"

"Whose side are you on?"

"You know that I'm always on your side, big guy, but he has told you to stop poking your nose into this case. Remember?"

"Of course I do, but I've got a client to look after, I can't just drop it 'cause he'd prefer it."

"I know, I know. And I'm not suggesting you actually do let it go. I'm just pointing out why Ed might not be too enthused about helping you out of the mess you get yourself in to."

"Uh huh. Thanks for the bail money."

"No problems. Though if you fail to show up to court and I lose that ten grand, I'll take it out of your ass. You know that, right?"

"If that's an attempted come-on, I'm not really in the mood, babe. But I appreciate the offer."

I winked at her and we rode in silence for a little while.

"Are you going to be all right?" she asked.

"Oh yeah, sure. I'll be fine."

"But?"

"Huh?"

"There's always a 'but' when you let your voice trail off like that."

"Well, I have to face the possibility that if I'm found guilty, and *that* will depend on how much shit Hernandez wants to throw my way, there's a distinct possibility they'll yank my license."

"Oh honey, I hadn't even thought of that. What will you do?"

"Not even going to think about it right now. Too much to do just working out the whole Bradley-Imani thing. If I get lucky and give Hernandez something to be happy about, that might help."

Hilda nodded. She clearly had no idea how I was going to get lucky. And, based on the way this case had gone so far, neither did I.

Hilda rolled the car up to a traffic light. "Home for a shower and nap?"

"Just the shower. Time to get busy. Gotta get out to Wright's house so I can bust this damn thing wide open."

I called Paul Eindhoven before I left the house. I needed to find out what he knew about Imani and make sure I wasn't being played again. According to the secretary the good counselor was attending court, so I asked her to have him call me back at Charlene's house as soon as possible.

The Wright vigil crowd had grown again. People were spilling onto the road as they jostled for space on the verge, making it hard to drive down the street without stopping. I couldn't get the Pacer even close to the driveway, but that didn't matter. Mimi's cherry-red Jeep with the black soft-top was taking up the space on the driveway behind Cowboy's truck.

I didn't want to fartass around today. Parked, locked the car, and got the Winchester 12-gauge out of the trunk, where I'd put it before leaving home. Chambered a shell. *Snick, snack.*

Some people love birdsong, others music. I'll be honest, the sound of a shotgun getting ready for work is the one that stirs my loins.

Walked through the crowd, with the shotgun at high port. They parted like the Red Sea for Moses. I continued up the front lawn and onto the porch, all eyes in the crowd following me with feet rooted on the crushed grass.

Made it inside.

"Rafferty, you old so-and-so." Mimi jumped up from where she was sitting on a sofa with Charlene and Ray. Came over to give me a hug. "Ain't seen you in too long. How are ya?"

I stood the shotgun in a corner and bent down—a long, long way—to return the hug.

Mimi is short. Real short.

But she was the perfect human argument for why size doesn't matter, as more than a few men had found out too late after making the decision to not take her seriously.

"I'm doing fine," I said. "Glad you're here."

"You're not worried 'bout those folks outside, are ya? P'shaw. Nothing out there but a bunch of folk with a lotta hot air."

"For the moment, yeah, but that's not gonna last. Plus, we've got the small matter of Charlene's son on trial for murders he may not have committed."

Charlene joined Mimi's side, brighter than I'd last seen her. Maybe even with a hint of momma lion starting to show again. "What did you say?"

"In a moment, Charlene. Hey," I said to Cowboy, who was leaning in the kitchen doorway, "The lawyer call here yet?"

"Yup. 'Bout five minutes ago. Figured that since he was lookin' for you, you were coming out this way, so tol' him jes' to keep tryin'."

"Great. While we wait, tell me about the kids you spoke to."

I grabbed beers from the fridge while Ray joined the four of us at the kitchen table. Cowboy ran through the calls he'd made to the other six kids not marked off at school on the day of the shooting.

I listened as he described running down each kid's reason for avoiding the carnage, and watched the others as they sipped beer and heard the stories of some of the luckiest kids around.

Charlene's face swung from joy at hearing that the other kids weren't involved, through terror at suddenly remembering that her own son hadn't had the same fortune, then to grief when she remembered why we were all sitting in her kitchen.

Mimi hung on Cowboy's every word, not even breaking eye contact when she tilted her beer bottle, and gave a secret little smile at a couple of places during the re-telling.

Ray looked like he couldn't wait to get back to Galveston, that the type of stuff that happened in Big D would be best left in the rearview mirror.

"What's your gut feel?" I said.

"They's all tellin' the truth," he replied. "I made enough phone calls to doctors, mechanics, and track coaches to make sure that each one of those kids was where their folks said they was. Goddamn ear was 'bout to fall off after that."

"Welcome to my world."

"You can have it, boss-man." Cowboy leaned back in his seat and swigged.

"Yeah."

Charlene took up the conversation. "Did you say that you think Bradley is innocent?"

They all looked at me.

"Honestly, I'm not sure." Wished I had more than that, but I had to play the hand I'd been dealt. "Firstly, and you need to know this whether you want to or not, there's nothing yet that proves Bradley innocent."

Charlene's face fell, but I watched her resolve break the fall and she started shaking her head. "No, no, n—"

The phone rang and I snatched the receiver off the wall.

"Yeah."

"Rafferty?"

"Uh huh. Paul. I need to know, now that Bradley's awake, what's going to happen?"

"He's awake?"

"He's awake?" Charlene and Ray parroted behind me. Mimi started talking. I waved an arm at them and turned my body so I could hear Paul better.

"Yep. Came out of the coma sometime late Sunday or Monday. I assumed you knew. When I saw him yesterday, he was still pretty grog—"

"You saw Bradley?"

"You saw Bradley?"

I was going to go 'round the bend if I had to keep listening to Paul's words on a two second delay, and in Charlene's voice, so I said, "Hang on, Paul." Covered the mouthpiece. "We'll talk about this in a second, Charlene, but right now I need to hear what Paul has to say."

Charlene and Ray stood, paced, and glared at me but I stayed strong.

Turned back to the wall, "Okay, Paul. Go."

"Well, if he's conscious again, the DA will swing into top gear getting to court. She's already got the indictment, so it'll just be a matter of getting a date for the preliminary hearing and making sure that she's ready with her case. Given what I hear about how many bodies in her office are working on it, I wouldn't expect her to have any problems in that area."

"How much time?"

"They'll get a judge out to the hospital as soon as possible for the arraignment, if they haven't already, so let's assume the clock is ticking. Nine days, max. Could be as little as a week. Which means that I need to get busy finalizing our defense. Charlene will need to start prepping in the next few days, so that we're ready to go. As far as evidence goes, tell me that you've got something I can use."

"Hold on, Paul. Our deal was for me to find you evidence connecting Bradley to the shootings, not exonerate him." I heard Charlene's breath and Mimi's whispers behind me. "But putting that aside for the minute, I need to know what's going on with the Laweles girl."

"What? Who?"

"Imani Laweles."

"Who's that?"

"Are you trying to play me again? Because, if you are counselor, you need to get acquainted with Rafferty's Rule Eighty-five: Fool me once, shame on you. Fool me twice, don't go complaining about the busted nose I give you."

"Seriously, I don't know who you're talking about."

"Imani Laweles? The girl who keeps cropping up in the papers?"

"I don't know her from Eve."

"I hope that turns out to be the truth, because if I find out that you told her to keep quiet so it helps your case, I will be very disappointed. And you do not want me disappointed. I guarantee it."

"Okaay, but I really don't know what you're talking about." His voice changed and I heard the dimples coming up to full power. "Can she help our case? Maybe I should talk to her."

"Don't go anywhere near the girl, Paul. You hear me? She's spooked and I don't need her going to ground, or hiding behind her family before I get her to tell me the truth."

"Keep me informed with what you find."

"It may be nothing."

"I'll use whatever I can, so let me know anyway."

"Uh huh."

I hung up, sat back down at the table and reached for my beer. Warm. Damn.

Before I could get to the fridge and grab another, Charlene and Mimi started in.

Charlene was standing in the corner with her arms crossed over her chest, as far away as she could get while still staying in the room. She looked at me like I was the family pet who'd contracted rabies: a mixture of revulsion, horror, and fortitude. She wasn't going to like what she might have to do, but she'd stay strong, get it done, and clean the blood away later.

Ray stood next to her, rubbed her shoulder. Charlene shrugged and he dropped his hand.

"My son's awake and you didn't bother to tell me! Probably because you think he shot those people. And you're trying to find evidence of that when I thought you were trying to prove his innocence. I knew you weren't really trying to help him. I knew it. Don't know why I let Paul talk me into hiring you in the first place. Maybe it's time for you to—"

Mimi looked up at her. "Charlene. I've known Rafferty a long time, and he's one of only two people I would trust with my life—with *my son's life*—to do the right thing. It might not look obvious, or even logical, but he'll prove Bradley's innocence. If there's evidence, he'll find it."

Cowboy hadn't moved a muscle, but it was his turn for a secret smile as he watched Mimi from under the brim of his Stetson. Then he looked at me, saw me watching, and raised his eyebrows.

She makes you sound good. Are you?

Prick.

Mimi sat, leaned in, reached up to lay a hand on my arm.

"Rafferty, we're here to help these people. Right?"

I could take Charlene's anger and blind devotion to her son despite evidence to the contrary, but the disappointment I saw in Mimi eyes with the mere thought that she couldn't rely on me, cut me to the core.

If Hilda ever laid a move like that on me, I'd be a broken man.

I patted Mimi's hand. "Charlene. Ray. Sit down. Please."

They cautiously joined us, sitting with chairs pulled out, not yet ready to commit.

I filled them in on the last seventy-two hours. Hilda and I getting jumped on the street, my conversation with Imani, and subsequent ejection from the house by her father. Imani's background in Houston, my aborted visit to Bradley, and a stirring account of my overnight stay in the DPD hotel.

About the time I was finishing, the same time I realized how thirsty I was, fresh beers and a bottle of scotch appeared on the table courtesy of Cowboy.

Good man.

"Before we go any farther," Charlene said, "I need to know what you're doing here, Mr. Rafferty. Are you trying to help my boy, or not?"

I blew out a breath. "In the beginning, when you hired me, I figured it was going to be easy to connect the dots between Bradley and the shootings."

"You took my money and deliberately tried to prove that my boy did this?" Charlene screeched.

I met her glare. "If you remember, I was quite adamant about not being able to help you, but you and your lawyer insisted." Charlene looked like she wanted to deny that, but sat there with an open mouth instead. "And you need to start listening to what I actually said before jumping off the deep end like that."

The open mouth turned to a hard line.

"I said that I wanted to connect the dots, not that I would deliberately make it look like he was guilty. This isn't a cheap crime novel, for chrissake."

Charlene said, "What are you talking about?"

"I'm saying that it shouldn't matter to you what I'm looking for, only that I'm looking at all. It makes sense, if you think about it." Now it all started to get clearer in my head. "I'll even bet that's something else Paul had in mind." Cowboy nodded almost imperceptibly. "You're so convinced that your son is innocent, so Paul didn't much care how he got me on the case. He just wanted me to find whatever there is to be found. And if you're right, then all my work should give Paul what he needs to defend Bradley in court."

"That still doesn't answer my question. Are you here to help Bradley?"

"I'm trying to find the truth. Whatever that is."

"Are you here—"

"Charlene. I can't decide what you think about what I find, and whether it helps Bradley or not. But think about this … I'm the only one looking. And, if Paul's right, he needs something quick, before Hernandez gets to court."

"He didn't do this. I just know it. He couldn't have."

"Unfortunately," I said, "that's not enough. Even if Paul hasn't said that to you." Charlene drew in a breath. I rolled on. "The cops don't have a lot. But, a duffel bag left behind at the scene makes it look an awful lot like there was a third shooter. Bradley's the only one who fits that role and the other two shooters aren't around to say different. And his prints were on the gun that killed four people. Circumstantial it may be, but it doesn't paint a great picture."

As some moments are wont to do, we all reached for our drinks at the same time.

"So, you're asking the wrong question," I said. "What you should be asking is whether you want me to keep digging, or not. I hope you can tell that I don't much care either way." That wasn't totally true, I wanted—needed—to get the Mustang out of hock, but I didn't want to seem too eager.

I sat back and waited. Ray touched Charlene on the shoulder and jerked his head. They both stood and walked to the front room. Now that I'd stopped talking, I could hear the low murmur of the crowd out front.

It took a while, and another beer, before Charlene stood in the kitchen doorway again, Ray hovering behind her.

"Keep digging, Mr. Rafferty. Save my boy."

———

Half an hour later, we'd hammered out a plan.

I couldn't go anywhere near Bradley; it'd be a race to see whether Ed or Hernandez would be faster coming down on me like a ton of bricks, but I still needed to hear his side of the story.

Charlene and Ray, with Paul's help, would get in to see Bradley and get as much of the story as they could from him. I still didn't share Charlene's staunch defense of the boy, so I pulled Mimi aside and told her to tag along and bring me back the unvarnished truth. She told Charlene that she wanted to meet Bradley and the last thing I heard was them concocting a story about Mimi being an aunt from Abilene so that she could be passed off as family, just in case anyone asked.

Geez, people who don't have to rely on subterfuge as often as I did seem to find it a lot more exciting.

Cowboy would look after the house while we were all out. He sounded like he hoped the crowd outside would decide to storm the place while he was there alone.

I deliberately didn't go into detail about what I'd be doing while everyone else was otherwise occupied. My plan was to peel back Imani's surface and see what was underneath. I still figured she was lying to protect Bradley, but I didn't need Charlene to start up with the histrionics again. I'd had enough of those for one day.

Also, I'd only know what the truth was once I'd managed

to get it from Imani, so I could report that the following afternoon.

Ah, my ignorance is truly magnificent to behold.

Revel in its glory one and all.

———

"That's a plan then," I said. "We'll hit it bright and early tomorrow." Turned to Cowboy. "Since you're gonna be here all on your lonesome, what say we head out front and lean on these turkeys, show them the rules of the game when they play with the big boys. Make sure they don't get any bright ideas."

Cowboy grinned like a split watermelon.

"No, I don't plan on shooting anyone," I said.

The grin fell.

"For the moment."

"Atta boy. Day ain't over yet."

———

I left my jacket draped over one of the dining chairs. It was getting cold as the day leaked away, but I wanted the assembled multitude to see the shoulder holster, and the ensconced .38.

I figured the crowd couldn't miss the Ithaca, as I stood on the front porch and thumbed shells into it. Yeah, I had to go through the process of emptying it inside the house before we stepped out, but there's nothing like a good bit of theater to brighten up the day.

Thought about pulling out the .38, breaking it open, checking and then spinning the magazine, decided that would be overkill. Plus, Cowboy was already doing the same thing with his Ruger Super Redhawk and I didn't want him to think I was copying.

"You ready?" I said.

"Shore thing, boss-man."

"Let's do it then."

"Ah yuh."

I touched down on the first step as Cowboy laid his hand-cannon on the porch top rail, eyeballed the crowd, and worked the slide on his shotgun.

Goddamn, I loved that sound.

By the time I made it down the steps and was standing on the grass below, and a little to the side of Cowboy, the crowd had congealed and started to move towards me. I hefted the shotgun and they slowed a touch.

"Okay," I called. "This ain't a gang bang. Who's the stud duck here? That's who I'll talk to."

They all stopped moving at that. Feet bone connected to the brain bone, and only one could work at a time. Lots of glances sideways and I felt the individual righteousness dial back to a simmer. Some murmurs here and there, more glances, and quite a few people backpedaling away from being volunteered for a major role in the proceedings.

"It's not a difficult question, people," I said. Heard Cowboy chuckle behind me. "Either someone's in charge, or none of you have the faintest idea why you're here. If that's the case, you've gotta be the dumbest bunch of people I ever laid eyes on."

They thought about that for a while, then a bunch of them turned their backs on Cowboy and me to discuss it.

Simple shits.

I breathed a bit easier.

The crowd parted, and Dark Hair and the fat, middle-aged woman I spoken to on day one stepped out. The space they left filled and the wall of people followed their duly-appointed dignitaries slowly up the lawn. They got to about ten feet and I worked the slide on the Ithaca. Tried not to laugh at the combination of the thrill that went through me and the reaction from all the faces looking my way.

"Hey smart-ass," Dark Hair said. "You gonna start by telling us who you are?"

I didn't need to look at Dark Hair for long before he dropped his eyes.

"How's your buddy's shoulder?" I said. I registered movement on the far right, which I guessed was said Buddy reaching for said shoulder. I didn't look. Cowboy would have it covered.

"Listen," I started again. "This is not the Treaty of Versailles. We are not going to engage in meaningful discussion and arrive at mutual agreement. I'm going to tell you how it is, and you're going to listen. That's all. Got that?"

No answer from the two in the front row.

"I'll take that as a yes. The time has come for this occupation to end. You've had your fun, you've made your point, you've ..." I ran out of things they may have accomplished. "It's time to piss off."

"And if we don't?" Dark Hair tried for belligerent and missed.

"Not a whole hell of a lot I can do to make you ..." I shrugged. "But ... if anyone moves closer to the house than this truck ..." I swept the shotgun across the crowd towards Cowboy's truck parked sideways on the drive. The collective intake of breath lowered the oxygen content within a block. "... or makes a move with, or towards a gun ..." A few men buried in the crowd dropped their hands from their belts "... then we will assume you intend to attack."

A bird called in the silence and I noticed for the first time you could hear the low drone of the freeway, fifteen blocks away.

Dark Hair crossed his arms and looked at me. Big Butt decided she'd take the lead.

"And what? I suppose you'll shoot us."

I thought about trying to move this whole mess into an intellectual sphere, explaining the concept of actions and consequences, then remembered where I was and who I was talking to.

"Yep," I said. "So, I'd be real careful about where you walk and what you hold in your hands. Okay?" About half the crowd tried to step backwards. More than a few of the skittish were standing in front of people who wanted to hang tough so the whole crowd kind of stumbled and jostled while they tried to get their feet back underneath them.

I brought the shotgun back front and center.

"Make sure you're not moving toward those sidearms, boys." I put a touch of country twang into it. Cowboy would appreciate that. "Things could get real ugly real quick."

Stepped forward and looked Dark Hair dead in the eyes.

"And I'm holding *you* responsible for any shit that goes down here. Got it?"

To his credit, he nodded. And swallowed. Maybe he was smarter than he looked.

I started to step backwards up the lawn.

Hell with it. I turned my back on the lot of them and walked back to the porch. By the time I was headed up the steps, the majority had moved back curbside and seemed to be huddling a touch closer than before.

The door of one of the news vans banged open and a guy dropped out hefting a camera to his shoulder.

Day late and a dollar short.

He looked around at the crowd, now mumbling a lot more

softly than before, decided there wasn't anything going on that would make good footage and stepped back up and into the van.

I stood on the porch next to Cowboy, our shotguns below railing level, and watched the armed guys in the group do this weird interpretive dance movement. They'd start to reach down toward their hip, unconsciously, realize what they were doing, jerk their hands away, palms out, fingers spread, and exhale a huge breath. After I watched the third guy do it, I nearly busted out a laugh, but held it together. Didn't want anyone down on the lawn to get the wrong idea.

"You think they'll give up now?" I said.

"Dunno. My guess is they took you serious and all. Depends on how stupid they be. A'course you were a candy-ass. Didn't shoot no-one or nothin'."

I looked at the sunset shimmering off the bottom of the clearing cloud and wondered if that would change during the dark hours.

"I guess we'll find out," I said.

"Ah yuh."

25

I left before sunrise the next morning, sneaking over the back fence and tip-toeing my way down alongside the neighbor's house. I couldn't give a rat's ass about pushing my way through the crowd out front, but I didn't want them knowing exactly how many people were or weren't inside.

Might give them ideas.

I made it around the block to the Pacer unnoticed, and tooled through the pre-dawn streets, drifting toward the Park Cities and Imani Laweles. Had the window cracked, trailing pipe smoke behind me, thinking about my approach as compere of the latest installment of everybody's favorite game: 'Truth or Consequences.'

She was clearly scared of her foster-father, or of what he might think or do, so I'd have preferred to get Imani alone and give her the space she needed to tell me what I needed to know.

Only problem was, I didn't know how to do that. I figured Donald would have her buttoned down pretty tight. Enough that walking up to the front door and asking to speak with her privately wasn't going to work.

As it turned out, it was academic.

Being in front of peak hour meant that I made it to the house quicker than I expected, and I pulled into the curb across the road and one house up. It was a beautiful morning, blue sky and dewy grass glistening in the sun, birds hopping about on the tract of parkland alongside the Beckett house as they looked for an early meal.

I was enjoying the peace and quiet and still thinking about how to play my next step when I realized the figure standing near the garbage cans and squinting across the street at me was the aforementioned Donald Beckett.

Next thing I knew he was in motion. I made it out of the car before he closed the gap and met him on the sidewalk under the branches of a large oak tree.

"Good morning, Mr. Beckett. Spring is definitely on the way. Terrific weather, isn't it?"

He rumbled through a scowl at me. "I told you to leave us alone."

"Can't do that, I'm afraid."

"I could call the police, right now."

"And tell them what? That there's a man here minding his own business, enjoying the sunshine? The last thing DPD needs is another scandal about frivolous call-outs. The Chief has enough on his plate as it is."

He side-eyed me for a few seconds.

"How's Imani doing?" I asked.

"None of your business."

"Raising teenagers is a tough gig." I'd heard that from someone a while ago.

"Hmmph. Like you'd know." Looks like my Doctor Spock impression wasn't going to fly. But I waited. "Imani's been through hell and back, Mr. Rafferty. I won't go into the details, but suffice to say, no-one deserves to see what she's seen in her young life. And now, just when we're able to be the ones taking her away from that awful mess, this happens to her."

I wasn't yet sure if we could agree that this had 'happened' to her, or whether she was involved in more ways than Donald figured, but I wasn't about to let him in on my thinking just yet.

Leaned back against the fender, relaxed. Two guys shooting the breeze. "That's tough, all right. I'm sorry to hear it."

"Hmmph." The shocks creaked under his weight as he took a spot next to me and looked at the ground.

"Mr. Beckett … Donald. Despite what you think of me, I'm not a threat to Imani. You and I both want the same thing."

He swiveled his head and looked at me. "How do you figure that?"

"We both want to know that the kids are safe when they go to school. Right?"

He nodded slowly. "Of course."

"Then let me speak with Imani so I can find out what happened on the day and make sure it doesn't happen again."

He pulled in a huge breath, and stood.

"I don't think so, Mr. Rafferty."

"Donald—"

"I said no." A sigh. "Actually, Mr. Rafferty, I don't harbor ill will against you. In fact, what you're doing is noble, in a way. I truly don't think that you'll succeed in your efforts to save that boy though, and yes, no matter what he did, I still believe he is due a just process, so your effort is commendable."

"Then why not—"

"But you'll be doing it without Imani's assistance."

"The lawyers will be doing it anyway, so what's the harm?"

"Let the lawyers come with their subpoenas, if they must. But no-one gets to speak to her while I have any say in it. Good day, Mr. Rafferty." He headed across the street to his driveway.

"What are you afraid of?" I called after him.

He reached the driveway, ripped the lid off one of the garbage cans and rummaged inside. I patted my hip pocket and cursed myself for not packing a blackjack. Thought automatically for a second about where the Colt was and made a mental note to stop doing stupid things like heading out the door unarmed.

He was back, jabbing a soggy newspaper in my face. Good thing I didn't have a gun to draw. I would have looked over-reactive.

"This, Mr. Rafferty! This is what I'm afraid of."

I took the paper and peeled it open. Today's date and another front page exclusive by Monica.

WHAT IS COLUMBUS SURVIVOR HIDING? New documents reveal holes in story about dramatic rescue from school shooting.

Damn, Monica was fast. I had hoped I'd bought myself more time by burying the attendance registers deep inside the mountain of information I'd asked her for. Whether she'd been through all of it or targeted those first was immaterial. But dammit, I wish she'd waited a few more days.

"I don't know where they get these lies from, but I will protect Imani from people who cause her harm, even unintentionally. And that means you, Mr. Rafferty."

I was about to answer him when I saw movement over his left shoulder. It took me a couple of seconds to work out what it was, and I turned my non-response into an over-exaggerated yawn and stretch, so he wouldn't follow my eye-line.

Imani had come out of the treeline at the rear of the parkland and was halfway across the open space to her yard when she noticed us. She froze like the proverbial deer in the headlights, then crept forward as Donald continued talking.

"Am I boring you?"

I locked eyes with him and shook my head, trying to keep Imani in my peripheral vision. She didn't move her stare from her foster-father's back, while she crouch-ran across the last thirty yards of the parkland, pushed through the side hedge, and disappeared into her yard.

"It's not boring to me, Mr. Rafferty. I'll be seeing my lawyers later today to start the process of suing the paper for defamation. And, as long as Imani does her part to fit into our family, I'll do whatever I need to do to protect her. She deserves that much."

"So there's no chance that I can talk to Imani?"

"None at all."

He snatched the paper from my hands, stalked across the road, and threw it back into the garbage can.

I leaned on the car for another ten minutes, wondering if there would be an Imani encore, but all I saw was the curtains in the living room twitch a couple of times.

Watching me, watching them.

The sun was starting to get hot, so I jumped in the car and headed for the office.

Bad move. Managed to nail peak hour dead center, but at least the Pacer was comfortable for the forty-five minutes I spent stuck in traffic. It still looked stupid, though.

Feet up on the desk, coffee cup swirling steam, and a pipe drifting smoke to the open window. Ah, my happy place.

Don't let anyone else know that I actually said that.

Stared out the window in thought. What was Imani doing this morning? Whatever it was, she clearly didn't want her foster-father to know about it. He talked a lot about protecting her, but he also said that she had to live up to her end of the bargain. I assume that referred to his dictums about drugs and school attendance. Too early for school, so what else was I to assume?

I found an old Dallas city map in the bottom desk drawer, underneath a handful of .38 cartridges, two empty Borkum Riff cans, my braided leather and shot blackjack, and a stack of gun shop catalogs. Almost got sidetracked flicking through the catalogs, but instead spread the map out and located the Beckett house.

According to the map, behind the adjacent parkland and treeline, a narrow greenbelt followed a small stream west for a few hundred yards before opening out into a lake and more parkland.

File that one away for later.

With Imani effectively out of the picture for the time being, I grabbed a fresh cup of coffee from the percolator and gently prodded my thoughts toward Bradley, hoping his mother and uncle could get something useful from him.

I'd take anything from specific details on how he wasn't involved through to a full confession. *Yeah, I gunned them all down, copper. I did it, and I'd do it again, too.*

Cheesy lines from movies notwithstanding, that scenario just didn't play for me. And, as much as I liked my soundbite of 'three bags for three shooters', it wasn't that hard to conjure a scenario where the two dead shooters humped all their weaponry to the school, hid in the service area while they got ready, and decided that they could cause enough destruction even with leaving some of their play toys behind.

Plus, I just didn't see Bradley as the gun-wielding type.

Maybe it was the stories that Ray had told me about the aborted family hunting trips. Maybe it was the way he handled the gun when I watched him in the schoolyard.

Still, not being confident, or cocky, with a firearm doesn't preclude a person from firing it. I watched him fire off a round, even though he didn't look particularly comforta—

Wait a minute.

Took me a couple more to get Ricco on the phone.

"I shouldn't be talking to you."

"Yeah, yeah. I get that all the time."

"No, seriously, Ed will have my guts he finds out."

"Well, shut up and let me tell you what I need so you can get off the phone. You guys cataloged all the ballistic details from the rec-area, right?"

"Yup."

"How many casings?"

"What? A shitload."

"No, not how many total, just how many different types?"

"That's a little easier. Let me check." The low hum of the DPD machinery—both human and mechanical—blew into my ear for a few minutes until Ricco came back. "We found casings from four different calibers: Twelve-gauge shotgun, nine mill and five-point-seven mill, and forty-five."

"The forty-five would have been the one that Bradley dumped."

"Ballistics says so."

"How many forty-five casings did you find?"

"Ummm, it says here, one."

"Only one?"

"Outside, yeah. That's what you were asking about, right? Inside, there were, ahhh, six casings found. Inside that hallway. You know the one that looked like a knife fight inside an abattoir." Ricco chuckled.

"Never mind that. So, the shot from the forty-five fired in the rec-area ... what did it hit?"

The chuckle turned to a full-throated laugh.

"Man, we picked up over three hundred casings throughout the school, and you want to know where *a single one* of those bullets went? Must be true what they say; you are the last of the dreamers."

"C'mon, Ricco. You said there was only one forty-five slug fired in the rec-area. It can't be that hard to work out which of the impact points or injuries out there was caused by that bullet. I assume the techs ran the trajectories."

"Ha! More than three hundred rounds fired, over a hundred bodies running around all over the place, some got hit and dropped, some got hit and kept running, some got hit by ricochets or bullet fragments. You *actually* think we strung the entire scene for each and every shot?"

My mind was trying to picture what that looked like and ground to a halt. I couldn't blame them.

"'Sides," Ricco said, "don't forget that there coulda been someone hit with one of the rounds from the forty-five *inside*, who then ran *outside*. What do you think then?"

"Christ, Ricco, I don't know! Can you at least just look into it for me?"

"Like I don't got better things to do. I ... Fuck, here comes Ed. I'll get back to you."

Not much more that I could do at the office, so I drained my coffee cup, flicked off the lights, then—heeding my words from earlier in the morning—went back to grab my blackjack from the desk drawer, and headed out to lunch.

26

After lunch, and as I turned into the Wright's street, I thought everything looked the same. The closer I got to the front yard, the more I realized I was wrong. The crowd had swelled in the last twenty-four hours; there must have been nearly eighty bodies on the front yard and standing space was at a premium.

I parked as close as I could, reprised my shotgun routine from a few days earlier, and walked towards the house. The crowd didn't part this time, as much as swell away from me.

Realized my brain was now thinking 'mob' instead of 'group.'

No smiles, no singing, no-one carrying signs. I saw Dark Hair and Buddy front and center of the group, heads together and whispering as I walked past.

I made it up on the porch before the first rotten tomato whistled past my ear and *shlupped* against the front window. A few little spatters of tomato blowback got me on the side of the face. I turned, pumped a round into the chamber, and pointed it at the crowd. The skinny guy at the front of the crowd, with a Peterbilt cap and a dripping fistful of tomato, became my focus. My gunsights found him, he found the gunsights, and stopped mid-motion. I tilted my head and backed up against the front door, kicked at it with my boot heel. Felt it open behind me, and backed my way inside.

Cowboy closed the door and a fusillade of grocery items spattered against the house. The front windows splashed red and trembled under the onslaught.

"Seems like the discontent of the huddled masses might be on the increase," I said.

Cowboy nodded. "Ah yuh. And here I din't think to bring my potato gun."

I walked through to the kitchen, keen to get away from the windows. I didn't expect they could do much more than make a mess with their greengrocer-inspired version of The Blitz but, the less we were in their face, the better.

I slumped into a chair, shotgun across my legs. Cowboy peered out the back windows. "Don't look like they've got to the chapter 'bout outflankin' the enemy." I nodded. "But I reckon it might not be long, 'fore one or more of them tries sumpin stupid."

"You got anything left in the truck you wanna bring in before it gets dark?"

"An old monkey wrench and a pocketknife. Don' imagine they be much use."

"All right, then. We'll get this place squared away and hope those folks out there ain't as stupid as they look."

"Hope in one hand, spit in the other," Cowboy said. "See which fills up faster."

"I know. That's what worries me."

Charlene walked past us to the sink with an empty glass.

"How did it go at the hospital, Charlene? How's Bradley?"

Charlene set the glass down on the countertop as softly as

laying a newborn into a cot, stood there with her hands flat on either side of the sink and bowed her head.

I waited.

She shook her head, and I could see teardrops landing on the edge of the countertop.

"Charlene," I tried again.

She reached across the counter and plucked a tissue out of a box, turned around to face me and dabbed at her eyes.

"It was terrible, seeing my boy lying there. I'd almost forgotten what he looked like with the bandages and the machines but to see him like that again ..."

"What did he say?"

"Hardly anything."

"That can't be right. How long were you there?"

She sighed and took a seat at the table. "A long time, Mr. Rafferty. Almost four hours, all told."

"He's more out of it than I thought."

"It wasn't that. The majority of the time we were trying to get in, the policemen were stopping us, Paul was yelling, the hospital staff were telling us to quiet down or they'd call security ..." She gave me a wan smile. "Lucky Mimi was there to calm everyone down."

I imagined Mimi's method of diplomacy to involve less peace talks and more Uzi but, hey, whatever works.

"In the end, I think Mimi got the policeman to take pity on me and he let us in for ten or so minutes. I was so frazzled by then that I spent most of that time just holding Bradley's hand and crying."

"He must have told you something."

"He told me to stop crying."

"And?"

"And that was all."

"What?"

"I tried. Ray tried. Hell, even Mimi talked to him before we got thrown out again. She's so sweet, and she looks so young, you know. Like the sister Bradley never had." She leaked a sad smile. "But, nothing."

"He's not thinking clearly. He's just come out of a coma."

"Maybe, but I don't think so." Charlene blew her nose.

"Does he understand that he's been charged with murder?"

"We tried to explain that. Said he didn't care, didn't want to talk about any of it. Then stopped talking altogether and wouldn't say anything else. Just lay there and stared at the wall."

"He doesn't care?! What the hell?" I needed to move so I got up, handed the shotgun to Cowboy, and went looking for a scotch bottle. He and Charlene watched me with fascination, like an exotic zoo exhibit. Found the scotch, poured a glass, and knocked it back. Blew out a breath and turned back to Charlene.

"Tell me this. If he doesn't care about what happens to him, and you're sure you were clear about the consequences …" She nodded, wiped her eyes. "Then why should I give a rat's ass about what happens to him? This is bullshit and a waste of time." I grabbed the bottle and glass and sat down again.

Charlene dabbed at her eyes and sniffed. Pulled her feet together, stood up straighter, pushed her shoulders back and looked me in the eye.

"Because he's my boy," she said. "I'm not giving up on him. And as long as you're here, and I can find a way to pay you, you're not going to either."

"Uh huh."

"Don't give me that, Mr. Rafferty. You work for me, remember? And you act all rough and tough and sassy. What is all that? Just a lie? A sham to get people to hire you, but you bail out when the going gets tough? Well, that's not good enough for me. Or for Bradley. You claim that you're the best there is. Here's your chance." She stepped forward, looked down at me and bored her eyes into mine. "Fucking prove it!"

Charlene gave me five more seconds of glare, then marched out of the room head held high. She padded up the stairs, the bedroom door closed softly, and footsteps creaked above our heads.

I poured and knocked back another scotch, tried to ignore Cowboy.

"Boy howdy, she's as feisty as all get out."

"Yep. She's a pistol."

"She just wants her son to be okay." I hadn't noticed Mimi standing in the doorway.

"I might go check on Ray," Cowboy said and stepped out, pausing to cup Mimi's chin in his weathered hand, then bent down to kiss her on the forehead. Mimi beamed, stepped into the kitchen, sat down beside me.

I brooded.

"C'mon Rafferty, where's that grouchy old tomcat that I know and love?"

"Is she telling the truth about what went on at the hospital?"

"Yeah. It went just like she said it did."

"Then I don't know if I can do this."

"Why not?"

"I don't see what the point is. The kid doesn't want to be helped. Practically begged me to shoot him the first time I met him. Maybe he did it, and the guilt is eating him up inside. That's why he's given up."

"Look at me. Rafferty, I said, look at me." I met her eyes. "You really believe that? Tell me right here and now that you believe that he shot those people and we'll all pack up and go home."

"I can't prove that he didn't."

"I didn't ask what you can prove. I asked you what you believed."

She waited while I got there.

"No." I heaved a sigh. "No, I don't believe that he did it. But that's not gonna be enoug—"

"That don't matter. You gotta start with what you believe. The rest is just hard work. You think that it's easy for Cowboy and me to be parents to Adam? With what we do? Hell's bell's Rafferty, I lie awake most nights wondering whether we're doing the right thing or if he'd be better off with someone else."

"You two are the best thing in the world for that boy," I said. "Nothing surer."

Mimi smiled, a big grin that lit the room.

"That's what I keep coming back to. We sure ain't perfect, but neither's anyone else. I will love Adam, and protect him, with every breath and every bullet I have until I don't have none left. And if it was him lying in that hospital bed instead of Bradley, no matter what he said and no matter what it looked like, I'd want good people fighting for him, right alongside me."

Mimi dabbed at her eyes.

"That's all Charlene wants. I'm gonna give it to her, and I know you're gonna, too."

I looked at her.

"Once you pull your head outta your ass and stop your bitchin', that is." She grinned, slapped me on the shoulder and headed out of the kitchen.

I sat for a few minutes longer then grabbed the phone off

the wall and called Hilda. No answer at her place so I tried mine.

"Hey Ugly," she said. "I was beginning to think you'd skipped town without saying good-bye."

"Never happen, babe."

"Uh huh."

"I'd say good-bye," I said. "From a long way away, but I would call. I'm no coward."

Hilda laughed, and some of the tension seeped out of my upper body. "And me with a casserole cooking, and sitting here on your sofa—naked, I might add—waiting to show you how much I've missed you." When I didn't jump on that like I wanted to, she spoke softly. "You're not coming home tonight, are you?"

"'Fraid not, babe. It's starting to look like it might get ugly out here."

"That's okay. I can wait. I'll just be here, eating casserole by myself and sobbing silently into my pillow. Still naked, of course."

"Atta girl." Damn!

"Before I forget though, that sergeant called looking for you."

"Ricco?"

"That's him."

"Did he say what he wanted?"

"Nope. Just to call him back."

"Thanks, hon."

"My pleasure."

We sat and listened to each other breathe for a little while.

"I'd rather be there with you. You know that, right?"

"Of course I do, Ugly. It's okay. You do what you need to do. Look after that woman and her son and come back to me safely."

"Will do."

"I love you, Rafferty."

"You too, babe."

———

"Man, you're lucky you caught me. I was halfway down the steps outside when the desk sergeant yelled I had a phone call. Lucky that he didn't tell me it was you, 'cause if I'd known that I might not have come back in."

"You called me."

"True enough. Well, you're not gonna believe it, I mean I can hardly believe it, but we found that bullet."

"The one from the forty-five?"

"Uh huh. Guess where it ended up?"

"Fucked if I know, Ricco. That's why I asked you."

He chuckled. "In an apartment across the street from the school. Second floor too, so it was like the kid was trying to shoot down a fucking pigeon or somethin'."

"Really?"

"Check it out. The damn slug went across the street, missed the balcony and everything on it, went through an open window—an open fucking window, Rafferty—crossed the room, missed everything else and plugged a hole in a big fucking plastic tank of water. You believe that shit?"

"Not really. You're sure that this is the same bullet? Sounds more like the result of a close shot to me."

"Yep. 'Cause it hit the water it was still in almost perfect condition. Easy to match."

"Okaaay."

"But you ain't heard the best part yet. Wasn't even our guys that found it. Couple hours after the school shooting, the neighbor in the apartment below calls the super, 'cause there's water running down her walls. From the tank, right?

"So the super goes up to the apartment above, knocks. No answer. Uses his key 'cause it's an emergency, right. Walks through the door and sees that the tenant has turned the whole goddamn place into a reefer farm."

"Bullshit."

"I shit you not. The guy had pulled up all the carpets, ripped doors off the cupboards, and had trays of pot in every available space. The place was rigged up with lights and hoses and pipes and all sorts of valves to water all the plants. Obviously been doin' it for a while, too. Some of the plants were nearly five feet high. Anyway, once they find the leaking tank, and the bullet, one of the bright sparks on the team thinks maybe it'd be worthwhile checking if it was anything to do with the Columbus shooting, asks ballistics to check for a match."

"How come I never get that lucky?"

"Born under a bad sign, prob'ly." Ricco didn't break stride. "So the report only turned up on my desk yesterday and I hadn't seen it yet. So I get to file that little bit of info—not that it makes any difference to your kid, we've still got him for the four vics in the hallway—Narcotics gets to take seventy, eighty kay of dope off the street, plus a good-sized stash of angel dust they found in one of the bedrooms, and this guy goes down for a long time. I swear, there are some days I fucking love this job."

"Lemme ask you something else."

"Hell, why not. I'm in a good mood."

"You guys ever run those duffel bags?"

"Huh?"

"Where they came from. Who they belonged to." It had

already been a long day and I was getting tired of not making any progress.

"What the hell you want me to say? Three khaki duffels; surplus, by the looks. Coulda come from any Army Navy store in the country."

"Detail on the owner, or owners?"

"The mom of one of the dead shooters said something about her son having 'too many book-bags' laying around his room. We took that to mean the duffels. *Book-bags*! Since when does an Army duffel look like a fuckin' book-bag. Some people."

"That's all you got?"

"And most likely they were all bought at the same time and place, based on the tags and the wear."

"*Most likely*?"

"You heard me."

"That ain't much."

"Fuck you. I'm not lettin' you ruin my day. We made a major dope bust, all 'cause your kid couldn't shoot straight."

I left Ricco to his self-congratulations and hung up.

Poured another scotch and sat back in the chair. Listened to soft murmurs upstairs and the white noise of the crowd out front.

So Bradley didn't hit anyone in the schoolyard with his shot. Why not? What would make him shoot four people in cold blood; six bullets, six hits, four kills, and then miss so badly with his seventh shot? Nerves? Adrenaline? I doubted it. They would come first, not once he'd started gunning down fellow students.

Maybe it wasn't his seventh shot. What if it was the only shot he took on the day, with similar results to those ill-fated hunting trips Ray mentioned? If that was true, then there was the question of why he was shooting at all.

But looming larger in the background was, if not Bradley, then who?

The kitchen was growing darker as the tag end of the day arrived and it was time to do something about fortifying Casa de Wright before full dark arrived. I'd have rather sat there with a few more drinks, but I didn't want to get into the wee hours and wish that we'd done something earlier.

So we got busy.

Organized for Charlene and Ray to hunker down in Bradley's room. Humped the mattress from the master bed in, so they both had a place to sleep, at the back of the house and out of sight, in case things got ugly. Chocked the windows in the master bedroom and the sitting room up a couple inches for makeshift gunports and made sure all the drapes on the downstairs windows were closed. A laundry window over-looked the back yard which left us with first floor options in case the mob got brave enough to jump the side fence, but the back of the garage hid a blind spot on the other side of the yard and I didn't like it.

"I could rig a coupla grenades and a tripwire 'tween the side fence and the house, boss-man."

So that's what was in the green bag.

"I don't want to hurt any of these people if we can help it."

"Pussy."

"That's harassment, you know. There was a seminar about it at the Annual Private Dick's Symposium. *Trying to Stay Sane in a World that Isn't.*"

"Sounds like fun, boss-man. Shame I missed it. Yore still a pussy, tho."

"Whatever. See if you can find a hammer and nails. Bang a few through the top of that fence and gate. That ought to slow down anyone trying to crawl over. While you're at it, that pissy little lock can be snapped easy enough, make sure that gate is nailed shut good and tight. Same on the other side, too."

"Ah yuh."

I could hear more traffic and voices out on the street and saw more than one face peering at me from behind windows in neighboring houses. There was a buzz in the air that felt like that around a smoldering pile of logs in the split second before you see the first lick of flame and the whole stack erupts.

I hoped we could snuff it out before it got to that point.

Cracked open the garden shed and moved all the tools inside the garage. Last thing we needed to do was give these clowns more things to hit us with if they did make it over the fences.

I was finishing the final load from the shed when Cowboy walked around corner of the house. "All done. Anyone tryin' to get over those fences now, gonna be able to strain tea through their palms." He grinned. "I bashed a few in down lower too. Jes' in case."

"All right." I did another visual around the back yard. Couldn't see anything in the gathering gloom that would come back to bite us in the ass. "That'll do," I said. "I still don't think they look smart enough to try anything stupid, but I've been wrong before."

27

C owboy shook me awake.

"Unnnhhhh," I mumbled. "My turn already?"

"Nope. Thought you'd wanna see what's goin' on."

I wriggled out of the sleeping bag and sat up, blinking in the gloom. "What time is it?"

"Little after four."

"Uh huh." I rubbed my eyes and cracked my shoulders. Stood. Followed Cowboy to the sitting room. "What's happening?"

"Take a peek for y'self."

I squatted near the left-hand corner of the window and eased the curtain back a couple of inches to look out over the front yard.

"Yore little Gettysburg address got to some of them, I reckon," Cowboy said.

He was right; the crowd on the front lawn had dwindled during the night, with maybe a third or less of the protestors remaining. Dropped signs and garbage wafted around in the pre-dawn zephyrs. The last of the news vans had disappeared and I guessed the neighbors would be happy about being able to park in front of their houses again.

"You woke me up to look at fewer people?"

"Shore. Thought you should see the results of a job well-done."

"Really?" I started to stand, deciding whether to clock Cowboy on the way up.

"A'course not. Look further 'round to the left, boss-man."

I wriggled around on the floor, opened the curtain wider and twisted my head to look toward the front left corner of the Wright's little piece of suburban paradise.

A flickering glow bent out from behind a large elm and illuminated a group of men standing there. I blinked again, trying to get the focus working, trying to work out whether the guy in the center of the group was Dark Hair or not.

"That the guy was in the front with the fat chick?"

"Got it in one," Cowboy said.

"Uh huh."

Couldn't hear what they were saying, and I wasn't yet ready to open the window further, but the body language was clear enough. Six guys, four with flaming torches, two others with long weapons, all facing Dark Hair. He was doing the majority of the talking, based on his arm waving and pointing at the house. The others shuffled a little, changing weight on their feet, and looked like they were unconvinced about whatever he happened to be saying.

"How long they been at it?" I asked.

"Ten, mebbe fifteen minutes."

"What's your read?"

"I think they might be plannin' to see whether yore a man of yore word, boss-man."

"Poor fools them."

"Ah yuh. How you wanna play it?"

"Much as I don't want to, I'll get outside and stop them before they get those torches too close to the house. This place is all wood and it wouldn't take much for the whole shebang to go up."

"Better you than me, boss-man."

"Where's Mimi?"

"She's watching from the other end of the house. Mom's room."

"You two stay inside. I don't want to provoke them if we don't have to, but keep 'em honest, okay?"

"Got it."

I made sure the door to Bradley's room was closed, heard soft snoring behind it. No point in waking Charlene and Ray if we didn't have to. They'd be awake soon enough if the night turned to crap.

Step-hopped into a pair of jeans, shrugged a T-shirt and windbreaker on, thought about the shoulder holster, and settled for tucking the .38 into the back of my waistband. Grabbed the Ithaca, confirmed that I had swapped out the buckshot rounds for birdshot before I went to sleep, and headed downstairs.

By the time I'd flicked on the porch light and made it outside to the top of the steps, the would-be posse was starting up the lawn.

"Cowboy?" I called into the night.

His reply floated back from the dark sky. "Right here, boss-man."

"Mimi?"

No spoken response, but the night air rattled with what sounded like the metallic clack of an Uzi being primed for action. Good enough.

I stepped off the porch and met the gang across a thirty-yard wide DMZ midway between the curb and the house. Far enough, I hoped.

Dark Hair was four steps behind the torch-carrying, rifle-toting group, like a Field-Marshal surveying his troops from a safe vantage point.

I worked the Ithaca. The sound mixed with the crackle of the torches and floated away in the night air.

"Hold it right there boys, and tell ol' Uncle Rafferty what you have in mind."

Dark Hair looked like he was about to speak. The blond, rifle-holding kid left of center beat him to the punch.

"Thought we might have ourselves a little fun tonight," he said. He was younger than Dark Hair, college-age maybe, as were the rest of the group. Lots of buzz cuts and thick necks. Looked like an Aggies offensive line after practice. Blondie continued. "Mighty kind of you to come out and make it easy for us." The dumb shit smiled and nodded at me.

I shot him.

He went down in a heap, the rolling echo of the shotgun drowning out most of his screams. By the time the second rifle guy had brought his weapon up and was starting to work the bolt, I'd chambered another round and zeroed the barrel on the middle of his chest.

"Be very careful about your next movement," I said.

His Adam's apple worked three times and he removed his right hand from the rifle bolt, one finger after the other. Once his hand was free and away from his body, he let the rifle tilt downwards until the muzzle hit the ground. He dropped it then and sank to his knees, covered his face with his hands.

I felt comfortable enough to look at the rest of them then, not yet ready to lower my gun.

Dark Hair had his hand over his mouth, a decidedly feminine move, which wasn't gonna win him points at his next bar-room skirmish.

The four with torches were giving me an amusing combination of open mouths, narrowed eyes, one clenched hand and a bunch of movements that looked like they wanted to drop and run but weren't ready to leave their friend. One thing they all had in common—the torches were no longer steadied by righteousness and testosterone.

Blondie was on the ground. The rifle had fallen out of his hands towards me. I stepped forward and picked it up. Remington. Nice. Tossed it behind me, made sure it landed on the grass. No point nicking up the woodwork.

Dark Hair started up then. "I told them not to … They …" He ran out of steam.

"You shot him, man." That came from the guy who I guess played tight end. I looked at him, then back at the group.

"Of course I shot him. What did you think I was gonna do, play patty-cake?"

"But you shot him."

I shoved my chin at Dark Hair. "These guys don't catch on too fast, do they?"

No response.

I moved toward Blondie, his friends stepped back. He moved from sucking in huge breaths to whimpering as I got to him. I lowered the shotgun and squatted. The whimpering intensified.

"Not so tough now, huh? Lemme take a look at that."

I duck-walked around to where I wasn't blocking the porch light. Blondie's face was pale and he was sweating a lot. His Nike trainer was a write off, and the lower half of his right jeans leg was shredded. There was less of a divot in the lawn than I had hoped—I'd tried to put most of the shot into the ground—but it looked like I'd been a touch high.

Whoops.

I parted the ribbons of denim to look at his ankle. His

once-white tube sock was soaking up a lot of blood, but he wasn't leaking enough to put him at major risk. Couldn't say the same for his bones. There wasn't a lot of protection in that sneaker.

"Looks like you're gonna have an extended off-season, pal. Who knows though, with a good orthopedic surgeon, you might make it back onto the roster."

Almost patted his foot. I know that I've been accused of overdoing it at times, so it was a good thing to show restraint now and then.

I looked up. "For chrissake guys, will one of you get him a jacket or something. He's not gonna bleed out, but he is in shock." I shook my head. Fucking amateurs.

No-one moved for about ten seconds, then the four torch-bearers decided they wanted to footrace to their cars.

I stood, cradled the shotgun, and stepped towards Dark Hair. Pointed at him.

"I warned you."

"But … but … but …"

"Take your motorboat impersonations and your friends and fuck off."

He looked at me like that was the best idea he'd heard all day.

Now that the threat was over, my vision widened and I could see faces reflected in the light from the front porch. A few standing, a lot down at ground level, and a whole bunch looking back at me as they moved to their cars. More than a couple other porch lights on up and down the street.

"I mean it. Go on."

Dark Hair snapped, stepped in and picked up Blondie from under the armpits. He tried doing it while staying as far away from me as he could, causing Blondie to lurch and put pressure on his beat-up foot.

He shrieked.

The guy on his knees with his head in his hands threw up.

The other four guys had dumped the torches next to a couple of cars, where they sputtered and charred the few remaining blades of grass. They arrived back to our trio with an assortment of blankets, jackets, and what looked like a tent fly, which they all tried to put on him at the same time. They whole group lurched again.

Scream.

Vomit.

Damn, they made it hard not to laugh.

The caravan was about halfway to the curb when they realized they'd left their now dry-heaving buddy behind. Swiveled heads, a couple of hissed "No way"s before one guy jogged back up the lawn, pulled his puking friend upright, looked at me, then at both rifles laying on the damp grass, thought about it, and shrugged. The two of them joined the rest of their ill-conceived group at the curb, got haphazardly into their cars and drove off. Rather sedately, actually.

Over the next five minutes, the rest of the remaining group did the same.

I leaned against the front of the house, patted my shotgun anytime I saw a face looking my way, and helped them through the process.

As the last car turned the corner at the end of the street, the eastern edge of the sky was growing faint. The clouds had receded, and my pipe smoke drifted into what looked to be the coming of a mighty fine day.

The front door opened, and Ray walked over. Handed me a mug of coffee, steam rising. Took a long, deep sip. Ahhh. Mirrored Ray and leaned my hip against the railing.

"Is it over?"

I looked sideways at the yard turned to mud, the lawn

chairs left behind, signs, food wrappers, piles of garbage, and the group of trees on the far side of the driveway with the dark hole underneath that smelled like a makeshift latrine. Shook my head.

"Not yet, Ray. Not until I can prove Bradley didn't do what they think he did. Maybe not even then."

Ray deflated like a punctured balloon.

"But, for the moment, it'll make them think twice about coming back. Let's enjoy the empty front yard and a quiet morning."

Ray grimace-smiled and looked out over the demolished yard.

"Sounds like a good idea."

We toasted our mugs and coffeed our way into a new day.

28

I t was turning into a beautiful day and I thought I could do with a dose of fresh air.

Mimi had cajoled Charlene into the idea of going to the hospital to see Bradley again and I'd left a message on Paul's service to make sure that they got a good chunk of time together. No matter what. Whether that worked or not we'd have to see.

After that I deftly avoided the task of cleaning up the Wright's front yard and drove to a local park, where I sat in the cool early morning sun and watched waterbirds on the lake, and a father and young son conning a remote control yacht around in the light breeze.

Decided a walk could lead to good things, so I followed a crushed gravel path as it meandered through a greenbelt alongside a small stream for a few hundred yards. When I thought I was more or less in the right spot, I melted into the trees, sat on my duff and waited.

Should have had a pipe earlier, but it was too late; no point in scaring the wildlife away.

About the time I figured I was too late, I heard rustling in the brush away to my left. It came and went, so I stayed still until I heard a match strike and the sweet, cloying smell of marijuana wafted its way through the pine trees.

Time to get moving.

Imani was sitting in the shadows of the tree line, leaning back against a solid trunk, eyes closed and looking like she didn't have a care in the world.

I got to within ten feet and she had no idea I was there.

"Good morning," I called jauntily.

He eyes flew open, she blinked a couple of times and finally dialed in some focus. "Oh fuck," she said, trying to hide her exhale, palm the joint, work out who I was, and decide how much trouble she was in. Once she realized it was me, and that I was alone, she started to relax.

"Fuck! You scared the shit out of me. What're you doing out here?"

"Looking for you. But first, what happened to 'Yes sir, no sir'?"

She shrugged. "Gotta keep the 'rents happy. You don't think I talk like that all the time, do you? Fuck, couldn't think of anythin' worse."

I nodded. I was more than happy to have Imani relaxed, away from Donald's gaze, and feeling like she could be herself. Might give me a fighting chance to get what I'd come for.

I sat down under another tree, about eight feet away, wriggled around until I found a comfortable position for my back against the rough bark. Pulled out my pipe and tobacco pouch and raised my eyebrows at Imani.

"Fucked if I care. You said you were looking for me. Whatcha want?" She took a hit on the joint, closed her eyes.

I made her wait while I went through the usual pipe

ministrations and got the nicotine starting to surge through my body.

"Thought we might have a little follow-up chat after I got thrown out of your house the other day."

Imani's eyes flew open again and she looked like she'd forgotten I was there.

"Whatever."

Another toke.

"I know you're lying about being in your class during the shooting."

"I am not."

"Don't bullshit a bullshitter, Imani. You're good, but you're not *that* good. Besides, I've got the attendance registers. I know you weren't there. Where were you?"

She gave me a minute of sneer before my silent treatment got the better of her.

"Okay, yeah, you're right. I weren't at school yet. I were running late and class had already gone in by the time I got there."

"Whoah, back up. Where were you?"

She hit the joint again, inhaled it almost down to her fingertips, and blew out a massive smoky breath.

"You can't tell anyone else about this, okay?"

"Imani, I don't give a damn about the newspaper stories and the whole brave survivor schtick you've got going on. I just want to find out the truth of whether Bradley Wright did this or not."

"You think this is about the newspaper stories? You have no idea."

"Tell me about it then. Where were you that morning?"

———

It took nearly forty-five minutes and another joint before she got it all out, but it was there, it made sense, and it fit with everything else I knew and felt in my gut.

Imani had left home early that Monday morning, 'headed for school' she told Donald and Martha. They were proud of her for applying herself to her studies but would have been less so if they'd known that instead of hitting the library before school, she would be stopping at a friend's house and getting high.

It sounded like that was a fairly typical morning, and she would have usually been keeping a close eye on the clock, because she didn't want to be late to school. As long as Donald and Martha knew she was at school, then they'd have no reason to ask difficult questions.

But, that Monday, the weed was good and she lost track of time.

Once she finally noticed the clock, she grabbed her book-bag and hauled ass towards the school. Still a couple of blocks away when the school bell rang and starting to panic that she might be busted.

But there was nothing else she could do so she ran as fast as her stoned body would let her.

By the time she made it to the school grounds everyone was inside and she knew she was too late. She couldn't risk being caught by the custodian, so she snuck into the rec-area —actually climbing over the pallet with the duffel bag, weapons and ammo underneath—and hid, trying to work out how she was going to get into her classroom without being seen.

She knew it was going to be damn hard to pull off and at some stage she'd probably have to sweet talk her way onto the attendance register, but she hadn't been busted yet, so she tried to keep moving forward.

While she was coming up with a plan on getting into her classroom, she heard pistol shots from inside the school. She knew exactly what the sound was, had heard it too many times in her childhood. Now she no longer cared about being busted but just wanted to stay alive.

She stayed hidden behind the ivy screen, only just choking down a scream when a bunch of students ran out of the school door, with the two kids in overcoats close behind. One of the Overcoats dropped a pistol like he was done with it, pulled a rifle from under his coat, and worked the action. The other let out a war whoop, then they high-fived and took off after the fleeing students, towards the other end of the rec-area.

She thought that might have been her chance to make it inside the school. Besides, she also wanted to be wherever the guys with guns weren't.

Imani was trying to build up the courage to stand and make a run for the nearest door, and thinking that maybe, in all the confusion, she might actually be able to say that she was in school the whole time.

But before she could do that, she saw Bradley sneak around the perimeter of the rec-area, staying in the shadows. He made it to the steps and, while another burst of gunfire went off at the far end of the rec-area, he ran up the stairs and inside.

Imani figured that he was doing the same thing she wanted to, and she was almost ready to follow, but the door swung open again and Bradley came back out, covered in blood, and looked around nervously.

She watched as he crept down and around the bottom of the stairs and picked up the dropped pistol.

"Wait a minute," I said. "You saw the kid in the overcoat drop the gun, and then Bradley picked it up?"

"Uh huh."

"Did he go back inside the school once he had the gun?"

"Nope. Went off towards where the other assholes with guns were."

"Okay. What happened then?"

"Umm, while everyone were down at the other end of the playground, I ran inside through a back door, snuck through the cafeteria, and got as close to my classroom as I could. When the cops got there, and they were helping everyone out of my classroom, I just kind of blended in and came outside like I'd been there the whole time."

"And that's what you told the police."

She laughed. "Fucking A. No way was I gonna tell them what actually happened. Too much chance that it would get back to Donald and then I'd be up the shit."

"You have to tell them now."

"No I don't. I don't got to do nothing."

Pulled myself to my feet. "C'mon, Imani. We're going for a ride. There's a couple of cops and a District Attorney who need to hear your story."

I took a step towards her. She took a huge breath.

"One more step and I scream." Grinned at me. "And I can scream pretty loud. Wanna hear it?"

I stopped, cocked my head. "What's that gonna solve?"

"It'll stop you botherin' me while I'm gettin' high."

Looked around. The stream-side path hadn't been highly traveled while we'd been sitting there, but the morning was growing later and I thought I could hear voices and the yipping of a little dog getting closer.

I tried to bluff her. "So what? I'm a P.I. Wouldn't be the first time I've talked my way out of a situation where someone thought they were smarter than they actually were."

Lots of teeth now. "Maybe, but have you ever had to do it

when you've been caught in a secluded area with a sweet, vulnerable, teenage girl? A girl also happens to be the 'hero survivor' of a school shooting. Try your luck if you like, but I can be pretty persuasive."

When I didn't have an answer for that, she ignored me and started to roll another joint.

Rafferty's Rule Sixty-seven: When you're out of options, keep 'em talking.

"Nothing else to do today?" I said, resuming my pine-needle seat.

She got the roach lit and squinted at me through the smoke. "Nuh."

"Uh huh." Looked like she didn't want to play the other side to my approach. A bird twittered somewhere back in the tree line and I tried to be just as soft and gentle. "So, you know Bradley Wright?"

The weed was working well by now, and Imani seemed to be relaxing with each breath. "Umm, yeah. I guess. Not real well, but I'd seen him around school."

"What was he like?"

She gave me the same story that I'd already heard from a dozen different students. Quiet kid. No classes together. Didn't exchange more than a couple of words over the whole semester.

"You know that he's been charged with murder?"

"Duh."

"That doesn't bother you?"

Shrug. "Why should it?"

"Because you know he didn't do it. You might be the only one who knows that."

"So what?"

"So what? You're gonna let an innocent kid go down for murders he didn't commit?"

"Not my problem."

"I've met a bunch of evil people in my time, but that's got to be the coldest thing I've ever heard. Just to protect your hero image? What are you getting out of it?"

"Again, and like all grown-ups, you don't have a fucking clue what you're talking about. Always missing the point." She leaned back against the tree trunk and closed her eyes.

"'Splain it to me, then. What's the point?"

She sighed and took a while to open her eyes and come back to me.

"I'm not going back to the shelter. End of story."

"You really think Donald will send you back if he knew the truth about that day?"

She nodded. "You heard him yourself. 'Two rules for living in my house, child ...' All that shit."

"If it's so bad living under his roof, maybe you'd be better off back there anyway."

I'd only seen one other face as frightened as the one she gave me then, and that had belonged to a young man arriving at the realization he was going to die from his gunshot wound.

"No fucking way," she spat, and despite her professed desire to bliss out, she stood and walked in wobbly circles. "Never going back," she hissed to herself. It was like I wasn't even there. "Never going back."

"Going back to what, Imani?"

She jerked, stared at me with wild eyes and shook her head, braids whipping around her face like a little cat-o-nine-tails.

"I know about your family," I said. "And what happened to them. Is it your stepdad? Are you worried about him?"

Shook her head. "I wasn't nothing to him."

"Then what? What are you afraid of?"

She stopped pacing and wobbled a little more until deciding it was time to sit down again. Tried to roll another joint, but her hands were shaking so badly that she couldn't open her little baggie of grass. She kept picking at it, growing more frantic until the bag ripped open, scattering the contents over her lap and the pine needles.

"Fuck!"

I looked across the stream at the silver-haired woman walking a fox terrier wearing a little purple coat—the dog, not the woman—who had stopped and was peering at us intently.

"Sorry," I called. "My niece just stubbed her toe. I've been trying to tell her about her language, but ..." I shrugged a 'what can you do'. The woman smiled, gave me a little wave and moved on.

Imani was scrabbling around on the ground but only succeeding in re-filling her bag with more pine needles than marijuana.

"Imani." I reached out to grab her by the shoulders, help her focus. She recoiled, scampered five feet farther away, curled into the fetal position against a tree and whimpered. Glanced up at me with those terrified brown eyes.

I gave her room, scootched myself to another tree, and packed a pipe. Before I had got it going well, Imani was curled up, asleep, snoring softly.

———

In the hour of thinking I got done while Imani was asleep, all I managed to come up with was that something at the shelter scared her so much that she would do almost anything to not be sent back there.

As the kids say, "Duh!"

That didn't give me a long list of choices when it came to being able to use her testimony to exonerate Bradley.

I could feed her to the wolves, get the DA to make her testify and leave the consequences from Donald to fall where they may.

Perhaps I could lean on him, soften the blow, and give her a fighting chance on staying in Dallas to play happy families and sneak out for the occasional joint by the creek.

Maybe.

And speaking of creeks, Bradley was a long way up one without a paddle if neither he nor Imani would tell the truth. One of them was going to have to come clean if there was any chance that he was going to get out from under the DA's train of justice.

I could sympathize with the innocent-looking sleeping girl, with her 'him or me' situation, couldn't really blame her for thinking the way she did.

But if it came down to a choice, where only one of these families was going to come out of this unscathed, it would be the one which had a neat little folder with their name on it in the 'Client' section of my file cabinet.

As if I had such a thing.

———

"Umm?" Imani sat up like a new fawn peeking out from behind the bushes.

"Good morning, sleepyhead."

"You're still here."

"Of course. Did you think I'd take off once you passed out? Never leave a man, or woman, behind."

"I don't need your help."

"Yeah, sure. You and everyone else."

Imani stood up, looked around. "I'm gonna go." Dared me to make something of it.

"It's a free country." I blew a smoke ring. Nice shape.

"Okay then."

"Okay then. Be seeing you, Imani."

"Hope not."

I'd heard that so many times it barely even registered.

Once Imani was beyond the treeline and out of sight, I stood, brushed the pine needles off my jeans and stretched. Strolled my way back to the car while I whistled a happy tune.

It really was a beautiful morning.

29

That didn't last long once I arrived back at the Wright house.

Mimi was hard at work trying to straighten the front yard and it was already starting to look better, but Cowboy's work on the dark patch under the large pine tree sent a stomach-turning odor across the yard and house.

He leaned his shovel up against the tree and met me before I made it to the porch.

"Mighty fine job you're doing there," I said.

He shrugged. "Hell, nothing much different to mucking out the horse stalls, really. Mind, horses ain't got anythin' else they can do. I pure don't understand how humans can be so goddamned filthy."

"Keep it up," I said, making sure that he knew I wasn't interested in helping.

"Almost done. Anyways, you got better things to do. Missus Wright and Ray tore inside like their asses were on fire after gettin' back from the hospital. 'Bout ten minutes ago. I reckon they got somepin on their minds."

"They say anything?"

"Naw. Gut feelin'."

Cowboy's gut feelings were better than the weather forecaster's, so I went looking. Didn't have to search far, they were both sitting in the kitchen cradling half full glasses, the open bottles of wine and scotch on the table testament to a good afternoon ahead.

I leaned against the door frame, neither of them noticed me.

"Day drinking now?"

Ray looked up. "Sorry. A million miles away."

"Mr. Rafferty, thank god you're back. You have to hear what Bradley said."

I pulled out a chair, sat down. "Hit me with it."

Ray nodded, glanced out the window. "While we were at the hospital—".

"It was better today. We could stay in with Bradley for longer. He still didn't say much, well, not while I was there, but Ray told me in the car on the way hom—"

"Charlene." Ray reached across and patted his sister's hand. "Do you want Mr. Rafferty to hear this?"

"Of course. Sorry."

"Bradley finally talked to me while we were alone in the room. We'd already been there a while and he hadn't said much. Charlene was getting upset, so she said she needed to use the bathroom and left. Mimi went with her. I was sitting there, didn't know what to do or say, when I hear Bradley say in this little voice, 'I deserve to die, Uncle Ray.'"

Here we go.

Charlene swallowed wine and refilled while she watched Ray lay it all out for me.

"I was sure I didn't hear him right, so I moved the chair a bit closer and asked him what he was talking about, and he repeated exactly what I thought he'd said the first time. Obviously, I told him that he deserved no such thing and that he shouldn't be saying crazy stuff like that."

"Did he say why?"

"It took a while for me to get it out of him, but yeah, in the end he did. Turns out we were right about him having a girlfriend." Ray smiled wistfully. "Her name was Becs ..." *Love U 4 Ever Bradley! B. xxx* "... actually, Rebecca and she was one of the students killed on the day."

"Rebecca Gibbons?" I said, knowing it had to be.

"He didn't say a last name, just Rebecca."

Well that explained why he didn't want to talk. Classic survivor's guilt, compounded, I guessed, by the typical intense teenage love affair. I was about to ask Charlene if she knew about the girlfriend, but Ray was still talking.

"... and because he didn't stop them, he—"

"Whoah, back it up there, Ray. *'He didn't stop them.'* What made him think that he could have stopped them? The schoolyard may have looked like the O.K. Corral, but Bradley sure as hell isn't Wyatt Earp."

"Because he saw the two kids with guns before it all happened."

"Wait. What?" Maybe I still had it wrong. "He knew the other shooters? Was he part of this whole shit-show and just pussied out at the last minute? I don't have to tell either of you that I will be very fucking unhappy if I've backed the wrong horse here."

"No, no, nothing like that. He was just late to school on that day, was trying to sneak in through a hole in the fence that all the kids know about, and he bumped into the two other kids, getting ready ... ready for ... well, you know."

"And they decided not to shoot him either? Come on."

"Honestly, I think that's the thing that's bugging him the

most, aside from Rebecca's death. That he got lucky enough to get away and not everyone else did."

"How does that work?"

"He said that one of the kids just looked at him and said, 'Go home. Today is not a good day to be here.' I think he sold something to the kid in the past, maybe. He was crying pretty good while he was telling me all this."

"Uh huh. What happened then? Did he say?"

"Yep. Said he pretended to go back out the way he came in, but hid and hung around, so he could try to get back into the school and warn Rebecca." Ray sniffed. "But he didn't get there in time and, because of that, he deserves to die."

"He can't really believe that?"

"I don't want to think that either, but he does. The only two things he said after that were making me swear I wouldn't tell his Mom, and then he said he was sorry. Charlene walked in only a few seconds after that he didn't say another word."

Ray downed his scotch and reached for the bottle.

I hated teenaged angst enough when I was going through it myself, but even more so now. This kid had nothing to apologize for and, other than being heartbroken about losing his first love, should have everything to live for. Yet here he was, ready to let a bunch of people who didn't know the truth use him as a scapegoat.

Not on my watch.

"Anything else?"

Charlene jumped in. "He doesn't deserve any of this. He's my son who should have his whole life in front of him. Can you help him?"

"Watch me."

Thirty minutes later I was also sitting at the kitchen table, coming up with plans for exactly how I was going to help Bradley and strictly observing Rafferty's Rule Fifty-Seven: Any job worth doing, is worth doing with beer.

Whilst enjoyable, Rule Fifty-Seven hadn't led to any startling breakthroughs, though.

I flirted briefly with the idea of finding Imani again. Thought maybe I'd gone too easy on her and I should wind up the pressure to the point where she'd have to tell the truth. Remembered the look she'd given me while pretending to get ready to scream, about how smoothly she had played her self-protection role with her concocted stories, and decided it wasn't worth the risk. For now. If I had any chance of helping Bradley, I needed to stay mobile and not get bogged down in meetings with cops, lawyers, and judges.

But speaking of lawyers ... I leaned against the wall, sipped beer, and cradled the receiver in my shoulder while I waited for Paul Eindhoven to come on the line.

"Rafferty," he said his voice sounding like his teeth and dimples were at full capacity. "I'm assuming you have good news."

"I'm working on it. Let me ask you something. I've found a witness to the shooting who saw exactly what happened and can testify that Bradley had nothing to do with it."

"Now that's what I'm talking about! Okay, I can see you both, tomorrow at ... umm, let's see ..."

"Hold your horses, Paul. That's the problem. They won't talk. I've got a line on why they won't and I'm working on that, but in the meantime, what sort of protection can you organize for them?"

"That's more your area of expertise, I think."

"That's not going to work here. She's a teenage girl, and she doesn't want her father to ... anyway, I don't mean 'lock down, siege type' protection. What she needs is protection from …" Despite my morning rhetoric, I wasn't ready to throw Imani to the wolves just yet. "… from any repercussions of her testimony."

"This girl isn't going to be testifying against the Mob here. Tell her to get over herself and do the right thing. I'm sure she'll be okay from whatever boogey-man she thinks is after her."

Paul hadn't seen Imani's reaction about the idea of being sent back to her previous life. My silence wasn't clearing up the picture for him, but it also wasn't hurting.

He sighed. "Okay. I'm just a city lawyer, so there's nothing I can do on my own. But, I'll talk to the DA's office and see what they say."

"Thanks."

"Don't thank me yet. What's this girl's name?"

"Maybe later, once the DA agrees to protect her."

"You don't make this easy. I hope you know that."

"And spoil all your fun? I couldn't do that to you."

He hung up and I grabbed another beer.

If I couldn't protect Imani from whatever her foster-father might do when he found out about her class-cutting, maybe I could at least make the ramifications less scary for her to think about and therefore more likely for her to come forward and agree to help Bradley.

There was an old buddy of mine on the Houston PD— we'd been rookies together—and although we hadn't spoken in years, I was sure he'd be willing and able to help out if I asked. He could give me the skinny on the shelter where Imani had stayed and maybe throw some light on what terrified her so much.

But it was a distraction from the main task at hand. And it could end up being a long distraction, with all sorts of boring issues like privacy and sealed documents to navigate before I got near understanding the situation before even thinking about trying to solve it.

No, I was better staying focused in my own backyard.

And, although I didn't want to take the next step, I knew it was one I needed to take.

Suitably fortified myself and snagged the phone receiver. Sat down for this call. Figured I'd need to.

"Why the hell are you calling?" Ed growled into the phone.

At least he'd answered, so I thought things might be looking up. I ran through the same request as I'd put to Paul, leaving Imani's name out of it.

"This isn't a private protection business," he said, "I would have thought I didn't need to tell you that, but apparently I do."

"C'mon, Ed. This is a material witness to the shooting with testimony that will prove Bradley Wright had nothing to do with it, and that the DA's charges are bogus."

"Take it up with the DA then. Nothing I can do. Especially with the amount of detail you're giving me. None."

I didn't have anything else, so I was getting ready to hang up, when Ed cleared his throat, and voice got lighter than I'd heard it for quite some time.

"Who's the eyewit?"

"Thought you weren't interested."

"I said I can't help you, not that I'm not interested. You say you've got someone who is gonna blow the DA's case to pieces, I say that might be handy to know about *before* I get an angry phone call from the Chief."

"What's in it for me?"

"Nothing."

"Then no can do, Ed."

"Fine." The growl was back. Good. It was quite frankly off-putting to hear Ed wheedle like that. Didn't suit him at all.

I'd barely hung the phone up before it rang again. Christ, it was getting like a telethon here.

"Rafferty?"

"This is he of whom you speak."

Without drawing breath, Paul updated me on his unhelpful phone conversation with the DA's office, spending a little too much time on how much they laughed at his request.

"Say what?"

"I'll admit it, I lost my cool. And when the associate said that they'll be ready to go to trial inside a week, and they looked forward to crushing us into the dust and seeing Bradley put to death for what he did, I fired back. Really I just wanted the smug son-of-a-bitch to shut up, but as I think more about it, it's the right thing to do. It might put them off their game. Maybe only a little, and only if we're lucky, but it'll definitely give them something to think about when they realize that they've got the wrong kid."

Paul went on to explain the ins and outs of exactly when and how he was going to file suit against the city, talking about 'malicious prosecution,' 'false imprisonment,' and 'deprivation of liberty.' I wasn't really listening by that point, I'd already moved onto the next step in my rapidly diminishing arsenal. I didn't have the luxury of thinking about what was going to happen after this was all over, I needed to get hot and make sure that it ended the right way.

"Great, Paul. You go get 'em." He was still blathering on with lawyer-speak as I hung up, but I couldn't listen all day.

I had a trip to make.

———

Donald Beckett intercepted me on his front walk, about ten feet from the curb, long before I got anywhere close to gaining the porch.

"We've nothing to say to you, sir."

"Donald …" I'd planned out a little of what I was going to say on the way over, but I had to step carefully. For Imani's sake. "This is important. Bradley is going to be tried for, and probably convicted of, murder unless Imani helps him. She's the only one who can, and I know his family would be forever grateful if you would let her tell her side of the story."

He stood center of the concrete path, arms folded. "You're trespassing, and I'm telling you to leave my property."

Well, he started it.

"Okay then. I'm pretty good at what I do, and I bet there's something in your past that you're keen to keep private, isn't there? I can't promise what might happen once I make that public."

"Are you threatening me?"

"Do you feel threatened?"

"No." He gave me a tight smile, spread his arms, and took a step forward, herding me just as you'd do with an old, blind dog. I automatically moved backwards in time. Cyd Charisse in blue jeans.

"I'll take you off my Christmas card list. That'll teach you."

"Good-bye, Mr. Rafferty."

We were walking in lockstep now, him forwards, me backwards, and consequently he was the only one making progress.

"I'll prank call you every morning at 3am."

Stumbled a little as I backed off the curb, then I was standing in the street, watching Donald's back as he walked back to his front door.

I leaned against the Pacer's fender while I smoked the last of the day away. The sun dusted the tops of the shade trees lining the street and the air was so still that my smoke hung around me, a blue cloud following me with every step.

With nothing but doors slamming in my face for the whole day, I was forced to admit I was running dangerously low on options. But not yet empty.

Always kept one scrunched up at the bottom of my pocket for an emergency. Looked like the right time to bring it out into the light.

It wasn't the perfect play, carrying a high likelihood of pissing a bunch of people off, but it did get results. Since it was already deep in the fourth quarter and the home team trailed by five points, I had nothing to lose.

Hilda didn't like this one, and with good reason. It wasn't so long ago she'd borne the brunt of a would-be Molotov Cocktail after I'd used the same approach.

I still felt bad about that.

But I jumped in the car, headed for the Wrights.

Needed a phone. It was time to beat the bushes.

And the whole drive there, while I was planning the finer details, damned if I wasn't grinning like a teenager about to go on spring break.

30

"Are you sure you know what you're doing?" Hilda asked.

Again.

"Most times, no, but in this case, I'm actually pretty confident."

"You're 'beating the bushes' and you think you'll flush everyone out with this story?"

"What? Oh, I thought you were talking about the *huevos rancheros*. They're almost done, by the way, if you want to make coffee."

Hilda looked up from the newspaper spread across the dining table, a frown creasing her forehead. I checked the tortillas warming in the oven, made sure the eggs were ready, and tried not to laugh.

"Ed's going to be angry at you," Hilda said, standing and getting two coffee cups from the cupboard.

"Oh, I expect nothing less, but then he's angry a lot these days. Maybe needs to look at his salt intake."

"Yeah, I'm sure that's what he needs to worry about."

We sat with the sun streaming through the window that

overlooks Hilda's back garden, ate breakfast, drank coffee, and held hands.

Damn, I loved waking up with this woman.

Looked over at the paper pushed to one side, Monica's byline nestled underneath the screaming headline.

LOCAL P.I. TRIES TO PROTECT SCHOOL SHOOTING WITNESS. DA'S office and DPD won't help. P.I says Kid Killer is innocent.

Hilda saw my eyes. "You won't be able to joke around with the DA's office like you do with Ed."

I patted my mouth with a napkin and reached for my coffee. "Fuck 'em. They all had their chances, but thought it'd be better to double-down on their version of the truth."

"As erudite as always, big guy."

"I try."

"Yes, you do."

After breakfast, Hilda headed to the store to meet a collector who claimed he had Lee Harvey Oswald's wedding ring to sell. I made my thoughts about that clear before she headed out the door, and then puttered around the house until mid-morning when I decided I should just get it over with.

Parked the Pacer in a lot a couple of blocks further away from the office than I usually did. Didn't mind the walk, and made it almost all the way to the office before I knew I was right.

They jumped me as I rounded the corner.

"Mr. Rafferty, Mr. Rafferty," they shouted, thrusting microphones and notepads at me. "What do you say to the DPD's claim that this witness of yours is fake? Who's telling the truth? Mr. Rafferty, Mr. Rafferty."

I shouldered through the pack, climbed the stairs, side-eyed the two reporters leaning against my door until they gave me some room, went in, and locked myself inside.

"Twenty-seven messages," said the girl when I called my service. "Do you want to write these down?"

"Nope," I said. "On second thoughts, tell me who they're from."

"Umm ..." A snap of gum. "Looks like nine from an Ed Durkee, six from Randolph who says he's calling from the DA's office, a handful of individual calls from TV stations and newspapers, and one from a Paul Eindhoven."

"What's the message from Paul?"

"It just says, 'Nice work.' That's all."

"Thanks."

Hung up, cracked the window, and fired up a pipe. Listened to the news-hounds mutter and chat on the sidewalk below the open window. Every few minutes I'd watch the shadow of a figure appear on the other side of my glass door, knock several times, rattle the doorknob, wait, then leave.

Started to think that maybe I'd left my starting hours too late, then the phone rang and I knew I'd got it right.

"You've done it now, sir," Donald rumbled at me, his voice like a distant thunderstorm.

"Good morning, Donny. I trust you're hale and hearty on this fine Texas day."

"Your wisecracks won't save you, Mr. Rafferty. I'm instructing my lawyer to file a libel suit against you and the newspaper for your scandalous interview today. When I'm done, you won't have a pot left to piss in."

"I find that a little hard to believe. I don't recall mentioning your name at all. Neither did I give Monica your daughter's name, or those of any other members of your family. Extended or otherwise."

"It's obvious who you were referring to." His voice wobbled just a little and I knew I had him.

"A judge may take a very different view of that, but you do what you need to do, Donny. I should let you know that you've got bigger problems than what you think Monica's article did or didn't say."

"No, I don't," he said, but the thunderstorm sounded like it was moving away over the horizon.

"Yes, you do. Imani is going to tell her story." He tried to get started and I talked right over the top of him. "To the DA, I imagine, but firstly it'll be to the cops, and you need to think very carefully about whether you want to play the role of the nurturing foster-father, supporting his new daughter through a traumatic experience as she builds a new life ... or ..."

Pause. Nothing from the other end of the line.

"Or ... do you want to be seen as sitting on your hands and doing nothing while your daughter is arrested? I mean, once Bradley Wright is proven innocent, I'm not convinced that you could be charged with trying to obstruct justice but, again, any given judge may think differently. At the very least, I don't think your brother-in-law will be too happy with the optics, no matter what the courts may say."

Still nothing.

"See ya," I said jauntily, hanging up before Donald could re-engage his mouth.

Over the next twenty minutes I fended off phonecalls from all the major newspapers, a few TV stations, and a DJ from KRRV radio station in Sherman who wanted me as panelist on their daytime talk segment, *School shootings: The new scourge of America?*

It was a hell of a shame to pass up all those good opportunities, but there were a couple of specific people I was waiting to hear from, and I wanted to catch them while they were still hot.

The next call from the DA's office wasn't as hot as I was expecting. More lukewarm, like a reheated burrito.

They did threaten me with a jail term, but the associate conveyed his preference that I be incarcerated with the same enthusiasm as ordering an egg salad sandwich. Just something to be done on a very busy day and he needed to get it done as quickly as possible to be able to get onto the next thing on his burgeoning to-do list.

He asked me if I understood what I was telling him, I told him that I'd stopped listening as soon as he said hello and we both hung up at the same time.

What he lacked in personal engagement to his task was more than made up for by Ed Durkee.

I couldn't get the receiver near my ear for the first three minutes. Not that I needed to, I could hear Ed just fine from where I left the handset laying on the desk.

Plus, it gave me time—and both hands free—to pack another pipe.

"YOU HAVE GOT TO BE FUCKING INSANE! YOU REALLY WANT TO GO TO WAR WITH THE DPD? OVER THIS? YOU MUST BE THE STUPIDEST MOTHERFUCKER I'VE MET."

And more of the same. I won't bother giving it to you verbatim, I'm sure you get the drift.

The longer that Ed went on, the more he started to punctuate each word with a couple of heavy breaths between. When I figured he was exhausted to the point where I could hold the receiver to my ear without risking permanent hearing loss, I picked it up and spoke evenly.

"Hi, Ed."

"You got the guts to 'hi' me?"

"What does that even mean?"

"It means you've shat in your own nest this time, Rafferty. You sold us up the river, and I wouldn't be surprised if the whole force is gonna be looking for you. You'll be getting parking tickets and moving violations even when you ain't parked. Or moving. And, I'm not gonna be able to cover for you."

"'Sold you up the river'? Christ Ed, this isn't a re-run of *Dragnet*. 'Sides, tell me one thing I said that wasn't true."

"Because of you, this morning all of Dallas is reading that their police department is hindering an investigation by not interviewing a key witness."

"No, that's not what I said. Nor is it what Monica wrote. I have it here in front of me, if you'd like me to read it back to you." He started to protest and I rolled over him. "Actually, it's a little long but I'll give you the gist. The DPD was approached about an important witness, who has material information relevant to the charges against Bradley Wright, and they refused to provide protection for said witness. Well written, too. Some of Monica's best work. I'm thinking of getting it framed."

"Get stuffed. And anyway, what you just said is the same as what I said. Tomato, tomahto."

"No, Ed. No. It's not. There's a fundamental difference between what Monica reported and what you claim she reported. Now, what people glean from the story, well … I can't be held responsible for that."

"Wrap it up in fancy words all you like, the outcome is the same. You made DPD look like fools."

"To be honest, Ed. It wasn't that hard." I heard the intake of breath and almost felt Ed's spiking blood pressure against my ear. "But … but before you go off half-cocked at me again, and waste my time and your voice, you're looking at this the wrong way."

Needed to have him along for this ride, or it wasn't going to work. So I waited.

"I'm listening." Gritted teeth.

"Okay, so there's been a few things that haven't gone DPD's way on this case, right?"

A huff of breath.

"I'll take that as an acknowledgment. Well, right now, you're sitting on another one and this has the potential to be worse than all the rest. Worse than the missed phonecall, worse than missing Bradley Wright at school, the leak, the—"

"Get on with it."

"Yeah. Bradley's innocent. He—"

"So you say."

"Trust me, Ed. He is. And you don't want to be holding the bag when the truth comes out. Hernandez will let you guys take the fall for it. Nothing surer."

"And how are you gonna help with that? I assume you're not telling me all this just for the sake of it?"

"Of course not. I'll give you the witness."

"Uh huh. Forgive me if I'm not overjoyed by your offer. You know we already interviewed everyone, and I mean *everyone*, who was there, nearby, saw, or heard anything to do with the shooting." He let loose a big sigh. "Unless you've pulled someone off a United flight out of DFW who said they could recognize faces from four thousand feet." He chuckled. "I trust I don't need to tell you how interested I'm not going to be if that's the case."

"Nope, you've already interviewed this witness, but they've been lying to you the whole time. You'll have the chance to get the truth and deliver it to Hernandez and her team. If she uses it, then great. If not, then at least you're the one seeking the right outcome, not pursuing justice against an innocent boy at all costs."

"Are you trying to hand me Bradley Wright and make it seem like some huge gesture? You know that we've got him under control at Parkland, I can get to him anytime I want, so you're not doing me any favors."

"It's not Bradley, and you're not going to get anything out of him, anyway. Goddamn stubborn teenagers."

I sat and listened to Ed breathe for a long while.

"What's your angle here?" he said. "We've got all the witnesses already. We want to go back and re-interview anyone, we can do it anytime. You're throwing a lot of shit in the game, but I don't understand why."

"The kid's innocent, Ed, and it's up to me to protect him. Unless I can get you, or someone, to listen then he's gonna go down for something he didn't do. That does not sit well with me, and I'm going to take whatever steps I need to, to make sure it doesn't happen."

Ed went silent on me again. For so long I thought we might have been cut off.

"You might actually have a heart after all, Rafferty."

"Well, speaking of that, we're getting closer to what I need from you."

"Goddamn it, I knew you'd want something. What is it this time?"

"If I give you the name, you absolutely, under no circum-stances whatsoever, upon pain of death—"

"Get on with it."

"… can tell anyone, anyone at all, that I might be a soft touch."

Ed chuckled.

"I mean it, Ed. If rumors of my sentimentality get out, I'm done. May as well just pack it all in and start teaching meditation or basket weaving."

"Well, as hard as it might be, I'll do my best."

"That's all I can ask."

"You're on your own with Ricco, though."

"I figured."

"So now that we've uncovered your soft center, gimme the name."

"Imani Laweles."

"Newspaper hero chick? You sure?"

"Yep. Do whatever you need to do to get her downtown and talking. It might not be easy, her foster-dad might want to make trouble, but if you have to arrest her, do it. She saw the whole thing, you just need to get her to say it out loud."

"Shit, Rafferty, that's the Chief's brother-in-law."

"If it was easy there'd be no need for men like us."

"You may be right, but there's easy, and then there's working with you, which seems to be a goddamn long way in the other direction."

"I don't make these things up. I just try to unravel them."

"Yeah, yeah."

"Get on to it, Ed. With the DA moving, you don't have a whole lotta time."

"Yup."

"And don't let Imani go to ground. Behind Donald Beckett, or anywhere else. You're gonna get one shot at this, so don't fuck it up."

"I gotta go. Let you know what happens."

"Okay."

Ed hung up, another shadow knocked on the door, rattled the knob and left.

I left the phone off the hook, put my feet up on the desk, and took a nap.

31

hen Ed wanted to, he could work damn fast.

I'd only been asleep for an hour and a half before the pounding I heard in my dream morphed its way into reality to become Ricco standing on the other side of my office door thumping on the wood and calling my name.

"Rafferty. Get out here would ya? We don't got time to dick around."

On the ride to DPD he filled me in on the latest.

"Ed's got the Laweles chick in an interview room, just waiting on a lady detective to come in to do the talking. He wants you there, too. No talking for you, but you'll get to watch."

Even in my still-waking state, I knew Ed wasn't inviting me in as some sort of olive branch offering. He wanted me close by so that if things went head-over-ass, he wouldn't have to go far to yell at me.

When you've worked together for so long it was nice to understand each other's thinking.

Besides, it didn't matter, I'd been in plenty of worse places.

"Did you shoot a kid the other night? Over at the Wright place?" Ricco asked.

"I have no idea what you're talking about."

"Yeah, yeah sure. Momma was screaming fit to burst about wanting to sue someone for poor little Tyler's injury, lost earnings cause he's gonna miss the draft, and all that. Funny thing though, Tyler ain't saying much at all."

"Wish I could help you, Ricco, but I sleep like a log. Wouldn't have heard the 3rd Armored division if they'd come rolling through the living room."

Ricco grinned, stirred his toothpick and shrugged. We rode the rest of the way in silence and it wasn't long before I was standing on the back side of a one-way mirror watching Imani sitting in a bare interview room. Hard chair, hard table, single can of Coke.

They hadn't handcuffed her, so that was a good sign, I guessed.

The door to the interview room opened and a blond woman dressed in a suit walked in, carrying a clipboard and a recorder.

"Hi Imani, I'm Detective Lee." She sat at the desk, not opposite Imani, but kitty corner on the left-hand side. Opening up the space. Non-confrontational. Smart. "Can I get you anything else? Another soda? Food?"

"A sandwich?" Imani said, sounding like she didn't believe a word of it.

"Sure thing. I'll rustle up a couple of PB and Jays for you. Be right back."

About the time Imani was getting her sandwiches, the door to the viewing room opened. I turned, thinking I might be able to put in a similar request.

"You!" Donald Beckett rumbled.

Ricco followed him inside. "You two know each other?"

"This man's the reason my daughter's in trouble with the police."

"No," Ricco said, "your daughter's not in trouble. She's helping us with an ongoing investigation."

Donald stared at me. Clenched his hands. Gave no indication he heard a single word.

"Mr. Beckett, I know who you are, and that your brother-in-law could have my nuts without lifting his butt out of his office chair. But, since you gave us permission to speak to your daughter, I don't have to let you stay here to watch. You're in here as a courtesy and I can just as easy have you escorted outta here if you're gonna cause trouble. Got it?"

Pretty impressive, given how easily the Chief could derail Ricco's career. Donald ignored us both, went and stood next to the window into the interview room, hands spread wide on the bottom ledge.

Ricco winked at me and pantomimed mopping his brow.

Detective Lee's voice came through the tinny speaker. "Imani, I want to be clear. You're not being arrested. I just want to sit with you and have a talk to see if you can help us with some things. Is that okay?"

"Uh huh." She glanced up to the mirror, like she knew she was being watched. "Umm, do I need a lawyer?"

"You can have one if you want but because you're not being accused of or charged with anything, no, you don't need one. And please ... call me Grace."

Ricco pulled up a seat, lounged sideways in it, and played with his toothpick.

Detective Lee got the recorder going, stepped through the formalities—date, time, those present, made sure that Imani knew she could leave at any time—and eased them both into a conversation. Understated, calm, professional. Asked Imani about herself, found common points of interest, developed rapport, and got Imani to give several yes answers.

I would have given up long before then.

Or fallen back to pistol-whipping.

"She's good," I said to Ricco. "Where's she from?"

"Sex Crimes. Ed thought it'd be better for Imani to be interviewed by a woman. Less confrontational. Grace is as good as they come." I nodded. Waited for Donald to weigh in, but the detective was being so kind to Imani, so un cop-like that he didn't have anything to pick on.

They walked through Imani's background—Grace had obviously done her homework—and finally moved on to the day in question. Danced around Bradley Wright for a little while before starting to narrow in on Imani's whereabouts on the day.

Imani stonewalled and trotted out her by now well-rehearsed story.

Grace asked her if there was any reason that she wouldn't tell the truth to a cop.

Imani said that she would never lie to a police officer.

Grace doubted that, saying that there were plenty of times when it was easier to lie, going on to tell a story of the teenaged yet-to-be-detective lying to the cops so that she wouldn't get in trouble for stealing a top she wanted, but said the guilt just ate her up inside to the point where she had to get the weight off her chest.

I almost believed it; she was that good. Any other teenager might have swallowed it hook, line and sinker, but Imani had seen more in her short life than most people and her skepticism had proven valuable so far, probably keeping her alive once or twice.

So it took a while longer, Grace gently probing and backing off, circling around and leaving enough space for

Imani to feel comfortable. I was starting to zone out and I missed the exact point at which the logjam burst, and she spilled the truth.

"That's it!" Donald roared. "She knew my rules. That lying bitch will never set foot in my house again."

Grace glanced up at the mirror and I wondered if Donald's bass tones had rattled it in its frame.

I grabbed his bicep, shunted him to the back of the room, and leaned my left arm across his throat.

"Shut the hell up."

He glanced down at Ricco for backup. Ricco raised an eyebrow, swapped sides with his toothpick. Said, "Fuck's sake, Rafferty. Leave Mr. Beckett alone."

I ignored Ricco, shook Donald's arm, made him look at me.

"That girl is doing a brave thing right now. By telling the truth, she's saving another kid's life today. She knows it's going to be hard and she's hoping like hell that you're not going to find out. Because she's terrified of what she thinks you'll do."

Felt Ricco's hand on my shoulder. "Rafferty. Don't make me have to hurt you."

For the first time I saw the hardness in Donald's eyes waver. I grabbed that and ran with it.

"That's right, this girl that you congratulate yourself on saving from her pitiful life, is petrified of what will happen if you abandon her. You're not going to abandon her, are you, Donald?"

He looked past me, focusing his gaze through the window on his foster-daughter dripping tears onto the table in the other room, and telling the truth, the whole truth, and nothing but the truth.

Ricco must have seen something, too. I felt his hand drop

off my shoulder, heard the squeak of the chair as he sat down again.

I squeezed Donald's bicep and leaned into him.

"I said, *are* you, Donald?"

"No," he muttered, almost sub-sonically. Shook his head, which showed how strong he was, given that I was putting a fair bit of weight across his throat at the time. "No, of course not."

I let go.

He stood straighter—making no indication I had disturbed him in any way at all—grabbed the other chair, and pulled it to the front of the room to sit and watch Imani as she recounted watching Bradley run into the school during the massacre.

I leaned against the back wall and fired up a pipe.

"Umm," Ricco said. Pointed at a No Smoking sign.

"What are you gonna do, arrest me for smoking?"

He chuckled, leaned back, and tilted his fedora over his eyes.

It took another hour, with two breaks—one soda, one bathroom—before Grace decided she had all she needed and terminated the interview.

Imani had cried most of the way through it, apologized for lying in the beginning and begged more than once for Grace not to let her foster-father know.

Donald had remained stationery in the chair, shifting his weight only to wipe away his own tears.

Grace left Imani on her own, said that she'd be back in a couple of minutes, with the promise of another soda and maybe a doughnut if she could find one.

The door to our room opened and she stepped inside, followed by Ed.

"Someone been smoking in here?" he said.

"It was Ricco," I said. "I told him to stop but he wouldn't listen."

Grace ignored our attempted comedy routine and introduced herself to Donald and me.

"Most of it's there," she said after we were done shaking hands and while she extracted two sodas from a vending machine at the back of the room. "Of course we'll have to run her through it all again to make sure that the story doesn't change, and you'll..."—she swept an arm at Ed and Ricco— "... need to confirm that it matches the evidence. Someone from the DA's office will also need to hear this, and they'll have to work out how to handle the fact that she lied in the beginning, which could be interesting if it still goes to court, but that's not my problem."

"Mine neither," Ricco said and then shut up after the look Ed gave him.

"But overall, I'm not getting any red flags. My gut says she's telling the truth this time."

She turned back to Donald.

"Thank you, sir. As you no doubt saw, Imani's concerned about what happens now. It takes a brave girl to do what she did, especially given her background, and that can only happen with good family support. Please make sure she continues to get that. There's still some hard times ahead."

Like I said, she was good.

Donald looked like he was about to respond when the door banged open again and the Chief of Police walked through. More politician than cop, he wasted no time in shaking hands and back slapping, congratulating all on a job well-done.

I was conspicuously excluded from the mutual-appreciation society they had going on.

He sidled up to Donald, blew smoke up his ass about

what a great job he was doing with Imani and how hard it must have been to convince her to come in and tell her story, and … I'm not sure what else there was.

I'd stopped listening.

The room got awful quiet, and I realized that the Chief had only just noticed me.

"And you are?" he said.

I thought about half a dozen wisecrack remarks but, truth told, I was pretty tired.

"Rafferty. P.I."

"You're the one."

"That's me." I flashed him a winning smile.

"I ought to let Lieutenant Durkee run you out of town. The damage you've done to the good people of this department." He shook his head like it was all too much.

Donald was grinning fit to burst behind the Chief's left shoulder. I was trying to decide between letting the Chief in on a few home truths or stepping around him to pop Donald on the nose, or both, when Ed stepped in.

"Rafferty's been … uh … somewhat helpful to this case. In … the background, mostly … but still helpful."

"Right then," said the Chief. "That doesn't cut much with me, not after what you did with that stupid newspaper report, Mr. Rafferty. I'll leave it up to the lieutenant, though. You say he helped, fine. But if he's going to continue to make trouble for the force, Lieutenant Durkee you'll have my backing to do as you see fit.

"Now, Donald, let's go get something to eat."

"Wow," I said as the Chief led Donald out of the room and Detective Lee took the soda back to Imani. "Thanks for the massive vote of confidence, Ed. Don't know how I'm ever going to be able to repay you."

"Keeping your nose out of stuff that it shouldn't be in would be a good start."

Ricco raised his eyebrows at me.

"I'll try Ed, but you know what they say. 'All care, no responsibility.'"

"Hmmmphh."

"On that cheery note, I'm out of here."

And I was.

Drove to Hilda's, with the usual end of case thoughts and emotions wheeling around in my head.

It was always a weird time for me. Even when I'd managed to get things right, I felt a big let-down. Of course, there were the typical doubts—I'd missed something, the case would fall apart once it was in the DA's hands, that type of thing—but I'd been doing this long enough to ignore those.

No, the let-down feeling, more of a despondency, I hadn't yet been able to nail down the genesis of that one. I didn't spend a lot of time thinking about it to be honest, because I figured that it really meant only one of two things.

That I lived too much for the rough and tumble, I enjoyed the scrap and that I was already mourning the loss of that heady tang of investigation and danger until the next case came along.

Alternatively, it's possible that I never gave myself credit for helping the people that I did, preferring to remind myself of the ones who slipped through my fingers. And there were a lot who did that on this case.

So I turned my thoughts to happier places, and the car into a liquor store parking lot. Picked up two six packs of Modelo and a bottle of Chardonnay for Hilda.

It was time to celebrate.

32

I t was a Friday morning five weeks later and we were lying in bed, drinking coffee and reading the morning papers.

Hilda had decided to blow off work for the day and planned to ease our way into a long weekend. If I had any work to blow off, I would have done the same thing, but in my case it was more a matter of everyone having to be somewhere.

Monica Gallo had followed the shooting story through to the end, her latest missive covering the DA's announcement on the courthouse steps the previous afternoon.

DA'S OFFICE DROPS ALL CHARGES. BRADLEY WRIGHT INNOCENT.

"She sure makes it sound like it was all her idea," Hilda said.

I looked up from a cartoon where Hobbes was busy tackling Calvin.

"Huh?"

"Listen to this. And I quote, 'As District Attorney for Dallas, I have always striven for truth and justice, and it pleases me greatly to be able to announce today that, due to recent evidence coming to light, my office is able to dismiss all charges against Master Bradley Wright. It is clear that Kevin McKinley and Randy Wilson acted alone on the day of the Columbus High School shooting and that Bradley was merely in the wrong place at the wrong time.'"

"Uh huh."

"Shush up, there's more. 'I would particularly like to thank the hard-working staff of the Dallas Police Department who left no stone unturned to discover the truth behind this heinous crime and for being instrumental in bringing peace and closure to the many dozens of families affected.'"

"All right."

"I'm not done. 'And special mention must be made to a brave girl, Imani Laweles, who came forward with information on the case and was critical in helping us to exonerate Bradley Wright. We need more people like Imani in this world. I offer my thanks and predict a bright future for her.'"

I didn't need to hear it again, had read the whole article while Hilda was still asleep and the coffeepot perked. I thought Hanging Hernandez had neatly sidestepped the whole issue of Imani lying to all and sundry for nearly three weeks.

And the period where she wanted her office to drop the death penalty on an innocent boy.

"Wouldn't be surprised to hear her announcement of running for the governor's mansion," I said.

"There's nothing in here about that," Hilda said, "but it wouldn't be a big shock. The other thing that isn't in here is any mention of you, big guy."

"Aw shucks, it t'warn't nothing."

"It was too. You've changed that boy's life."

"Pshaw. The thing that's really going to change his life is

the settlement that Paul's going to get for making the wrongful imprisonment suit go away. That should set Charlene and Bradley up for a long time to come."

"Monica doesn't mention that."

"That's an indicator of how tight a lid Maria and Paul have on it, but he assures me that the DA's office has admitted they will settle, it's now just a matter of coming up with the figure. Which means ..."

"I know, you've told me before. But go on, say it out loud again. I know how much of a kick you get fr—"

"I get the Mustang back and I can finally get rid of that stupid-ass Pacer. I just hope Peter works Saturdays."

"I thought you were going to meet with Bradley and the family tomorrow. That's when he's getting out of hospital isn't it?"

"Uh huh."

"But you're not going?"

"Nope."

"Because ...?"

"They don't need me there, and I don't need me there. Besides, I need to get down to Peter's to—"

"You can pick your car up anytime, Rafferty. This boy will only come out of hospital once, and he's going home instead of to jail. Because of you. You don't think that's important?"

"Nope."

"How ...? Why ...? There are times I don't understand you at all, Ugly."

"You wouldn't be the first. Ed's head nearly came spinning off when he finally worked out that I was trying to help him. He kept thinking I had some sort of inbuilt mechanism for making his life hard."

"I can see how he'd get to that conclusion. And stop changing the subject. Even if it's not important to you to be there tomorrow, it will be for Bradley. He owes his life to you."

"Big deal."

"It is a big deal. No, don't start reading the comics again. Tell me what's going on."

"It's just a job, babe. It's not like we became best friends."

"Nice try, and that would probably work with Ed, but it's me you're talking to."

I lay down the newspaper and turned to Hilda. The sun came out from behind a cloud and squirted through a gap in the curtains, the room glowed bright and I could almost identify the colors swirling in her deep, dark eyes.

But they were gone before I could name them. Maybe I would never find out.

"Aw hell, Hil. It's hard to explain."

"We've got all day. Try me."

"It's not just the Wright kid. Once a job is over, and I've done whatever I'm being paid to do, I don't want to be around any of my clients. They might be great people, and if we met under different circumstances, who knows? But I'd rather just keep moving forward and leave them in the rearview mirror."

She sighed. "That makes no sense."

I broke eye contact, leaned back against the pillows.

"Never said that it did," I said after a long pause. "It's just that ..." Hilda knew to wait me out. She also knew that it was just what I needed. "I never told you about Edie Schuster, did I? From high school."

Hilda leaned her head down on my shoulder and spoke softly. "She was the girl killed in that accident, right?" I nodded. "The girl you said that Patty Akister reminded you of."

"Okay then. So you know that I felt like shit when she

died, 'cause I'd yelled at her in the hallway, embarrassed her in front of the school, and never got a chance to apologize."

"It's not your fault that she was killed."

"But I didn't tell you everything about that. It's a long story and I won't bore you with it chapter and verse, but while Dad was still on the force, I musta been four or five I guess, he let a woman and her young daughter stay with us. Hubby was beating up on them, and when the mother finally got the kid out of the house and to a police station, my old man wanted to make sure they were safe until they could get admitted to a shelter. It was only for a couple of weeks, but that was Edie and her mother. She would only have been three or so."

Hilda ran her fingers across my chest. I barely felt them.

"Dad would get a card every year on the anniversary of the night he took them in, with an update on how they were doing, and thanking him once again for what he did for them.

"Sometimes, especially when things were getting real tough at work, Dad would sit in his chair and re-read those cards. Over and over.

"And I took that all away from him. I wasted all the good work he'd done, just by being a stupid fucking kid."

I was almost whispering. Hilda's fingers stopped.

"So, once I've done what I need to do, Hil, I don't ever want to see any of them again. Too much chance for me to fuck things up, and no-one deserves that."

"You can't control what happens to people, you know."

"I know!" I breathed deep. "I know, and that's the problem. Fuck it, maybe I've just seen too much. Seen too many people, too many kids, die needlessly. Especially on this one. Maybe … ahh … I don't know."

"You helped two kids this time, not just Bradley. Remember that."

"Yeah."

"Speaking of ..." Hilda leaned up on one elbow and looked at me. "How did you know that Imani's foster-father wouldn't send her back to the shelter?"

"I didn't."

"You mean you were prepared to sacrifice that poor girl to whatever she was afraid of just to get Bradley cleared?"

"'Course not. After they left the Wright's house, Cowboy and Mimi headed straight to Houston. Poked around a little, found the source of the problem in the shelter. Let's say that the name of the problem was Earl, and that Earl had been a problem for a lot of other girls in the shelter, not only Imani, and ... well, let's finish by saying that Earl's not going to be a problem anymore. For anyone."

Hilda leaned in, hugged me, and grabbed my hand. Nuzzled her face into my chest. "You are, without a doubt, one of the best men I've ever met."

"One of?" I made to pull my hand away. She held on. "And here I thought ..."

She looked up, winked, stuck her tongue out between her beautiful, perfect teeth, smiled and broke into her wonderful, throaty laugh. Trailed her foot up the inside of my leg.

Whispered to me, "If you're on your game this morning, you might be able to break into my top five."

"But you think I should still go and see Bradley tomorrow."

"We'll talk about that much later ... but yeah, you should."

33

So I went to Parkland Memorial the next day to watch Bradley Wright take his first steps out of the hospital and into a new life.

Worst decision I ever made.

I put the Pacer in a lot further down on Harry Hines and walked back to the hospital. The media scrum was camped out in front, chatting, smoking, and waiting to get the money shot of the triumphant return of the boy they'd wanted to crucify two months ago.

Dummies.

I ignored them all, walked around the block and worked my way back to the Emergency entrance. Okay, maybe not all the newshounds were dummies. Several outlets had stashed a couple of reporters here too, looked like juniors charged with covering the bases in case their subject tried to elude the pros out front.

Paul had only let me know that Bradley would be discharged in the morning, hadn't given me a specific time. That the media were still there meant that I definitely hadn't missed him, but anyone I could ask wouldn't have any more idea than me on when we might be seeing his still-healing face.

I might have been wasting my time but, let's face it, there wasn't a whole lot else that needed doing.

So I leaned against a brick corner, smoked a pipe, and waited.

It had been nearly an hour and I was in the middle of a couple of deep knee bends to take the pressure off my back when the low murmur of the journalists started to rise to a crescendo, and I saw a few cameramen running around the corner from the main entrance, no doubt tipped off by radio.

Over the heads of the reporters I could see Bradley, flanked by Ray and Charlene, walking slowly towards the exit. He looked strong, a lot better than the last time I'd seen him, even smiling.

That boded well.

The trio stepped outside, the overhang casting a strong shadow across the top half of their bodies, and the media pack moved in.

Then the day turned to shit.

I left the screams and the *whirr-clicking* of cameras behind me as I chased Frank Gibbons out of the parking lot and on to the access road that looped back to Southwestern Medical Avenue. His denim shirt flapped as he ran, and I cursed my decision to wear boots instead of sneakers.

What the hell was I, a fashion plate?

Frank had already turned and started running before I recognized him, so I was twenty yards behind as he rounded the corner and ploughed right through a clutch of what looked like first-year med students.

I stepped on to the sidewalk and tried to hit the hole he'd

made, but they'd already regrouped and a petite blond woman and I waited for the other to move for three precious seconds, before I picked her up and manhandled her to the side.

Now I was forty yards behind and by the time I stopped and took aim, Frank would be well out of range.

So I ran.

Traffic on Southwestern cruised past us as we ran up the block—Frank not getting away, and me not gaining.

I wondered if any of the drivers and passengers were having the day they'd expected when they woke up that morning.

Yeah, Hil, you're right. I should be there to see Bradley when he walks out of the hospital a free boy with his whole life in front of him.

His name has been cleared and he'll finally be able to move on with his life. Get back to school, maybe find a new girlfriend. It's only upwards from here.

They say that if you want to make God laugh, tell him your plans.

While I'm waiting for Bradley to show, I'll ponder the case and think for the first time in a very long time, I'll feel like I made a difference. Yeah, there were a lot of kids left behind at Columbus High, but I helped this one. And Imani. And they'll get a chance to live a full life, and I'll feel like I actually did this one right.

Can you see it coming? Wait for it, it's hilarious.

I'll look up and see Bradley and his mom and uncle stepping out of the entrance doors and a few of the reporters will close in, thrusting microphones and questions at the Wrights, and I'll think that I'm happy to not be going through that shit, and then I'll see someone thrust something that isn't a microphone, and before I can do anything, Bradley will be lying on the bitumen, bleeding from the chest, and I'll be in a footrace against Frank Gibbons with no finish line in sight.

Terrific day, right?

And none of it needed to happen.

If I'd done what I should have done—what my better judgment told me to do—the first time I'd clapped eyes on Frank, I wouldn't be chasing him now, and Bradley wouldn't be bleeding to death in the parking lot.

So I ran.

It was happening again. I'd gone through the whole exercise just to have Bradley die a pointless death. To have protected him, to have made the powers that be see sense, so that he could come out of enforced hiding, only for him to be senselessly taken out.

Just like Edie. Just like Dad.

I didn't want to think about that.

So I ran.

Frank wheeled past a coffee cart parked on the corner, scattering customers like fall leaves, and pounded through a small loading area as he headed back towards the hospital buildings.

I thought that he'd already accomplished what he wanted to for the day, and that he wouldn't be a threat to members of the general public, but I couldn't be certain.

And I had nothing else I could do for the moment.

So I ran.

Followed Frank as he weaved between parked station wagons, and bounced off SUVs, and ran across Campus Drive. He swerved away from the main buildings, angled between two tennis courts, and disappeared into a small parkland.

Great.

If he pushed hard through the trees, he could be out to Harry Hines Boulevard and jacking a car before I had anything to say about it. Or he might grab someone doing nothing more than taking a walk on a nice day and try to bargain his way out.

Please don't let it be that.

I'd been wrong about too many things on this case, let me have this one, for fuck's sake.

Please.

I thundered across the verge and into the parkland, skidded to a stop, and whipped my head side to side, trying to pick a faded denim shirt and red beard out from the stands of trees.

Heard the pounding of my heart, and the clang of metal. I cut to the right, came upon a three-story parking garage, a rusted metal door at its base with the words 'Keep door closed at all times' fading into obscurity.

I eased over to the wall alongside the door, pulled out my .38, wished for more gun, and thumbed the hammer anyway. Took two deep breaths and hit the door, weapon up.

Carried my momentum through the door, in case Frank was waiting inside, ready to line up my silhouette in the doorway.

Swung left and right.

Nothing.

Slowed and placed my feet carefully, and quietly, as I moved to the main parking aisle. Listened hard and blinked, trying to get my eyes adjusted to the gloom.

Nothing.

I could see the whole length of the structure, one of those simple elongated corkscrew-type designs, as it rose to the far end about seventy-five yards away.

Leaves, paper, and other assorted garbage collected in the dead corners and, from the smell, I'd have bet that more than one family of rats called this little piece of paradise home.

Most of the car spaces were filled. Busy day at the campus. Mostly middle-aged sedans, only a couple of larger pickups, but then Frank could be lying on the dirty concrete and I wouldn't have seen him behind anything larger than a Radio Flyer wagon. He hadn't had enough time to get to the end up to the next level, and I couldn't hear footsteps, so he was here somewhere.

Hiding. Waiting.

For what?

I could move my way methodically up the aisle, looking between and under each and every vehicle, hoping to dislodge him, but I played a different card.

Wrapped both hands around the butt of the pistol, held it down and out to my right side, stepped about ten feet up the ramp, and focused on movement in my peripheral vision. Took a breath.

"What'd you want to go and do a thing like that for, Frank?"

Silence.

"You've just fucked up that family's life and you know how that feels, right? Why'd you want to do that?"

A breeze whispered through the structure, stirring the dead leaves from their slumber. I heard a raspy intake of breath underneath the scuttling.

"Did it bring Rachel back, Frank? Did it?"

The roar came from my right-hand side. A green Chrysler rocked, its car alarm went berserk, and Frank lunged at me.

He was too slow; I was already stepping back and raising the gun. Zeroing it on his chest.

"Her name was Rebecca, you piece of shit!"

He stopped a couple of feet short, panting, glaring at me

through his shaggy hair and beard. His gun was still pointed at the ground.

Reminded me of a dog that wanted to tear my throat out, if only it knew how to get off its chain.

"Ah, Rebecca ... that's right. And do you know what his name was? The kid you killed. Huh?"

He gritted the word at me. "Bradley."

"Yeah, that's right. Bradley. His mother is Charlene. His uncle, Ray. And you've just fucked up all their lives, big time."

He shrugged at me, which was not the best move.

"That's all you've got? A fucking shrug?"

"Like I should care. At least he won't do it again."

I gripped the gun tighter and ground my teeth. "He didn't do it this time, you idiot."

Frank shrugged again.

"But, let me guess, you didn't know. Or, maybe you don't actually give a shit."

Third time for the shrug and, as if to prove my theory about how much he cared, Frank perched his butt on the fender of the shrieking Chrysler and continued to glare at me.

I watched the gun in his hand, wobbling in the loose grip of his fingers like he'd forgotten about it.

Over the pounding in my ears, and between the pulses of the car alarm, I thought I could hear sirens in the distance. The cops would know that we couldn't have gone far from where Bradley was shot, but it would still take them a while to work out exactly where we were.

Thought about the situation.

From the brief glimpse I got before I gave chase, Bradley was dead or dying.

His killer wasn't going anywhere in a hurry.

The cops were on their way.

And this whole thing had been a colossal waste of time.

I'd busted my hump to prove Bradley's innocence and none of it meant a damn thing. Done everything I could to protect Bradley, thinking that once the DA got through admitting her mistake it would be enough.

But the only thing I was left with was more cold bodies—more people left behind.

I checked the hammer. The bright brass of five shells winked back at me.

Watched the realization dawn on his face, then the confusion of wondering what he should do about it.

He eased his weight on to his feet until he was standing. I was glad about that, at least.

Stared at me.

The sirens were closer now.

Time slowed down and I looked at Frank through a dark tube.

I'll be honest, he may have started his gun hand moving. He may have been raising it, bringing it to bear, or trying to throw it away.

Or maybe he didn't.

I didn't care.

I gave him two in the chest. He bounced off the Chrysler's hood, landed on the concrete, and didn't move anything again.

For a long time after I would wonder if I'd done the right thing.

— *THE END* —

Rafferty returns in
Down the Barrel

A firebombed car. A bloody package.
And a spoiled tabloid prince with a target on his back.

Rafferty figured it'd be a quick paycheck—babysit London
Baines, keep him alive, collect the fee. But London treats the
whole thing like a publicity stunt—and refuses to take his
own survival seriously.

Now Rafferty's chasing leads, dodging bullets, and trying to
figure out what London's not telling him.

Because keeping this kid alive is proving a hell of a lot harder
than it should be.

Fast, sharp, and loaded with bite—*Down the Barrel* never
lets up. Scan the QR code below to get your copy.

Read Now

DID YOU ENJOY THIS BOOK?

Reviews and recommendations are the best ways to help another reader have as much fun as you did.

And no matter whether you loved this book or not, I'd appreciate it if you could take the time to leave a review. It can be as short or as long as you like.

Scan to leave your review

And if you do leave a review, I'd love to read it!
Email me the link at **bill@duncanandlee.com**

DUNCAN & LEE

Bill Duncan & Catherine Lee make up the Australian crime-writing duo of Duncan & Lee. They have more ideas than time and their typing speed will ever let them create.

———

DUNCAN & LEE BOOK SERIES

Eden Cross FBI Mysteries

Detective Bonnie Hunter Thrillers

Rafferty P.I. Mysteries

Detective Charlie Cooper Mysteries

Scan the QR code for more information.

ACKNOWLEDGMENTS

I don't know if it's apocryphal that the second book is the hardest but, boy, did this one take some getting over the line.

There were too many times along the way I thought it wouldn't happen, and it was only due to the wonderful people around me (and possibly a strong stubborn streak) that this book is now in your hands.

Ongoing thanks and gratitude to:

My beloved Catherine for listening, offering sage advice and snacks, and laughs, and trips, and so much more. Let's keep doing this for a long while to come.

Lisa Cron, and her book *Story Genius*, for pulling aside the bushes to reveal the path which would allow me to write the book I always wanted to. Without Lisa, this novel wouldn't exist - end of story.

Amanda Spedding and Rebecca Heyman for thoughtful, honest, and sharp-eyed editing that made this a much better book than it originally was. It wasn't always easy to hear their insights, but it was worth it.

My team of loyal beta readers: Stew, Alice, and Grace, for slogging through first drafts and coming back for more. My sister Kelly, for her buoyant proofreading and belief.

The *Memories of Dallas Facebook Group* for the inside scoop on Rafferty's haunts and locales. You guys are great, and I'll be back to pick your brains for more.

Everyone kicking ass and taking names over at the *20*

Books to 50K Facebook Group for daily inspiration. Keep pushing up that mountain!

Jo Penn, Mark Dawson & Nick Stephenson for sharing their hard-earned lessons and their ongoing commitment to indie publishing.

My Sydney Indie Tribe: Samantha Grosser, Susan Mackenzie, Rachel Sanderson, and Angharad Thompson Rees. You guys inspire me with all that you do and make me want to work harder. I'm so glad we found each other.

As always, so much gratitude to Dad for starting this journey and creating a cast of characters who make me laugh, cry, and teach me more about myself with each book. I just wish you were still here walking this trail with me.

And finally, to yet again plagiarise one of my author idols, Matthew Reilly: *"To anyone who knows a writer, never underestimate the power of your encouragement."*

ABOUT THE AUTHOR

BILL DUNCAN lives with his wife, Australian crime writer Catherine Lee, in the coastal city of Newcastle, Australia and defines a great day as one spent plotting how to get away with murder and drinking coffee. Always coffee.

He was born in a small town just north of Dallas, Texas before the family immigrated to Australia when he was 7 years old. While he studied Architecture at university, his father wrote a six-book mystery series featuring Rafferty, a Dallas P.I.

In 2017, after 20 years working in the design and construction industry, Bill obtained a rights reversion for the Rafferty books and launched them in ebook format for the first time. He continues to write new Rafferty stories and the growing series has become a hit with over 300,000 readers around the world.

He has no dogs or cats, but two adult children he shamelessly adores, and a vinyl record collection with an unhealthy proportion of 1980's releases.

Get in touch with Bill at: **bill@duncanandlee.com**